the
**leaning
man**

the
leaning
man

ANNE HARRÉ

THE CUBA
PRESS

Edited by Mary McCallum.
Cover image: *Wellington skyline* by russellstreet / flickr
Cover design by Sarah Bolland.
Typesetting by Paul Stewart.
Author photo: Jane Harris.

ISBN 978-1-98-859541-2
A catalogue record for this book is available from the National Library of New Zealand. Kei te pātengi raraunga o Te Puna Mātauranga o Aotearoa te whakarārangi o tēnei pukapuka.

Printed in Aotearoa New Zealand by Ligare.

THE CUBA PRESS
Level 6, 138 Wakefield Street, Te Aro
Box 9321 Wellington 6141
Aotearoa New Zealand

for Simon

1

MAD-DOG BELIEVED IN ANGELS, Mozart and a good piece of cardboard.

If you had cardboard you had warmth; if you had warmth there was a better chance of a decent night's sleep. The weather would start to close in soon. It was almost April. Then it would be autumn, then August and winter.

He needed cardboard.

He'd found a skip, in a side street off Tory, but knew he had to go back in the deepest dark. Dark was good – he preferred the shadows – it lessened the chance of being hassled. Mad-Dog disliked hassle, that's why he didn't like going to the shelter. The shelter meant other people. He didn't mind the soup kitchen; they didn't mind him either.

Mad-Dog watched the sky slowly darken through the trees. He stayed sitting a while more. He was good at waiting; his camp on Mount Victoria was a good place, a safe place. Waiting was something he had perfected; life was too hurried for most people. They rushed, pushing forward, heads down. He saw them all the time, bodies leaning, striding along, always on to the next thing.

He tightened his coat around him, pulled a comb out of his pocket and dragged it over his hair. His hand went to his beard – it felt better now he'd trimmed it. From another pocket he took a pair of nail scissors he'd found in one of the skips. It still amazed him what people threw out. The light gently faded as he clipped each nail then carefully scraped underneath.

He held up his left hand and looked at it. His fingers twitched. Mad-Dog closed his eyes as the sound of strings drifted in over his right shoulder. A Mozart quartet floated in front of him. He hummed a few bars – yes, No. 16 in D Flat Major, no, E Flat. He flicked his eyes open, hurriedly putting the comb and the scissors back in his pocket.

The sky was properly dark. A light breeze played around him. It wasn't going to be too cold tonight, he thought, that was a good thing. Mad-Dog stood up, stretched his back a little and flexed his fingers. Picking up his bag, with a length of rope and other essentials inside, he hoisted it onto his shoulder and set off down the hill.

He wasn't a tall man, just average. People didn't see him, but if they looked at all, they would see an older man, mid-fifties maybe, thinning grey hair. They would see a dark blue suit jacket that was too big in the shoulders and trousers that bagged around his shoes. If someone was truly seeing, they would notice him walk with his right foot facing forward, understanding where it had to go; the other foot facing slightly to the left as if declaring an alternative agenda. If anyone caught his eye for long enough, they would see he had green eyes, like his mother.

A group of young people walked towards him. He stepped out onto the road as if to cross. He waited for them to pass then moved back to the pavement, keeping on down the hill towards Courtenay Place. His stomach grumbled as he walked past the cafés, the smell of evening meals drifting under his nose. His mind went back to the cardboard. He'd perfected this over his time out here, the art of diversion, the art of forgetting.

Now, on a Saturday night, Courtenay Place was fully alive. He waited at the lights outside the Embassy Theatre surrounded by chattering people who had just come out of a movie.

'I thought he was better in …'

'Yeah, but this one had far superior cinematography, you have to admit that.'

'I don't have to admit anything, mate.'

Then laughter.

He missed that, laughter. The lights changed – the wave of people washed over the street. Mad-Dog shuffled his feet. He eyed the drivers of the cars that were waiting for the pedestrians. A slip of their foot off the brake and mayhem would ensue. Cars were not benign; they were killers. Their shiny metal, their sleek lines, all designed as a weapon. We have been fooled all these years, he thought. 'Fooled, we're all fools,' he muttered. The light was red again.

He felt their stares. That couple over there, waiting to cross, were staring at him, and that young one in the leather jacket – he was doing it as well. He could feel them, he could feel them. 'You're staring, you're staring,' he muttered. 'You're all just waiting to be rounded up, like sheep, you're all sheep.'

They moved away from him. He felt the change in the air. Mad-Dog turned away from the crossing, then towards it, then away again.

'Make up your mind, mate.' A voice came from behind him.

He'd wait for the next one. Sometimes it took him several goes, but he had time.

'Cardboard, I need the cardboard,' Mad-Dog said.

Another crowd started to form at the crossing. He would go when they did. The lights changed, he held his breath and surged forward with the crowd and started up Courtenay towards Tory Street. He felt jangly, his nerve ends alive.

Groups of people were coming towards him, couples holding hands, a woman with a baby strapped to her front. He wanted to look, he wanted to peer at the baby and have it hold his finger. Instead, he kept out of the way, his head down, melting into the walls.

He turned into the side street. Yes, he thought, the skip was still there. The street lighting down this end wasn't that good, but that was okay. He stood there for a while, next to the skip. This one didn't smell so bad. Some of them were unbelievable, even for him. He was on the hunt for cardboard boxes, the larger the better. The best time to look was at night, less chance of being caught that way, less chance in the late, dark night.

Occasionally he found himself in competition with those who were part of the new trend of skip divers: freegans. Freaks more like it. They explained it to him, slowly and patiently. It was information. Mad-Dog liked information, information was tradable, like cardboard.

'We do it for food,' one of the freegans had told him, 'and to help keep our footprint down. There's so much wastage out there, man.' He had a wispy beard, his long hair held off his angular face with an elastic band. 'We just want to keep the planet alive a little longer.'

Mad-Dog stared, he tried not to laugh.

'Look at all this food, look at the plastic, all going to landfills. We can use all of this and give away what we don't use.' That was a woman, a girl really, muscular and fierce, a snake tattoo coiled around one arm.

Mad-Dog looked at those kids. They were educated, middle class and slumming it. They had no idea which side of their skip the bread and freegan butter was spread. Still, he figured that tonight he wouldn't bump into any of them; this was strictly a rubbish and recycling skip.

He threw his bag over first. Then reaching up, he gripped the metal edge. Even in gloves his hands were cold and seemed to have less strength than last time; his shoulder creaked and his right knee wobbled, but slowly he pulled himself up and over. *Bingo*, he thought, lots of flattened cardboard boxes. He had recently relocated to another patch. His last place had bothered him a bit; it was too close to a track up on Mount Vic where people walked their dogs. The people never noticed him – it was the dogs that caused the problem, sniffing around, barking. He didn't like that, he didn't like being barked at by dogs, or humans. He sat there for a while catching his breath. Dim sounds wafted through from Tory Street. It was surprisingly warm in the skip, out of the breeze and well insulated.

Eventually Mad-Dog stood up. Yes, there was cardboard, but it always paid to look a little deeper – you could never be sure what you might find. 'How do I do it, how do I do it? How do I get this lot up the hill?' he said. He grabbed his bag. 'I have rope and one of those springy cords, that ought to do it.'

A shimmer caught his eye. Part way up one of the buildings that backed onto the alley, the outline of a woman – an angel really. He counted, four storeys up.

Her dress was white and floated just a little. Her hair was long, loose and golden. Flicking it away from her face, she turned with her back against the glass sheets of the balcony. Even at this distance he could see she was pretty. So pretty, he thought, even if she didn't have wings. Mad-Dog sat in the skip and stared up at the balcony, up at the angel. Behind the tip of another building he caught sight of the moon, an almost perfect full sphere. Tomorrow, it would reach its peak.

He looked back at the angel, the moon and the angel, perfect. She seemed to be talking to someone, her arms were moving in time with the conversation. Mad-Dog began to hum some long-forgotten music in time with the angel's arms. He saw the other figure, just briefly, more of an outline really. Mad-Dog smiled; he was glad she wasn't alone. Someone as beautiful as that shouldn't be alone.

The air was cooler now, the breeze had picked up. How come she wasn't cold; she should have been cold. If Mad-Dog had been with her he would have draped something around her shoulders. The thought made him frown. He put his head down and busied himself with the cardboard and rope. After a few minutes he permitted himself another glance up at the balcony. Her arm moved over her head with another graceful ballet movement, like she was drawing a large circle in the air. Then, turning and leaning slightly forward towards the street, her hand let loose a star, a shooting star. The pretty angel-woman with the floating dress and golden hair dropped a shooting star.

With a small crack it bounced off the side of the skip and into the rubbish. Well, if some angel-woman was going to send him a shooting star, the least he could do was pick it up.

Mad-Dog reached forward to find it.

Then came the scream.

Angels don't scream, he thought, but that's what he heard. A scream and a flapping and arms and hair, and a noise he never wanted to hear again. He'd heard many things in his life: grown men cry, the silence of a baby, the inner workings of his own softly scrambled brain. The sound of a body hitting the ground was something else. Mad-Dog sat there on his pile of cardboard staring at the star the angel had thrown him.

He twisted around and peered over the side of the skip.

She didn't move.

No one came running.

He stared up at the building she'd come from and watched the shadow push something up against the balcony then retreat away from the edge. He knew there would be police. Mad-Dog was okay with the police and the police were okay with him, but he didn't want to be there when they arrived.

He grabbed his bag, pocketed the fallen star and pulled himself up out of the skip. The cardboard could wait; he could always go to the shelter if the weather got bad. Keeping to the shadows of the alley and with the faint sound of a siren curling its way into his head, Mad-Dog scurried into the night.

2

'You need to get ready; we'll be leaving soon.'

'I *am* ready,' said Stella. She smiled at her mum. They were in the kitchen, leaning against the bench. Stella was eating Vegemite toast and sipping a punishingly strong coffee. Her dad, clothed in a voluminous apron over his good suit, was finishing the dishes. He had long refused to get a dishwasher. 'I do my best thinking at the sink,' he said.

'Please tell me you're not wearing that?' her mum said.

'What's wrong with this?' Stella asked. She smoothed her hands down the front of her shirt, trying not to smile. She heard a gentle snort from her dad.

'Don't tease her, love,' he said.

'Well, you're clothed,' said Peace, 'but jeans? And that shirt, look at it. It isn't even properly ironed. This is a celebration, not an outdoor barbecue.' Peace, her mother's name was Peace. She was slightly taller than Stella, sixty-two, trim and fit and still very beautiful. Over the last few years she'd let her hair go to its natural grey, and now she swirled it up in an elaborate French chignon.

'Put your mother out of her misery and let her dress you.' Her father hugged Stella, giving her a quick kiss on the cheek. 'She's missed you. She really has. So have I.'

'Ew, Dad, you've just dripped dish water down my back.'

'You had me worried there for a minute,' said Mum. 'It's lovely you're here – you're part of the equation whether you like it or not. I'm sure I've got a little black dress that would work for you.'

'What's wrong with your mouth?' Dad asked, untying his apron.

'What do you mean?' said Stella.

'You're holding your mouth funny.' He was starting to stoop and his eyebrows were developing a slightly mad professor appearance.

'It's okay, Dad, just a bit of toothache, that's all. I'll take a couple of Panadol. It'll be fine.'

Peace took her arm. 'Come on, let's find you something to wear. You don't want Charlotte having a go at you. Besides, she said something about your giving a speech. I think that's a lovely idea.'

They started up the stairs.

Charlotte had mentioned something about a speech, hadn't she? Stella scrunched up her eyes and tried to remember. Travelling through time zones was a bitch; it always took time for the brain cells to line up in their right place again. Twenty-eight hours in an air-conditioned tin can was no one's friend. Honestly, Stella had thought she was joking about the speech idea, but Charlotte wasn't one to joke about stuff like that. Hang on, it was coming back to her. Somewhere after Hong Kong there was a delay, she'd been wide awake at that point and made notes in case she'd had to email them to Charlotte. There might have even been a joke or two in there. She patted the phone in her back pocket. Yep, all good.

'Don't panic, Ma. It's under control. It'll be great, you'll see.' She held out her phone. 'Just let me put this on a charger.' She plugged it in and followed, barefoot, into her parents' bedroom.

Stella stifled a yawn. God I hope that coffee kicks in soon, she thought. Her mother, a mild-mannered florist by day, demon in the clothing department at night, was expertly flicking coat hangers across the pole in the wardrobe.

'Not that one, not that one, what about this one?' She was holding up a lacy number.

'Ah, no, that's not really me.'

'You have such a gorgeous figure. You should make the most of it. There's nothing wrong with looking pretty.'

Stella rolled her eyes. Peace wanted the best for her daughters, she truly did, but she did have that habit of trying to tame anything she could lay her hands on. She'd straighten shirts, comb hair, tie shoelaces so they sat better, no doubt part of the 'Catholic guilt' hangover. Stella was always grateful her dad had won that argument: 'I will not have the church involved in my children's education.' It was one of the few times her Mum had acquiesced.

Still, Peace liked her children to put their best selves forward. Charlotte was great at it – she'd inherited the ability. Stella ... not so much, and Tim was a law unto himself.

'I can't believe you've still got that,' Stella said, pointing to one of the framed paintings.

'Of course, I'd never throw it out. I love it. You did that in high school. What about this one?' Peace was holding out another dress, peacock-blue with a swirling skirt.

The look on Stella's face made her hang it back in the wardrobe.

'I was trying to be arty,' said Stella. 'I don't think I succeeded.'

'Don't be silly, you had real talent. I love the line of that drawing and peonies are still my favourite. I always hoped you'd go into something a little more, you know ...'

'Creative?' Stella finished the sentence for her.

'I guess art was never going to work for you, you always needed more excitement. Timmy was always the sensitive one.' The hangers clinked as they were flicked to one side. 'Don't get me wrong, I love you all equally, you know that, don't you?'

Breathing in, out, in, out.

She would not have an argument with her mother, at least not tonight. All children disappoint their parents in some way or other, it's just life, isn't it?

'How is Tim?' asked Stella.

'He said he'd try to get here.'

Flick, flick, flick, that coat-hanger noise was starting to get to her.

'So you've spoken to him?'

'No, Charlotte's been in touch – he doesn't call here much anymore.'

'That's crazy, Mum, you know it is. I'm sure he …'

'What your brother chooses to do is his business.' She went quiet. 'Aha, this is the one.' She held out a simple black shift dress, three-quarter length sleeves and made of raw silk. Looking at the low square neckline, nipped in waist and minimal lace, Stella had the feeling that she may have worn it before. She nodded.

'That one I will do. I'll wear that – I may even tie my hair up.'

'Lovely,' said her mum, giving her a quick hug. 'Pop this little jacket on as well, you'll look fab.'

Stella started to get changed as her mother looked for shoes.

'I forgot to mention it, but thanks for inviting Teri. She sent me a text to say that she'll be at the party. It's going to be great to see her.'

'No problem at all. She called a few hours ago, but you were completely out to it. There's a few of your friends on the list, some of Charlotte's as well.' Stella turned around so her mum could help with the zipper. 'Besides, I knew you'd be wanting to see them. It's always nice to have some young people at these kinds of events. Can't have all the old fogies running everything.'

Stella smiled. Peace went indoor rock climbing every

week without fail and was a rower from way back. 'I'd never put you in the old fogie basket, Mum.'

Her mum held out a pair of sling-backs with a square heel. 'Here, these will go nicely.' She handed them to Stella.

'Mum, don't you dare.'

'No, no. I'm not going to cry. It makes me so happy to have you here, to have us all here, well apart from Tim. But ... anyway, you look lovely, sweetheart. I know – I've already said that. I'm rambling. I'm sorry.'

She gave her mum a hug. Her feet hurt, her tooth was throbbing, a wave of jet-lag exhaustion crashed over her. Catching sight of herself in the long mirror standing next to Peace, she smoothed her hands down the front of the dress. Stella thought they both didn't look half bad. It would be okay.

'Thanks, Mum, for the dress and shoes. We'll all have a good time, you'll see. Besides, look at how presentable you've made me.'

The smile on her mother's face said it all.

3

THERE WAS A SPONTANEOUS round of applause as they arrived at the Boat Shed. Stella moved to one side, letting her parents bask in the acknowledgement. A string trio was playing Mozart in the corner; waiters swept past with trays of champagne flutes. There were flowers everywhere and candles glowed from large glass containers. Grabbing a glass of juice from one of the waiters, she turned to see who was already there. She had to find Charlotte and let her know that the speech thing was all sorted.

She spotted her across the room with her husband, Ben. Even at a distance Stella could see Charlotte had made an effort. Her teal green dress moved with her body, her honey brown hair was shiny and fell in expensive waves down her back, all held with a band that glittered in the light. Beside her, Ben wore a pale blue suit with nonchalant style. He laughed, a warm chocolate sound, and placed a hand on the small of Charlotte's back. Those two truly defined the meaning of a 'beautiful couple'.

Her grandmother, ensconced in a chair and surrounded by bouquets, looked like an aged flower princess. She gave a quick wave to Stella and patted the seat beside her. Before Stella could move, an arm was around her waist giving her a wee squeeze.

'Hi you, I saw you come in with your parents – you look great. London life obviously suits you.'

Stella's Aunt Rita was in her late fifties, smart and hip in an urban 'I know my own style' kind of way. She wore interesting brooches. Her hair was cut in a sharp pixie style, with a streak of bright blue down one side.

'Thanks, Rita. Actually, the dress and jacket are Mum's,

so are the shoes.' Stella laughed. 'It's amazing I got here at all. I am woefully under-prepared.'

'Well, you look fab,' said Rita. 'Peace always did have an eye for fashion.'

Stella sipped her juice – it was very sweet and very non-alcoholic.

'How much longer do you think you'll be away?' asked Rita. 'I know your parents, and Charlotte, would love to have you home.'

'Can't argue with that,' said Stella. It was going to be a long night and she desperately wanted a cigarette.

'I'm working in the new library now. We must meet up for lunch one day.'

'That'd be lovely.'

'Did you bring a boyfriend back with you?'

'Not this time, but I'll be sure to keep you in the loop.' Stella grinned at her to make sure the subject was dropped. She looked over at her parents surrounded by their friends. Someone was telling a raucous story. The sound got louder and louder then burst into a waterfall of laughter. Her dad wiped tears from his eyes, and Peace patted him gently on the back.

They'd managed forty years together – forty years still married, still talking to each other, still actually wanting to be together. Christ, Stella had only half managed one live-in arrangement, which had ultimately failed – an affair with a married man that had ended in monumental disaster, and then (for repetition's sake) there was married man number two. By the time her mother was her age, thought Stella, she'd had two kids and been married ten years to the same guy.

'Your mother said you probably weren't coming,' said Rita, 'that it's such a long way for one night.'

'Yes, well, it was Charlotte who kept reminding me they'll only do this once.'

'Well, she's quite right there. Have you heard from Tim?'

'Not recently. I'm not even sure I have a current address for him. What about you, heard anything?'

'Nothing, no one has. Peace keeps up a good face, but it eats at both of them.'

'Yeah.' Stella was wondering how she could politely extricate herself. 'It's lovely to see you, and dinner, or a lunch, would be great, but I have to find Charlotte – let her know that my speech is all sorted.'

'A what?' said Rita.

'Yeah, a speech,' replied Stella. 'Apparently it's traditional at these kinds of occasions for speeches to happen. They usually come from the oldest child, and seeing Tim is AWOL, that means me.'

Trust Charlotte to do what's traditional, she thought. Her wedding had been ultra-traditional right down to the tears the bride had shed while walking up the aisle. That was the last time Stella was back in New Zealand. She gave Rita a quick hug. 'Can you excuse me – I *really* need to find Charlotte and say hello to Grandma.'

The Boat Shed sparkled and hummed – guests swirled around; a swoosh of cooler air came through as more people pushed open the doors. It was Saturday night in New Zealand, and Stella had arrived in the country as fast as her credit card was racking up interest. We're not designed for it, she thought. We're not designed to be packed into a metal tube and shot thousands of kilometres to the other side of the world. London would be waking; her flatmate would be with someone in the next room. In the normal course of events Stella would be subjected to the dull, rhythmic thumping of Saturday morning sex. She smiled to herself – at least she was missing that display for once. She rubbed her jaw; her mouth still hurt. It wasn't right, she thought. Her big brother should be here as well. Talk about the elephant in the room.

Where the fuck was Charlotte? Stella had been back in the country less than thirty-two hours and jet lag wasn't her friend. Her brain and her other senses weren't managing to keep up with each other. The time/space continuum between the hemispheres was in a blurred state. Eventually her body clock would reset itself, but for now her head and her mouth were not in sync.

Her tooth really wasn't settling down. Bloody international flights, the surest way to stir up any dental problems. But it was there, her bottom left molar beginning to throb again. As Stella's hand went to her face, she spied her dad through a gap in the crowd. He mouthed 'Okay?' towards her, she smiled and nodded. Stella looked around for Charlotte; she would be sure to have a decent first-aid kit in her bag. It was times like this when a quick vodka, or three, would be heaven. There was Ben, through the crowd, maybe he could tell her where Charlotte was. Stella started to make her way over to him. Many of the faces surrounding her she half recognised, but there was the odd sense that there'd been some kind of time warp; they all looked so old. How the fuck am I going to get through this whole event, she thought.

A waiter whistled past holding another tray of long-stemmed glasses. She eyed them. Like the tongue of a frog, her hand wanted to dart out and replace her empty juice glass with a full alcoholic one. She wanted to feel the tingling bubbles work their way down her throat, wanted to sink into that pool of forgetting.

Stella scanned the room.

The crowd moved slightly and she caught sight of a profile: long blonde hair, a floaty white dress that wasn't off the peg. Immediately she relaxed; thank the sweet baby

Jesus, sanity would be restored and the evening would be bearable. She planted her glass on a table and dodged her way through the crowd to be enveloped in a huge hug. Her friend's arms were tight around her, rocking her from side to side. She smelt of vanilla, expensive vanilla. Her hair tickled Stella's face. They were both laughing, bouncing up and down and a little out of breath.

'Teri, thank goodness you're here.'

'Stellanova, I knew you'd come home.'

'Teri, honey, I need to breathe,' she said. Teri let her go but hung on to her arm. 'I almost didn't make it, but the stars collided and here I am.' Stella knew she had a dopey smile on her face, but Teri was one of the few people that accepted her completely, shit and all. Her friend – her good, kind, beautiful and wonderful friend – was truly pleased to see her.

'It is good to be here,' said Stella. 'I wasn't given a huge amount of choice from Commandant Charlotte.' She stood back and looked at her friend. 'You look amazing, Teri.'

'This old thing?' Teri giggled and twirled around.

'Yeah, that old thing,' said Stella, laughing with her.

Teri's floating, white dress wasn't too far removed in style from the one Marilyn Monroe wore in that famous 'over the grating' photo shoot. Her friend was all halter-neck and cleavage, with an infectious smile. It was fantastically difficult to dislike her. She had that effortless beauty and style, the kind the rest of the world tried for and seldom succeeded at.

'The best thing about this dress is that I can do this.' Teri tucked her hand just inside the strap on one side and pulled out her phone. 'It gives a whole new meaning to the term "good vibrations".'

They laughed. Stella started to feel the pain pills might be working.

They'd met in the first week of uni and clicked straight away. Where Stella had been dark and sarcastic, Teri had been light and funny. She was tall, that always helped, and a natural golden blonde. They were perfect opposites. Stella was smaller, with usually unbrushed hair hurriedly tucked behind her ears. Teri always had lippy on and invested in regular manicures. Stella managed a chapstick half of the time and bit her nails, sometimes until they bled. Teri had stood by her when the shit hit the fan, one of the few people who had. Stella loved her for that. But the best thing was she wore her style with charming nonchalance. Teri slipped her arm back through Stella's.

'Stellanova,' she said, 'it's just so lovely to see you again, in person.'

'You know you're the only one who calls me that.'

'Well, they run together perfectly, just like you and me. I called you earlier, but Peace said you were shattered and having a lie down.'

'And I was,' said Stella. 'Still am, I think. Teri, you know I'm really bad with the Facebook messaging or WhatsApp or whatever … but hey, I've missed you, and I'm here now.'

'How long are you back for? Tell me everything.'

'That's the big question. I don't really know this time. It kinda depends.'

Teri gripped the top of Stella's arm.

'Really, really? Do you think you may come back for good? That would be super-deluxe. I'd love that, Stell, so would Kate.' Teri hugged her again. The noise in the room made it difficult to talk. She leaned in. 'Listen, Stell, in one of your emails ages ago, you said you'd got back into some kind of police work in London. Did you get my email? I sent it a couple of days ago.'

'Sorry, hon, what with travelling I haven't had the chance to get online, and calling it "police work" sounds a little more than it actually is.' She snorted. 'Trust me, it's just grunt work. PI stuff. Not that exciting.'

'Maybe, but I really need to talk to you,' said Teri. 'I was relieved to hear that you were going to be here.' She started fiddling with her bracelet.

'Teri, what is it?'

'Ah, sweetie, sorry, now's not really the best time.' She grabbed a glass off a passing waiter and took a mouthful. 'By the way,' she said, giggling. 'You know Mitchell is here … what can I say? Your mother has plans. Just promise me we'll talk soon.'

A man arrived at Teri's side. He put his arm around her waist and stared at Stella. Stella stared back. His eyes were startlingly blue. In her heels, Teri was a good ten centimetres taller than this new arrival. She made the introductions.

'This is Maurice Ravosky. Maurice, this is my brilliant friend, Stella.'

'A pleasure to meet you.'

'Oh, no, my dear, the pleasure is all mine.' He took the hand she offered him, raising it to his lips and kept hold of it. His fingers were warm, the nails professionally buffed. He stood a little too close; Stella caught the strong whiff of very expensive smelling aftershave. 'I've heard so very much about you,' he said.

'And I've heard nothing about you,' she replied.

'Teri told me you didn't mince words.'

Maurice Ravosky finally let go of her hand. He was bald in the insouciant, sexy way that some men carry baldness. The cut of his dark grey suit screamed bespoke tailoring. His shoes had the high gloss of footwear the Italians favoured; an antique diamond ring sparkled on his pinkie finger. Theresa Mossburn, her friend Teri, with an older, wealthy man. Stella hadn't pictured that ever happening. She'd come across enough of this situation in London to last her a lifetime. As a PI she'd made a decent living dealing with spurned first wives. They would hire her to tail their exes. Unhappy wives – suspicious wives knowing there was something going on – were bread and butter in Stella's line of work.

'So how do you know Teri?' she asked.

'My angel.' He placed his arm back around Teri's waist. 'She came to me in a dream and we've been together ever since, haven't we? Teri, my dear, I'll leave you two to chat – but you'll join me soon?'

'I'll be right over,' she said.

Ravosky smiled at Stella then turned into the crowd. He shook hands with someone, his left hand on their forearm. He laughed, leaning in to the conversation. She turned to Teri and raised her eyebrows.

'Um, are you going to fill me in on this chap?'

'It's not what you think. I've been doing some work for him. There's been so much going on, things have been moving fast.'

'You could have called me.'

'It's not the sort of conversation to be had on the phone, Stell. We need to catch up properly so I can fill you in,' said Teri.

There's no accounting for taste, Stella thought, as Ravosky slid through a gap in the crowd.

'You're not in any trouble are you?'

'Trouble? No, not at all, quite the opposite.'

'Promise me you'll call tomorrow, we'll have a good long lunch, without any interruptions.'

'Absolutely.' Teri hugged her again. 'I miss you, my friend, but I need to check on Maurice. There was someone he wanted me to meet, some work thing, besides you've got family to meet and greet.'

'Go, go,' said Stella, 'but tomorrow you're mine!'

Then Teri, too, was gone.

Clearly Stella had been in the police game for way too long. She smiled to herself. Here she was at the Boat Shed function room, on a Saturday night in little old Wellington, surrounded by family and friends celebrating her parents' fortieth wedding anniversary. Her best friend wasn't in trouble. This wasn't London or New York, for god's sake. Things don't happen here. Teri probably wanted to know how to ditch Ravosky and not hurt his feelings. Stella would check that email when she got home. Hang on, what had Teri said about Mitchell being here?

Charlotte was at her side. 'You look nice,' she said.

'Thanks. Mum had her usual way.'

'We'll have the speeches soon. You'll need to get closer to the front. Uncle Ivan is first, then you. You have prepared something, haven't you?'

Stella patted the pockets of her jacket for her phone. 'Sure, of course I have,' she said.

'I need to find Ivan,' said Charlotte. 'I'll see you up the front soon, okay?'

'Absolutely,' said Stella. The palms of her hands felt clammy. She was trying not to hyperventilate. Her skin prickled and shallow breathing wasn't helping.

Shit, shit, shit.

Where the fuck was her phone? She jammed her hands into the pockets. Oh god, no way, she'd done it now.

They'd rushed out the door, the taxi was waiting, Peace had been on a mission to time it all to perfection. Her phone – it was on the bench back at her parents' house, plugged in to the charger. How the fuck had she missed that, and how the hell was she going to manage a speech without any notes?

Stella grabbed another glass from a passing waiter and took a gulp. It went down the wrong way and she doubled over coughing; bubbles of juice spurted out onto the floor.

Fuck, she was going to choke to death at her parents' party, way to go, Stella. Her eyes were blurry. All she could see was a pair of elegant shoes and a hand proffering her a handkerchief, a real one not a paper tissue. She straightened up and took the handkerchief.

'Hi, Stella, it's been a while.'

'Hey, Lassie, only you'd have a real handkerchief on you,' she said, dabbing her face.

Mitchell Lassiter. The only person on earth who managed to carry off having a surname for a first name, something Stella had mercilessly teased him about.

'Well, it's the small things that count,' he said, placing his hand firmly under her elbow. He steered her to the side of the room and removed the glass from her hand, setting it on the window ledge. Stella felt herself growing red in the face. She hated that she did that, especially in front of Lassie. He was standing close and bent his head to her ear.

'I hear a rumour Charlotte has roped you into a speech,' he said.

'Yep, that'd be right,' she said, dabbing the handkerchief at the front of her dress. Her mind was working furiously, how was she going to make this speech without notes?

Lassiter took a step back and put his hands in his pockets.

'What are you looking at?' she said.

'Nothing, Weston. It's just really good to see you, that's all.'

She was in a borrowed dress, damp from spilt juice, her phone was twenty minutes' drive away and friggin' Mitchell Lassiter was smiling at her.

'Give me your phone,' she said suddenly.

'What?'

'Just give me your phone.'

'Yes, but …'

'Come on, hand it over. Trust me, I'm not after your

search history or anything – please. I've left my phone at home with my speech notes on it. I can get them from the cloud. Don't give me that look.' He fished his phone out of his jacket pocket. 'I'm tired,' she said, 'my mouth fucking hurts, I need a cigarette and I'm off the booze.'

'Okay, okay, here you go.' He keyed in his security code and handed it over.

It felt like forever, but Stella finally found what she needed. She scanned through it quickly. It was all there – enough of a speech so that she wouldn't make a complete tit of herself. Actually, some of it wasn't half bad. Uncle Ivan was wrapping up his speech. There had been laughter, a smattering of applause at one point. He obviously knew what he was doing.

'Thanks for the phone and sorry for snapping at you. Once again, Lassie to the rescue.'

'Occupational hazard, I guess.'

'You're a lawyer, Lassie, not Indiana Jones.'

'Quibble if you like, but you're about to be introduced.'

Stella turned towards the front of the crowd. She held Lassiter's phone in a death grip.

'So, it is with great pleasure,' said Ivan, 'that I ask Stella, Peace and Clive's eldest daughter, to come and say a few words.'

There was applause. He was scanning the crowd for her. Stella felt Lassiter's hand on the small of her back pushing her towards the front of the room. The crowd parted like the red sea. It was the slowest walk Stella had made. She tried smiling but her face felt as though it were contorting into a death mask. She was perfectly able to stare down all kinds of low-life in her job, but public speaking … fuck that for a joke.

The next three minutes she had very little recollection of. She was there, in front of a microphone, gripping on to

Lassie's phone. All at once she was finishing.

'On behalf of Charlotte, myself and our brother, Tim, who was unable to be here, I'd like you all to raise a glass to our parents, Clive and Peace. They've crossed every sea imaginable and come through it with the wind in their sails, the sun at their backs and, most remarkably, still talking to each other.'

Not too shabby, thought Stella.

She didn't have a glass in her hand. One was quickly put there by her aunty Rita, who was sniffing and dabbing her eyes with a tissue. Stella looked over at her parents, who were in some kind of clinch she didn't really want to see. Stepping back into the crowd, her knees threatened to give way. Stella felt relief wash over her like a soothing mouth rinse. Teri was giving her the thumbs up and Charlotte was steaming towards her.

'Stella, that was great, thanks so much for doing that. I knew you'd come through in the end, but you do always seem to leave it to the last minute. I couldn't do that.'

'Yeah, well I wish I didn't either, but there you have it.'

Charlotte hustled her to the side of the room. Large windows framed the lagoon, and lights were strategically placed to play on the water under the bridge. Stella looked out. Wellington could be stunning at night – the lights around the waterfront, the curve of the harbour. A boat was coming in. Her head was feeling quite strange, but the jelly feeling in her legs was receding. The main problem now was the spinning room.

Stella was trying to remember the last time she ate a proper meal. She couldn't. Had she had lunch? Had she even been awake at lunch time? Charlotte was talking to her; she could see her mouth moving but she couldn't make out the words.

'What was that?' she asked.

'I said, Stella, that I was thinking you and I should spend some time together. You know, quality time.'

'Quality what?' Stella said.

'I've booked us in for a "cleanse and renewal" day, up the coast. Hey, Mum wants a word with you. She's coming over. I'll give you a call about it – you'll love it.' She swept away.

'That was lovely, darling. I know speeches aren't your forte,' said Peace.

'What's this spa day I've just been roped into?'

'Charlotte?'

'Yep, get me out of it, and fast,' said Stella.

'Darling, I can't. If Charlotte wants to spend time with you, you're just going to have to deal with it. She misses you, that's all,' she said, giving her a quick hug. 'We all do. I see you were talking to that lovely Mitchell Lassiter.'

'Not now, Mum, please not now,' she said. 'Actually, I still have his phone, and I hate to be a party pooper but I'm completely shattered. I think the jet lag has kicked in for the evening. Would you be horribly offended if I made my way home?'

'Of course not. I've just seen Mitchell go outside, so you can give him his phone on your way,' said Peace. 'You take yourself off and get some sleep. Do you have keys? Here, take mine.'

'Thanks. You enjoy yourself. I'll see you in the morning.'

'Well, not tomorrow morning, love. Your dad and I have a hotel room across the road, you know, for a bit—'

'Yeah, okay, Mum, too much information,'

'I have no idea how I managed to produce such squeamish children.'

4

OUTSIDE THE AIR WAS COOL but not cold.

There was a smell of salt off the sea. After the stuffy inside of the Boat Shed it felt refreshing to be out. The night was clear, but her head was floating – she still felt her eyes weren't managing to focus together. Resting a hand on a bollard, she closed her eyes. It didn't make any difference.

Everything was still moving.

She spied Lassie on some steps that led down to the sea. Making her way over, Stella searched in her jacket pocket and found a cigarette packet. Lighting up she inhaled. A fresh wave of light-headedness washed over her. As she inhaled again, Lassie reached over and gently removed it from her hand.

'A foul habit, Weston, I thought you would have kicked it by now,' he said before taking a deep drag.

'Fuck you, Lassie,' she said. 'Hand it back, I need my vices.'

He passed the cigarette over and they both sat on the steps. They were quiet for a while. The sea sloshed against the concrete, the lights from the bridge reflected in the water.

'You look good,' he said.

'You're joking, right? I look like crap, I feel like crap, but hey, thanks for your help back there.' She handed him his phone.

'You're welcome.'

'It's nice to see you. It's been way too long.'

'Three years if my memory is correct.'

'Yep, Charlotte's wedding.' She inhaled, then exhaled a plume of smoke. 'Now there's an event seared onto the back of my eyeballs and not in a good way.'

Lassie laughed. For as long as she could remember Stella had loved that sound and she'd loved making him do it. There was the beginning of grey at his temple; it suited him, gave him an air of gravitas that he'd previously relied on clothes and a briefcase to provide. But she was tired, very, very tired. All she wanted to do was lean into the person beside her and sleep. Trouble was it was Lassie, and there was way too much water under that bridge. They sat there, companionably side by side. The door to the Boat Shed opened and, for a brief moment, cheerful party sounds filled the air.

'So how long are you back for?' he asked.

'Not sure.'

'How's life in the big smoke?'

'Not too shabby.'

'How's your love life?'

'Not sure.' She looked at him. 'Seriously, I'm not sure. I'm never fucking sure. How's yours?'

'You haven't heard?'

'Clearly not – what's going on with you?'

'Another time, Weston.' He gently bumped his shoulder against hers, and she bumped him in return.

Stella thought about her friends. Not the ones in London, but the friends that truly knew her. Stella had known Lassiter and Teri since uni. Those two, along with Kate, were her oldest friends. They'd all flatted together, travelled together, got drunk and broken hearts together. Shared history gave them a shorthand; it meant they could be relied on, even if the communication across the years wasn't always that good.

'That's a thought,' said Stella. 'Where was Kate this evening? I'd heard she'd been invited.'

'Kate's on a tour at the moment,' Lassie said. 'There was

a gig up in Auckland this weekend that was too big to give up. She's meant to be coming back sometime this week. She has some shows organised at a club here.'

'Fair enough. It was great to see Teri though; we've planned a decent catch-up tomorrow. She looks amazing, as per always, but who on earth's that bloke she's with?'

'Ah, I see you met the charming Maurice Ravosky. He's okay, sort of, but I wouldn't want to get too caught up with him.'

'You know him?'

'Only in a professional capacity. He has an office in the same building, so I see him from time to time.' He took the half-finished cigarette from her hand for another puff.

'Yeah, but what's she doing with him? I can't picture Teri with a sugar daddy.'

'I'm not sure that it's a "sugar daddy" situation,' said Lassie, handing it back. 'She works for him, I believe. I tried to talk to her about it once, but she just laughed and said that for now she was having fun.' He ran a hand through his hair and stifled a yawn.

'She never mentioned him in emails,' Stella said.

'She probably knew you wouldn't approve.'

'Teri never needed my approval.'

'Are you sure about that, Weston? You can be pretty harsh at times.'

'Ouch, speak for yourself.'

She shivered slightly. Lassiter removed his jacket and put it around her; immediately the warmth enveloped her. She rested her head lightly on his shoulder. She was close enough to smell his aftershave, a warm, slightly smoky scent. He crossed his arms across his chest. Stella looked at his hand resting on his forearm. The nails were close cut and clean, the light caught the hairs on the back of his hand.

Stella could feel her hand moving to take his.

Shit.

'I need to get home,' she said sitting up and squashing the butt with the toe of her shoe. 'It's been a long night.'

'I'd offer to drive you, but I don't have my car here.'

'Thanks for the thought, I'll just grab a taxi …' Stella stood, swayed slightly and sat down again. 'I think I'd like to visit the leaning man.'

'Who?'

'You know, the leaning man, the chap who's leaning out into the water. He's still there isn't he? He'd better jolly well be. I'll be pissed off if some bureaucrat has removed him.'

'Oh right, you mean *Solace in the Wind.*'

'What?'

'That's what he's called.'

'You're such a pedant,' said Stella, rolling her eyes at him. She stood up again. Slowly this time, her hand resting on his shoulder for support. 'Are you coming, or not?' She started off, slightly unsteady. He caught up and tucked her arm into his; she lengthened her stride to match, grateful the wind wasn't whipping along the wharf like it sometimes could. They walked slowly along the waterfront, over the bridge, past the high-diving platform. It was an almost full moon, the sky clear of any cloud. Lights sparkled at Circa Theatre. No doubt the show would finish soon, patrons spilling out into the night, satiated with culture.

'Look at that,' she said. 'He's still there, still leaning.'

She loved this sculpture. It was like a fine pencil drawing. She loved the lines of it. Maybe her mother was right, maybe she did need to do something creative again. Stella admired the sense that here was a person, an artist, who knew something, who understood longing, striving, the act of reaching out for something – anything. She wanted to be like that. She wanted to be the person that knew things, a person that could lean fearlessly into the unknown, forge ahead, get things done.

That had been her. Once. But that was a long time ago. Now she was here, huddled into a borrowed jacket, not leaning into anything of note, not having any kind of anchor to hold her. She walked over to the statue and trailed her hand down his arm. It was smooth in places, rough in others. Cold to her touch. Stella rested against the cool arm, her face on the surface of his grainy, pitted skin.

Just along from the leaning man a pair of kid's jandals sat perfectly placed, side by side. They were pink with a little flower that would rest between the wearer's toes. Cute, she thought. The sea was gently sloshing and sucking around the piles under the wharf. They were the only two people there. Well three, if you count the leaning man.

Stella straightened up.

She wanted him to come alive, to tell her what he knew. Instead, she turned to the sea. Leaning forward a little she tried to find the same angle that he was at. Her arms were straight by her side, just like his, raising her chin she stretched her neck out to mimic his. If she leaned just a little further she would reach into his unknown. She wobbled, her arms flailing into nothing.

'What are you doing, Weston?' Lassie grabbed hold of her.

'What do you mean? Let me go, you idiot. I was just, I don't know, ah fuck it.'

She sat on the side of the wharf and looked over to the other side of the harbour. The concrete was cold. Cranes stood silent while piles of containers waited to be carried off. There were lights on in some of the buildings, cleaners working late, or people just forgetting to turn the lights out. Maybe there were couples up there fucking each other's brains out, only to forget the next morning in a Sunday fog. She stared down into the black, oily water. Slosh, slap, slosh,

36

slap. Here the sea had a rotten seaweed tang to it, carried on a breeze getting up. She needed another cigarette. Stella couldn't help wondering who owned the jandals, would they be missed, would the owner of them get into trouble for losing them?

Everything she'd tried so hard to leave behind had just sat here waiting for her return. Her head was still in London trying desperately to catch up. She felt she was on the back foot, that she didn't fully understand the lay of the land anymore. She had another life, in another city, she had friends and work colleagues. Well, friends might be stretching it, but there were people that she cared about and hoped cared about her.

Why hadn't Teri told her about Ravosky? Both of them had all the available means to communicate anywhere, anytime, but they didn't. Had Stella become so removed from her life back in New Zealand that even her closest and oldest friend couldn't talk to her anymore?

She could feel herself slipping into the morose part of the night, that time where the ability to fake it slides away leaving a raw edge.

Being back unsettled her.

Wellington unsettled her.

The kitchen was quiet when she got home. The street outside, quiet. Stella leaned against the bench as she finished a glass of wine. Everything here had its place – her dad's apron hanging on the back of the door, the tea towel folded neatly by the sink, the perennial stack of books and magazines at the end of the table topped with a pair of reading glasses. Where was her place in it all? Strange to think she could be in her early thirties and still be a worry to her parents. But they'd always worried, probably always would, that's the prerogative of parents, she thought.

She needed bed and sleep.

Stella checked the door was locked and started up the stairs to her old room. The lights were off, but there was plenty of light from the street and the moon. She could find her way in this house in pretty much any state – sick, drunk or just plain exhausted. After a perfunctory visit to the bathroom, Stella wriggled out of her dress, fell into bed and into a long, deep sleep. Dreams swirled around her. Teri featured at one point, then her dad, then Ravosky, who morphed into Lassiter talking into a phone, calling her.

5

STELLA WOKE TO THE SOUND of a phone ringing somewhere outside the room. For a moment she thought she was in her flat in London, but she couldn't be – the sun was streaming through a gap in the curtains. Her head was thick, her tongue dry, a dull thumping in her ears.

The phone stopped.

Then started again.

She rolled over pulling the covers over her head, London, another life, another time. Stella groaned. She loved her parents, she honestly did, but she wished like hell they would invest in some modern technology, maybe a bloody answerphone.

Eventually it stopped again. She lay there, an arm draped over her eyes in the mistaken belief that maybe, just maybe, she would go back to sleep. Nah. She opened her eyes. Stella squinted. Had they painted the walls? It looked like it. Maybe she'd just forgotten their original colour. The curtains were the same, she was sure of that. Psychedelic purple and orange flowers raged across the fabric that she'd thought cool as a fifteen-year-old.

She needed to drink water soon or she'd shrivel up. Probing around in her mouth with her tongue, she pushed against her gum on the left. Yep, her tooth was still hurting. She would need painkillers and a dentist. One of her credit cards was maxed out with the airfare, but the other one was in pretty good shape. The dentist's bill could go on that one.

Stella sighed and rolled over – god, her tooth hurt.

Sleep wasn't going to happen any time soon. Pushing off the covers she sat up, very slowly. She rubbed her eyes with the heels of her hands, picked up an elastic band from the table and tied her hair back. She took a deep breath and stood, putting her hand out to rest on the bedside table. Her grandmother last night had more energy than this, Stella thought. Last night. Fuck, what a night. All she'd wanted to do was to jet in, attend the party and piss off again. No such luck.

In the bathroom the hard light made her eyes look as bloodshot as they felt. Her skin was London pale. That's the arse end of a winter for you, she thought. The cabinet yielded the usual suspects, along with a box of Panadol. She popped a couple of pills out of the sheet and drank a large glass of water to get them down.

The phone rang, again. This time she picked up.

'You're there.' It was Lassie.

'What the fuck time is it?' said Stella.

'It's after eleven. You weren't answering your mobile. I'm outside the door. We need to talk.'

She hung up. Walking down the stairs to the front door, she was trying desperately to remember if she'd said or done anything inappropriate last night. She flicked the lock and let him in.

'I need coffee,' she said. 'Don't talk to me until I've had coffee.'

Stella went into the kitchen and stared at the coffee machine – too many moving parts. Filling the jug, she found the coffee plunger and proceeded to dump in four large spoons of coffee from the grinder. She sniffed the bottle of milk. Lassie pulled up the blinds to let in the sun, then took the steaming mug Stella offered and sat at the kitchen table.

'I'm sorry to have to do this,' he said. 'I've been knocking for ages.'

'What's so bloody urgent?' She leaned against the bench.

'It's Teri, I had a call early this morning – a mate in the

force who knew that I knew her. He phoned me. Shit.' He didn't look at her. 'There's no easy way to say this, Stella. Teri's dead.'

There are moments when life splits in two.

Life before the event and life after.

She started pacing up and down in front of the sink, one hand holding on to the bench for support, the other clutching her coffee mug to her chest.

'Say that again,' she said.

'Stell, I ...' He was crying.

She looked at him. 'No, no you're wrong.' She put her cup down and lashed out hitting his arm. 'Is this some kind of sick joke?' She hit him again, harder this time. 'Don't be fucking ridiculous.'

'I'm so sorry ...' He grabbed her to get her to stop, then the grab became a hug. She felt his body shaking.

'What happened?' she asked eventually. 'Was there an accident?'

Lassie struggled to speak.

'Was there an accident?' she repeated, pushing him away.

'No.'

'Then what? I don't understand, you're telling me she was murdered?'

'No, Stell, it wasn't murder,' he said. 'They found her – in the alley, another tenant coming back into the building saw her ... it looks as though she ... Her apartment was on the fourth floor. There were no signs of forced entry.'

'Teri would never do that.'

'You can't know that.'

'And you can?' she snapped.

'None of us ...'

'I know her, Lassie. I know she wouldn't do that.'

'Stella, I'm really sorry, I know it brings up all kinds of stuff for you, but ...'

'Fuck that. I talked to her last night – she was great. There is no way she went home from the Boat Shed and threw herself off the balcony.'

'I'm telling you all I know.'

'This better not be your idea of a fucking wind-up.'

'Why in god's name would I do that?'

'I don't believe this.' Stella sat down on one of the kitchen chairs, then immediately stood up again. 'I don't believe you,' she said again. 'What about that fucker Ravosky – where was he?' Stella asked. She brushed her cheeks, her face was damp.

'Ravosky? That's a stretch isn't it?'

'Why? He was all over her last night. You said she works for him – maybe it was a business thing gone wrong … Teri knew too much about something … or an affair gone wrong.' Grabbing a couple of tissues from the box on the table she pressed them into her eyes.

'Look, I don't know many of the details. I probably shouldn't even know this much. Stella, you need to know … there was a chair up against the balcony.'

'Oh great,' she said. 'So it's signed, sealed and delivered to them on a platter.'

'That's a bit harsh. The police will be thorough and professional – you of all people should know that.'

She blew her nose, threw the tissues in the bin and took a swig of lukewarm coffee. There was a small piece of skin around her right thumbnail she picked at with her index finger. 'Was there a note?'

'Not that I know of – all I know is that they're notifying next of kin.'

'What about Kate? Who's going to tell her?'

'I managed to get hold of her this morning,' said Lassiter. 'Awful to tell her over the phone, she was a wreck. She's going to try to get back here sometime Monday, but it'll more likely be Tuesday or Wednesday.'

Stella needed a cigarette to help unclog the zinging noise in her ears. She didn't know where to look. Her tooth was starting up again, the low throbbing extended itself along her gum. She was having trouble focusing her eyes on anything, anything at all.

There were too many questions, the hamster in her head was back and it was running at full speed. She looked at Lassiter. He ran his hand over his head. Dark smudges sat under his eyes. He'd probably been up most of the night.

'Have you eaten?' she asked. Stella opened the bread drawer, found the Vogel's bag and banged a couple of slices into the toaster. 'Hang on, Teri had one of those ICE numbers in her phone, I know she did. I set it up for her, I told her it was one of the things that emergency workers look for when they get to a scene, so why the fuck did they call you?'

'Like I said, a mate on the force. He didn't say anything about her phone.'

Bloody hell, thought Stella. Unless things had drastically changed, it'd be McCarthy doing the investigating. Shit.

Her mind was jangling now. She needed to move. She needed the pool – she needed water, she needed to feel it on her skin. Lassiter could believe what he liked. Stella knew Teri wouldn't jump. But there was something she was missing. She had to think – to sort out the details, the facts. The toaster popped. Grabbing the hot slices she started to roughly butter them.

'Wait a minute,' she said. 'I need to check something.'

Stella raced upstairs, grabbed her laptop, opening it on the way down, pushing buttons and willing it to start up faster.

'Here it is, see?' She put the laptop on the table next to him and read out loud:

'Hey Stellanova, I hear you're coming back for the PARTY. It should be good and I can't wait to see you. I'm working on something at the moment, it's a bit hush-hush (sounds a bit James Bond, don't you think?) Anyway, I'd love your opinion on exactly how to proceed. I'll fill you in on the details when you're here. Safe travels, see you soon, xxxx T.'

'And that proves what exactly?' said Lassiter.

'That something was going on. We need to take this to the police.'

'Hush-hush could mean anything, she could have been working on a new recipe for cupcakes for all we know.'

'Don't be flippant.'

'I'm not. I'm just pointing out exactly what your mates in blue would say.'

Stella rubbed her eyes. He was right and he fucking knew it, so did she. It meant nothing. For a moment they were both quiet.

'Where are your parents?' he asked. 'We should let them know.'

'They booked a night at a hotel in the city, you know, for a bit of …'

'Yeah, I get the picture. I admire them actually.'

'Really?'

'Well, there's a lot that is admirable – they're still together for one thing.'

Stella fixed her eyes on the last of her toast. 'I can't sit here all day, what can we do to help?'

'There's not much we can do. We'll need to wait for the autopsy, the police report, the coroner's report.'

'I don't mean about those things, I mean what can we do to find out what happened?'

'It's not up to you, Stell. It's not your job.'

'Thanks for the reminder,' she said. 'Oh god, there'll be a funeral.'

'Yeah.'

'Something isn't right, Lassie. It's not fucking right.' She stood up and put her plate in the sink. 'I need to go there – I need to understand what's happened.'

'It won't solve anything or prove anything.'

'Maybe not, but I need to see it for myself.'

It was taped off when they arrived.

Stella stared up at the balcony, then down to the alleyway. Teri's apartment was four floors up. The balcony was clear glass topped with a metal railing. Could she have had too much to drink and lost her balance? Unlikely. So, who'd been up there with her?

Lassiter had said there weren't any signs of forced entry, so it had to be someone Teri knew. Stella knew the police would want to talk to those who'd had recent contact with her. Fuck, that would mean she'd have to go over it with McCarthy.

They'd removed her body, but the white tent was still in place preserving the scene. A couple of police cars were parked further along; no doubt the police would be going door to door to see if anyone knew or had seen anything. A lone skip sat along the street. The wall of a warehouse had a mural painted on one side, penguins marched up and over the side of the building. There were no pavements, the alley wasn't wide enough. Water dribbled off to one side down a grate where someone had washed the road clean.

One of the doors into the apartment building opened; a couple came out, green shopping bags in each hand. They paused, taking in the fluttering tape, the cars. The man shook his head. They hurried away.

It was a beautiful morning. The sun bounced off the windows up high, a shimmering, glinting light. A breeze scudded the clouds across the sky like bubbles in a bath.

Sunday morning shoppers swirled along the footpath on their way to the market. The coffee cart across the road was doing a brisk trade. A steady stream of affluence turned off the main road to visit Moore Wilson's food emporium.

Life continued. She felt Lassiter's hand on her back.

'Let's get out of here,' he said. 'Let's go up Mount Vic.'

6

MAD-DOG SHIVERED. The sun didn't reach down here. It had taken him a while to find this new place on the hillside. There were lots of trees, a bit of scrubby bush, then a dip in the land. It had been dug out years ago, a small quarry maybe, but was now totally overgrown. He needed to keep away from the main paths. Dogs could smell him. They'd come rushing down and he'd have to move again.

As usual he hadn't slept that well, worse last night though. He kept seeing the angel falling, fluttering, the sound she made, the smell of the bin. Each time she hit the ground he woke with a jolt.

Sitting up he peeled off his gloves and took the phone out of his pocket. The cracks on the front were still there, a permanent reminder in the shape of a broken spiderweb. It had buzzed a couple of times but he'd left it, it wasn't his to answer. She had thrown it to him, hadn't she? She had asked for his help, but what could he do? What was he supposed to do with it? Mad-Dog wasn't good at asking for help. He was invisible – he had no friends – unless he counted Rita. Well, Rita and Warren. Warren was a friend of sorts, helped him out when he needed. Trouble was, Warren needed the drink, which made him unpredictable. Mad-Dog wasn't always keen to spend large amounts of time with him.

Mad-Dog understood if he kept away from the drink he wouldn't hurt anyone again. He couldn't go there. Nonetheless, Warren was a good bloke and Gus, Gus was definitely a friend, but Mad-Dog didn't like to think about people too much. Thinking about people made him remember things. The fallen star didn't belong to him; he didn't like having something that wasn't his.

Now that he had it, he wasn't sure what to do. The angel had given it to him – like a runner in a relay race she had thrown it to him. He could take it to the police station, but they'd just start asking him questions. He could leave it at a bus shelter, but then he couldn't be sure that someone else would do the right thing. No, it was up to him to sort it out. Rita, Warren or Gus?

I'll go and see Gus, he thought. Gus didn't push him, didn't question him too much. He just made cups of tea and fed him warm pastries. Mad-Dog shivered. Mornings were always the worst out here. He felt stiff and cold. He shuffled a few things around and found the last of some food. Pulling his hat down over his ears he lay down and burrowed deep into the sleeping bag. Cardboard would definitely help. Sometime today he would leave his camp and head back to the skip – he needed to walk to warm up – but later, he would leave later. Eyes closed, his mind drifting. Mad-Dog started to hum, then whistle lightly through his teeth, 'Là ci darem la mano' from Mozart's *Don Giovanni*.

Such beautiful music. It had been a favourite of hers, of theirs. He continued to hum … and she's there, being seduced on stage by the Don.

The orchestra plays with her – cradling her voice as they meld into one. He can't see her – he's in the pit at her feet – but he hears her. His songbird, up in the trees, with a voice so exquisite it makes grown men weep.

7

STELLA AND LASSIE WOUND their way through the narrow streets up to the Mount Vic lookout. They passed the monastery on the corner and the million-dollar houses nestled smugly into the hillside. The afternoon stretched out in front of them – through the trees the harbour glistened and sparkled.

They drove in silence.

She leaned her head back and closed her eyes. That's the thing about being away for so long, she thought, life just chugs on without you. The city moves and diverges but you're not there to see the changes, no matter how small they might be.

Cities move on, just like people.

Stella wondered if she could ever live here again and smiled remembering Teri's bear hug. Maybe she could, maybe she could put it all behind her, start again. Wellington wasn't so bad, trouble was there was always the other shit.

Stella's eyes were heavy. In her exhausted whirring brain she was in another car. A police car.

There had been a call to the station, a distressed woman, a suicidal woman. Stella was the constable on duty. She had to go. She'd driven this road countless times. She'd seen the body in her dreams. Occasionally the dream would be different. There might be a different person in the squad car with her. Sometimes there was a crowd of people she had to push through. Sometimes the scene would be transferred to a beach with the sound of gulls screeching, waves crashing onto a stony shore. Other times she walked into the room by herself. But the outcome stayed the same.

It was always the same body, with William somewhere in the room. He would turn around, tears streaming down his face. 'We did this to her,' he'd say. She would try to speak, but as with most dreams the sound never got past her throat. Dry, rasping sounds would be all she could manage. She would fill her lungs with air and try again, same thing.

She'd be left in limbo, unable to close her eyes at the sight of the body, hands hanging limply at her sides, the wedding band glinting in the pale light of the dream. Like a hamster on a wheel, it would start over, from the beginning.

Wash and repeat.

Wash and repeat.

I have nothing to say, thought Stella, there aren't any words for this. Were there signs? Did I miss something with Teri last night? She'd seen what I went through with Dee and William. Have I become so self absorbed, so absent that I don't notice the signs? Was Teri trying to tell me something and I just couldn't hear it?

No, this wasn't her, Teri was a fighter. She gave to life; she didn't take life away and definitely not her own. They'd talked about this, they had, especially after 'the incident' as it became known. Teri had soothed her, reassured her. She'd taken away the half-full bottles of whisky, tucked her into bed and told her things would get better.

Stella was lost. Her stomach wove itself into an intricate boy-scout knot. She cradled her cheek with her hand. The ache in her jaw was starting. She pulled a couple of tissues from the box on the floor and blew her nose.

Lassie parked the car and they sat there for a few moments.

'Come on,' he said. 'Let's just walk to the top.'

They got out of the car and walked slowly up the steps to the viewing platform. Wellington surrounded them.

The wind was stronger up here, the clouds pushed away to the north. It was clear enough to see the South Island, the inland Kaikōura range jagged in the distant haze. The turbine on Brooklyn Hill spun crazily above the Sunday walkers. Stella shrank into the collar of her coat, stood shoulder to shoulder with Lassie and watched as the Picton ferry lumbered into the harbour.

'You never talked about it,' he said.

'What?' She kept her eyes firmly on the harbour.

'You and William and what happened.'

'There was never anything to say,' she said. 'Besides, you never asked.'

'I was probably too afraid to ask. Did you love him?'

A strangled laugh died in her throat. 'I'm not sure that love was ever part of the equation.'

'So, how long will you keep punishing yourself for it?'

She leaned forward and put her head in her hands. Punishment, retribution, penance, they were all just words, designed to label something that would never go away. How on earth could she explain the night sweats, the shaking, the overwhelming waves of guilt that had threatened to drown her.

It wasn't love.

It was never that. Had she known his wife was pregnant? Yes, she had. Had she kept fucking him? Yes. Had she ever imagined his wife would hang herself?

At the end of it all the punishment for their actions was they both had to live with the images, the continuous flickering film. Cruellest was that moment of waking. Those brief seconds of calm before it all started up again. Stella was poison, she understood that. Everything she touched eventually turned to shit.

Now Teri.

Teri wasn't a suicide. She just wasn't. Stella didn't believe it. Wouldn't believe it. She needed to leave soon – London would be better than this. Anything would be better. Her jaw ached. Her head was clamouring with noise, fucking noise. Alcohol would help.

Lassie and Stella stood there. The wind tugged at their clothes. She shivered only partly from the cold. He put an arm around her shoulder, she didn't resist.

'Living is punishment,' Stella said. 'There's only one way out.'

They were joined by a couple – young and in love Japanese tourists – who posed in true tourist style. Stella and Lassie watched them giggle as they looked at the images. The recent past captured on their phones.

Stella found her anger and held it close.

It had power; it would keep her going.

8

By the time she surfaced the next day, both her parents were at work. Stella needed the pool. She needed to keep busy – she needed to push herself away from the freight train threatening to pulverise her head. Swimming was the one thing Stella could do anywhere, at any time, in any weather. It calmed her, allowed her to think. It worked like a moving deprivation tank – you couldn't talk, or sing, or whistle. You couldn't see people around you, and it made you work up a sweat. Mostly it allowed her to empty her head of the rushing sound that was building.

The funeral would be later in the week. Today she'd go to the pool, then see if her mum needed a hand. A fun few days in paradise, she thought. Hunting around in her mother's dresser she found a pair of togs that would fit. She'd buy goggles at the pool.

Stella let herself out of the house and made her way down to the city. The morning rush of people walking to work was over. She strode along The Terrace, took the steps to Lambton Quay, made her way to Ghuznee Street, then through Cuba Mall. Most of the shops wouldn't open until ten or later and the mall was still in shade. Stella got a takeout coffee from one of the cafés and kept walking towards the waterfront.

At the leaning man statue, she stopped to watch a single scull boat slide out of the lagoon into the harbour. Like a skater on ice, pull, glide, pull, glide. There was something hypnotic about that movement. A bit like swimming, a bit like falling.

It was balance, breathing, a complete body movement as smooth as a piece of glass worn by the sea. She glanced down at the bronze plaque, *Solace in the Wind*. That was her leaning man.

She tried focusing on the boat sliding further out into the harbour, pull, glide. But time and time again it was the image of Dee at the end of the rope, like slow falling. It sped up every viewing to become a movie newsreel spinning too fast. London had kept her busy, kept her away from anything that might trigger that reel in her head. Three days back in Wellington and it had started again. The hamsters on their shitty little wheel in her head.

This was where she and Teri had walked, or sat countless times, countless conversations, coffees and glasses of wine.

'Don't go,' Teri had said.

'I have to go, you know that,' said Stella.

'No, I don't. I can't help but think you're running away.'

'Of course I am. I need to get as far away from this crap as is humanly possible.'

'But London? Don't go, stay and face it.'

'She wanted me to find her, Teri. She phoned when she was sure I'd be at work, she set up the whole scene. She even left the front door unlocked so I'd go into the house. I keep seeing it in my head.'

'Have you spoken to Mitchell?'

Stella laughed. 'Mitchell Lassiter has made his disapproval of me quite clear.'

'Are you sure about that? He cares about you, he really does.'

'That's all a matter of perspective.'

'What about Auckland?'

'What do you mean?' asked Stella.

'I mean, go and live in Auckland or Dunedin, or anywhere for a while. It'll die down.'

'New Zealand is a fishbowl, Teri, you know that. I'd be there for a couple of months, maybe six, someone would find out and the rumour mill would start. There's Constable Stella Weston. The one who had an affair with a married colleague,' she said, 'wife hung herself in the garage, Weston found the body, yadda, yadda, yadda.'

'She was mentally unwell,' said Teri. 'He said so himself.'

Yes, she might have been, thought Stella. But Dee had also been four months pregnant.

She shook her head. Jesus, what the fuck was that? Teri wasn't here. Her eyes blurred with tears.

This may be home, she thought, but she knew she couldn't stay.

Outside Freyberg Pool the fountain pushed up a stream of water that sparkled in the morning sun; the pale sand, barged in from Golden Bay, shone in the light. She walked down to the small beach area. The light, so different from English sun, so sharp, stung her eyes, relentlessly cutting through everything. She watched as the Interislander ferry swirled past Matiu/Somes and disappeared to the South Island. Admittedly this section of waterfront was perfect on a day like this, but everything looked beautiful in sunlight.

Standing at the end of the breakwater, the city was to her left, and the Hutt Valley sat in a faint mist to her right. Like overbearing matrons, the moneyed apartments of Oriental Bay pushed against her back. She looked down at the water sloshing around the concrete foundations.

The pool was quiet; it would be busy in the very early morning, and again in the late afternoon. But for now there was an aquacise class under way and very few lane swimmers. The fit young instructor called out directions from poolside, while the older participants, like ageing mermaids, swished and swirled in the water.

Stella changed and slipped into the shallow end. The

chlorine smell, the heat mixed with the rush of cold air from opening doors was soothingly familiar. She stretched out, length after length freestyle, her arms slicing through the blue. A practised tumble-turn at the end of each length – then stretching out again she tried to emulate the smooth motion of the boat.

Pull and glide.

Pressure built in her lungs. Her arms were giving out, she reached the shallow end and stopped. Eighteen lengths, that was a joke. She could usually do at least forty before she had to stop. It was the smokes but hey, we all have our weaknesses.

Peeling off the goggles she leaned against the side of the pool, her head a mess of thoughts that she was having difficulty sorting out. Anger pushed against the lack of sleep and the dregs of jet lag didn't help. The exercise made blood thump through her jaw, a pneumatic drill into her head. She felt each heartbeat with each throb.

Fuck this tooth.

For the first time in a very long time, she felt her brain wasn't keeping up with events. Each time she turned her head there was a split second for her eyes to catch up. The light slanted through the windows, played off the water; a couple of other swimmers were doing lengths. Splashes echoed off the walls. The music from the aquacise class pounded along the tiles. She rubbed her eyes. There was no way round it, if she wanted to find out anything about Teri she'd have to grit her teeth and talk to DI Meathead McCarthy.

Putting her goggles back on Stella pushed off the wall. A little slower this time but still working at stretching out her arms. It helped ease the ache in her back between her shoulders. Her brain whirred into action – what was Teri playing at? Why on earth had she been with Ravosky? Stella had found nothing when she researched him; he seemed clean. She could see the attraction on one level and she'd certainly come across that mutually beneficial arrangement many times, but she never imagined Teri to be the type.

Her PI job in London had required her tailing men whose wives thought they were cheating on them, usually with a younger woman. Invariably, they were right – a woman's intuition and all of that. Trouble was a great many men were really stupid. Like little boys in a sweet shop dipping their hands into any jar they fancied, thinking the woman at home wouldn't suspect, let alone do anything about it. Maybe that's what happened. She needed to check if Ravosky was married. Maybe Teri had been threatened by a jealous wife. But suicide? It didn't add up.

She didn't think there was any way she'd be able to get her hands on Teri's phone or laptop. She didn't have any credentials in this country, not really. Her police work was long, long ago and best forgotten. Her PI work in the UK wouldn't stand for much here. But it was worth a try.

She needed to talk to Ravosky. Teri's death wouldn't change a thing in his life – he'd just get another pretty face to boost his ego. She finished in the water and made her way to the changing rooms. She checked her phone for messages. Nothing. Stella felt irritable, the painkillers she'd swilled before leaving the house were taking their own sweet time; if she was going to get to the bottom of Teri's death, she needed a plan.

Swimming hadn't really helped.

Walking might.

9

OUTSIDE THE POOL Stella zipped up her jacket. The wind had got up – the sea looked choppy. There wasn't any sign of the rower on the water and the early morning brightness had gone. Clouds swirled in over the hills, low and grey. Rain threatened the air, and the dark green bush covering the hilltops pushed the buildings down to the sea. Or maybe it was the other way around and the buildings were clawing a hold on the land. A dull thudding sound pulsated in the distance as the incoming Bluebridge ferry backed laboriously into its berth. Tourists would disembark, see a concrete-grey Wellington and think it was like this all the time. They'd tell their friends of the city's inhospitable hills and cool wind.

Everything fights for its place in this landscape: the hills, the bush, the people, the buildings, even the coastline and sea. It wasn't long ago that where she was standing would have been far into the harbour. Land reclamation had solved that little problem. Just push your way into the sea; it won't fight back.

Stella stopped by the leaning man and stared over to the CBD. She sat down by the sculpture and rested against his legs; they were cool against her back. *Solace in the Wind.* Solace – comfort in times of distress. She looked to the other side of the harbour. Boats came in, boats went out. Water sloshed around the piles. She was thirty-three, soon to be thirty-four. Childless, for all intents and purposes partner-less, in a job that covered the bills with not much more. She lived in a far-off city where, if she died, few would mourn her. Maybe Lassie was right – how long was she going to punish herself? This wasn't living. There would always be that limping sensation of having a stone in her shoe. That would never leave, but maybe it was worn down enough. Everyone deserves a second chance, don't they?

Then she saw her.

Partially submerged.

'Oh,' Stella whispered. 'Oh, shit.' She could see there was no need to jump in or climb down the ladder for a rescue. That would only disturb potential evidence.

Floating on her back, her eyes mostly closed; one hand rested lightly on her belly, the other outstretched, palm up – mouth partially open. Her delicate neck was wound around with tendrils of seaweed. She was small, pale and unmistakably dead. The sea had performed its duty and delivered her back to the world.

Salt water washed the small pearly teeth. She couldn't have been there long – her skin looked intact, not bloated. Long black hair melted into the sea. She wore a white T-shirt and short skirt, not enough clothing for this time of year. Her tiny feet were bare. The sea rocked her up and down, like a mother calming a fractious child. This was someone's daughter, someone's child. Their life, too, was about to be torn apart.

Stella stood. She could leave, just walk away. She could leave some poor sucker to find what she'd stumbled across. There would, most likely, be CCTV along this stretch of wharf. There was no way, on god's green earth, she wanted any involvement in this. Teri was enough of a shock. Not this as well. Stella looked again. She must be only eight or nine. A child. Why the fuck did this have to be a child. Stella's mouth was dry. Her fists tightly clenched. She felt herself start to shake. *Come on, Weston, pull yourself together. You've seen a dead body before.*

Pulling out her phone, she pressed 111 then sat next to the leaning man.

A seagull screeched overhead to its mates on the wharf, several made their way over to where Stella was sitting. 'Piss off.' She waved her arm.

A woman pushing a buggy ran past, oblivious to the drama about to unfold – the coffee cart up by the bridge was devoid of customers. Banners advertising the latest exhibition at the museum fluttered in the breeze. She looked down to the water, blinked and looked again, just to be sure.

They didn't take long. Soon the place was swarming with police and the whole area taped off. Stella stayed sitting on the wharf, resting her head on her knees.

'Well, well, if it isn't Stella Weston.'

She looked up. Oh shit. 'McCarthy,' said Stella. 'Or should that be DI McCarthy?'

'I heard you were back in the country,' he said.

'Keeping tabs on me, are you?' She stood up.

'Tabs? Not at all, but I bagged your friend the other day. You know we'll need to talk to you about that, and here you are again.' He folded his arms across his chest. 'You have a habit of appearing where there's dead bodies, Weston. Is there something you're not telling us?'

'Fuck you, McCarthy.'

A crowd was gathering with phones at the ready, all recording their version of events. Like the seagulls, they stood waiting to pick over the remains, take them back to their safe lives in the café or the pub. Stella felt a hand on her shoulder. He was there again, in her face, standing just a little too close. He needed to shave. The rancid smell of long hours in the office drifted off him; there were dark smudges under his eyes.

'I understand you found the body?' said McCarthy.

'Yes, I did.'

'Just happen upon it, did you?'

'Yes, I did.'

'Did you go down the ladder to see if she was still alive?'

'Of course not.'

'No? Why not?'

'There was no reason. It was obvious she was dead and I didn't want to disturb any evidence.'

'You're certain of that?'

'Yes, I am.'

'Have you been drinking?'

'Excuse me?' She took a step back from him.

'It's a standard question, Weston.'

'No,' she said. 'Unless you count the coffee I had.'

'Just out for a walk?'

'No.'

'What was your business on the wharf?' McCarthy asked. He was enjoying this. Any junior PC could have asked all this stuff, but he wanted to it. Arrogant prick. He wanted to keep her there for as long as possible. They were standing off to one side of the crowd.

The officials on the police launch removed the body from the water. They'd need to be careful to protect any evidence that might be useful. As usual the media was there in a heartbeat. A journalist stood to one side and primped her hair before presenting the tragedy on the night's infotainment segment that masqueraded as news.

'I said, what was your business on the wharf?' McCarthy asked again.

'My business?'

'Yes, why were you walking along the wharf at this time?'

'My business, as you put it, was that I was walking home from having been at the pool.'

'You have proof of that?'

'What? You want to see my wet togs, is that it?' she said, holding out her bag.

'We have procedures, Weston,' he said. 'I need to know

that you're not involved in this in any way.'

'You truly amaze me and I don't mean that as a compliment.'

'You'll have to come in for questioning and a formal statement. You know the drill, unless you've been out of the game so long you've forgotten.'

'Do you shit around with all your witnesses, McCarthy?'

He leaned his head down closer to her ear. 'No, no, just you, Weston, just you.'

The air was salty – she felt it on her tongue. The crowd was being managed. A light flashed from a camera. There was a body in the water, parents who would need to be informed, funeral arrangements made. Stella kept seeing the hand, upturned, loose fingers. The seaweed moving in time with her tiny body and the sea itself; the open eyes, a glimpse of her foot. There's something so vulnerable about bare feet, she thought. Such a small foot, no shoes, and a silver chain with the tiny bells around her ankle.

Eventually McCarthy stopped. 'You're free to go for now, but remember you'll need to come in for the formal chat,' he said. 'We'll expect to see you very soon.'

Stella saw the journalist heading in her direction.

'Were you the one who found her?' called the journo.

'Fuck off,' said Stella.

10

CHARLOTTE HAD HER HANDS on the wheel at ten and two.

She sat forward slightly; her head tilted towards the front window. She always drove like that, careful, aware. Charlotte was the younger of the two of them. Stella had always had that over her, being older, but Charlotte was all artfully streaked blonde hair, hints of perfume and soft hands. She had perfected the art of being perfect; she seldom raised her voice; she sent thank-you notes. Stella often thought that her sister was like some modern-day, misplaced, Jane Austen character. 'Why yes, Miss Charlotte, your carriage awaits.' Stella slunk into the seat, thinking that no doubt Charlotte saw her as a Danish crime novel wannabe, not that her sister read that sort of thing – too much blood and violence.

'I don't understand why you're so reluctant, Stell.'

'Well, it's a nice thought but I'm not sure a massage and a bit of pampering is going to solve anything.'

'I know, but especially now after what you've been through, y'know, with Teri … I thought it would be good to have some relaxing time.'

Stella looked over at her, then back out the window. Her jaw hurt from clamping it shut. Her lips were dry and a little cracked; she ran a finger over the rough surface. She certainly didn't want to talk to Charlotte about the girl in the water. It had been all over the news this morning, journalists talking to bystanders, microphones in faces: 'How did you feel when you heard there was a body?' How the fuck do you think they felt?

It was difficult enough for them both to deal with Teri's death. Like a jumpy film reel, images flashed in front of her eyes. How Teri would have looked on the pavement, her white dress like petals fanned around her. Her beautiful blonde hair over her face, her head at an unnatural angle, an arm awkwardly placed under her body. There would be the flash of cameras, a light drizzle, police, cars, people staring.

She'd been to enough crime scenes to know the drill, but this time her friend was at the centre of it. One thing we often fear, she thought, is a lack of control. Suicide is the ultimate control act. I will take my own life on my terms. That wasn't Teri; it just wasn't.

This morning the inlet looked like glass, the hills wetting their feet in the high tide. A shag dived and broke the water sending small ripples to either shore. The last of the morning's traffic was straggling into the city. Stella laughed when people talked about rush hour here; it was nothing compared to a decent-sized city. In London there was a constant rush, everyone all the time, straining to be somewhere else. Cars, buses, the Tube, bicycles, all of them rushing. Here it was pedestrian, in more ways than she could poke a stick at.

Stella knew Charlotte was trying to be kind with this spa day. 'You're right, and thanks for thinking of me, it's really thoughtful of you,' she said, 'but you didn't mention anything about, hang on let me read it out …' Stella found the pamphlet and ostentatiously cleared her throat. 'Here you go: *The Aqua Vitae Day Spa, where women will discover their own unique magic while experiencing a deepening sisterhood amongst the feminine spirits. You will be given the opportunity to live courageously, to embrace the unique mystery that is woman and the magic of self.* Oh, please.'

Charlotte laughed. 'And if I had, you wouldn't have come with me.'

'You're not wrong there.' Stella was dying for a smoke.

'Well, it's up to you. You don't have to do all of it. There's a café on site, you can sit there while I do my thing.'

'I should have brought a book.'

'Don't whinge.'

'I'm not whinging. I hate being bored, besides why did we have to leave at sparrow's fart? You know I don't do mornings.'

'Stella, it's 9 AM, hardly a farting sparrow around. Look, I'm sorry. I just wanted to do something nice, to spend some time together. We've all got to get through the funeral on Friday. How about we have a restful time today.'

'Sorry, Lottie, I didn't sleep that well and I don't mean to sound petulant. It really is very kind of you, but seriously what's the point?'

Charlotte took a deep breath. 'Not everything has to have a point.'

'Yes it does,' said Stella.

'What, like Teri's death?' said Charlotte. 'Did that have a point?' They were both quiet for a moment. Charlotte cleared her throat. 'Sorry, that sounded a bit harsh.'

'No, you're right, I'm not sure what the point of her death was.'

Anger pushed at Stella's throat, everything that came out was coloured red and she didn't know how to stop it. Sniping at her sister wouldn't help anything or anyone. Images of Teri appeared again, Teri at uni, at parties, with a hangover, laughing herself stupid. Those times when her relentless positivity could be just a bit much and Stella had to bite her tongue. Their trip to Thailand, where they'd hung out, been tourists, eaten cheap food and swum in the warm clear water. Stella could feel adrenaline building; it sat across her shoulders and down her arms. She needed the pool again – that would help, she thought. Moving through water, the feeling of weightlessness had always been her way of de-stressing. What the fuck was she doing sitting in a car?

The light was strong; she'd become soft with the hazy light in London, the morning glare hurt her head. You barely needed sunglasses in Europe, more for a fashion statement than anything else. The designer air freshener hanging from the mirror swayed backwards and forwards. Stella watched as it released the scent of acceptability with waltz-like movements. She didn't like travelling like this. She didn't like being a passenger, it meant she had nothing to do except think. The train whooshed past, heading back into Wellington, clicketty clack. Stella pushed her tongue against her dodgy tooth, as Charlotte pulled up to stop at the Plimmerton lights. A small fishing boat motored out towards Mana Island – the beach was empty apart from one lone walker.

'I need a coffee,' said Stella. 'Why can't we stop for a coffee?'

'You can have one when we get there.'

'Is that allowed, caffeine?'

'Course it is,' said Charlotte.

'I thought it would have been all herbal, organic and vegetarian.'

'Well, if you took better care of yourself maybe you'd feel not quite so rubbish.'

Stella looked at her sister again – she never used to be like this. Charlotte could knock back enough alcohol to fell a small elephant in her day. She also knew she'd smoked, and not just good old tobacco either. Where was all this healthy crap coming from? Stella leaned forward to check the glove compartment.

'What are you hunting for?' Charlotte asked.

'Have you got any chocolate, or mints?'

'Just sugar-free ones.'

'Jesus, next you'll be telling me that you've taken up yoga,' said Stella, 'and you're training for a marathon.'

'Well, if you must know, I do go to a yoga class and I'm training for a half-marathon in October.'

'Okay, that's it. Who are you and what have you done with my sister?'

Charlotte turned in her seat to face Stella. 'I keep busy. I work part-time. I try not to focus on it. I try not to let it consume my life. Ben and I have been trying to get pregnant for the last two and a half years,' she said in a rush, 'but nothing has happened. I need to understand why it's not happening; I need to find what the point of it all is.'

The lights changed and Charlotte returned her eyes to the road. For the longest length of time Stella stared straight ahead, the morning shadows on the hills gave them a surreal look. Patchwork shades, brown from the summer heat, jostled the emerging green. A few bouts of rain would change that.

'Why didn't you say anything?'

'Once again,' said Charlotte, 'it's not the easiest thing to put in an email. We've kept it pretty quiet really, I thought if I put it in writing it would be too real. I'm still hoping for a miracle.'

'You could have phoned.'

'I tried a few times – you always seemed too busy.'

'I'm sorry,' said Stella. 'I'm really sorry, I had no idea.' She reached over and stroked Charlotte's arm.

'Yeah, well that's life, isn't it?' said her sister.

The car crested the hill at Pukerua Bay. Kāpiti Island lazed in the early sun. The sea was shades of green and blue, calm with white frosting along the edges. Stella knew this view in her sleep, she'd dreamed of it many times the years she'd been away. As they neared Paekākāriki Charlotte drove into the left lane.

'Why are you turning off here? I thought we were going to Waikanae.'

Charlotte laughed. 'To be honest, Stell, I'm not sure they have caffeine where we're going. I'd hate you to have a full-blown tantrum when we get there.' She smiled at her sister.

'Bless you, my child. You've done a good thing.'

Stella stayed in the car while Charlotte got takeaway coffees from the local café. Yeah, this was Paekākāriki, she thought. Large sliding doors from the café opened to the street, and umbrellas shaded the brightly painted tables on the foot-path. A dog waited patiently under one of them. An old brown crockery bowl sat to one side, filled with water for thirsty pooches, and a hand-made sign read: *Free Canine Refreshment.*

Stella thought of the times she and Teri used to have Sunday brunch at the Fig Café on Tinakori Road, huddled inside out of the wind. They'd sit in the corner, away from the window, nursing their Saturday night excesses. Swapping stories, they'd vow to never indulge like that again; it stayed that way all the time they were at uni. Things changed a little when Stella joined the police training programme, but they always managed to find time for each other. That was gone now. She took a sharp breath in. Her shoulders tightened.

Teri was gone. The image she had of her at the balcony, that split-second moment when she went over …

No. Teri didn't do it.

Stella shook her head slightly and rolled her shoulders to try and relax them. She'd pretty much taken an instant dislike to Ravosky. She could be quick off the mark – she'd been told so many times before – but instinct is a power-ful thing; she could smell all kinds of bullshit at twenty paces.

They drove out to the seafront and, leaning against the car, sipped their coffee. The way the sun shone made Kāpiti

Island look like a solid shape on the horizon, a child's wonky cut-out from a sky-coloured piece of paper.

'How about you, Stella, do you want kids?'

'I'm not sure,' she said, 'I really don't know. Actually, I've never really given it much thought.' Stella was walloped by the image of Dee's pregnant body at the end of the rope, the PJs, the chair toppled over on the garage floor.

'Are you okay? You look kind of funny,' said Charlotte.

'No, I'm fine. It's just the bloody jet lag. It catches me out sometimes and I've got a bit of toothache.'

'Yeah, jet lag can be a bitch.' Charlotte sipped her coffee. 'I know it's not very twenty-first century, but all I've ever wanted was to be a mum.'

'Crikey, is this the bit where I volunteer to carry triplets for you?'

Charlotte laughed. 'No, but thanks for the thought, sort of. Triplets eww, no way.'

'I see myself as the fabulous aunty, y'know, telling them all the things that you won't, keeping them up late, spoiling them rotten, then sending them back home for you and Ben to sort out.'

'Mum's desperate for grandkids. She doesn't say much, but I know it's there. You're not much help in that department and Tim is AWOL – it seems it's up to me.'

'So where is he?'

'Tim?' said Charlotte. 'Goodness knows. Mum's convinced he's homeless on the street somewhere. Dad just looks sad whenever I mention him. Honestly, Stell, they both put on a brave face, I'm amazed we all managed to get through Saturday night,' she said, and quickly flicked her hair over her shoulder. 'The last time I heard from him he was in Auckland, but that was months ago, and even then he mentioned something about moving to Nelson. He doesn't have a phone, so we have to wait for him to contact us.'

Maybe Lassie was right, thought Stella, how well do we really know anyone? Her sister was longing for something that may or may not happen and she'd had no idea about it. Her brother was possibly a homeless bum – how the hell had that happened? We all keep secrets, she thought. We bend the notion of truth, the flow of information. She'd done the same thing herself, convincing those around her that life in London was great. It wasn't lying as such, just controlling the story, the narrative she wished to tell.

'So, what else do you get up to, Charlotte?' said Stella. 'I mean apart from practising making babies with Ben. What's this job you've got?'

'I've been working for Audrey, you know, in the antiques shop along from Mum's. She's been showing me how the business works. She travels a lot, so I fill in for her.'

'Sounds very *Antiques Roadshow*.'

'Yeah, it's quite fascinating really. I've been doing research on provenance and that kind of stuff. Who knows, I may become an expert in nineteenth-century colonial furniture. She's a funny old bird, I can't quite make her out.' Charlotte smiled at her sister. 'Bit like you really.'

'Thanks a heap, sis.'

Charlotte drained the last of her coffee. 'I miss you, you know. Is there a chance you'll ever come back?'

Stella shrugged her shoulders in reply. 'Come on, let's get this over with,' she said.

They tossed their cups in the bin and headed towards Waikanae. Stella had to admit it was a stunning day. Her shoulders were tight and the idea of a really good massage was beginning to appeal to her. It was amazing how her outlook could change at the consumption of a decent coffee.

*

Stella and Charlotte walked up the steps to the spa reception.

'Lovely to see you again, Mrs Fitzgerald.'

Confused, Stella frowned – when had Charlotte started using her husband's name? 'Have you been here before?' she asked.

'Yeah, a couple of times. I came with Teri. She wanted the company and I had the time. She's the reason I know about this place.'

Stella looked at her sister. There was a frailty about her she hadn't ever noticed before. Charlotte, perfect Charlotte, always-on-time Charlotte, toned-and-groomed Charlotte, was only just managing to keep things together. Stella felt as though all the people she thought she remembered were other versions of themselves; or that she was holding on to an idea of people that was slipping through her fingers. They looked the same, maybe a little greyer like Lassiter and her dad, but what came out of their mouths was unpredictable. It was unsettling, like landing in a parallel universe without a map. Or being in a play where everyone else knew their lines, but she was always a page behind.

Stella declined the Reiki session along with the rebirthing class but said yes to the massage and sauna. They agreed to meet in the café at lunchtime. 'For sprouts and green tea,' Charlotte said with a grin.

Flicking open the visitor's book that sat on the counter, Stella scanned her eyes down the list. Teri's name jumped out, the curve of her handwriting was unmistakable. She frowned at the name underneath. Snapping the book shut, she pressed her open palm firmly on the cover.

'Stella, are you okay?' Charlotte asked. 'You look a bit ...'

'I'm fine.'

11

MAD-DOG HOISTED HIS BAG and rope on his shoulder. He checked his camp was well camouflaged then walked down the faded lumpy track towards the communal garden. He waited, hidden in the trees to make sure the area was empty. He didn't want to scare anyone from the apartment blocks by lurching out of the undergrowth. At this time in the afternoon the place was empty. Today was Monday – he knew that. It was one of the things he kept track of: weeknights and weekends were busier, with people tending their plots or visiting the community room. His eyes roamed over the notices stuck on the door. Yoga on Thursday, a buggy for sale, a mindfulness meditation retreat from last month, an excess of feijoas on offer.

He liked this area.

He liked that it was used.

Sometimes he'd sit on the bench during the day and feel he was part of the garden, part of life. Occasionally he would harvest some of the produce: baby carrots, an apple off one of the trees, a handful of parsley. Always careful to rotate his way around the different gardens so as to leave little trace of his pilfering.

Mad-Dog thought about heading back to the skip where he'd seen the cardboard – he'd left before he could get any – but he worried there would be too many people. Best to go later when it was dark.

He was hungry again. He tried not to think about it, thinking about it made it worse. Walking helped. Helped keep him warm, too, kept his mind on other things. He didn't want to think about the angel anymore, or the sound she'd made, how she'd looked splayed out on the concrete.

Pulling his coat around him, Mad-Dog fossicked in the pocket for his knitted hat. It was soft and very warm. Rita had given it to him. He smiled when he thought of Rita.

He made his way out through the gate by the row of wooden compost bins and started walking down Majoribanks Street. The sole on his right shoe was starting to come loose, step, flap, step, flap. He'd have to be careful or he'd trip. In his other pocket was a pair of gloves; he put them on. It wasn't too cold now but he liked to cover as much of himself as possible

Mad-Dog turned left into Brougham Street. There were times he couldn't walk this route and he'd have to go all the way down Majoribanks, but tonight he was okay. Just before he crossed over Elizabeth Street he stopped. Elizabeth.

Elizabeth.

Behind his eyelids there's light, a woman across the table, he's cutting up some meat, she's holding a glass, her small hand over her mouth trying to stifle a laugh, lots of laughing and he's gazing back at her.

A motorbike roared past and he was back on Brougham Street. Mad-Dog carried on. Number thirty-two had that music playing again. It wasn't really music, just bass notes thumping a sad excuse, but he waited for a minute before moving on.

Step, flap. Step, flap.

Brougham Street had big houses with fancy letterboxes. He could smell cooking. Mad-Dog stood with his eyes closed, enveloped himself in the warm kitchen smells.

Step, flap. Step, flap.

Mad-Dog turned right into Pirie Street, then cut through a couple of the back streets towards the skip where he'd been the other night when the angel fell. He screwed up his eyes, not wanting to hear that scream again, or the thump. He stopped for a minute to catch his breath then took the phone out of his pocket and looked at it. The fallen star he called it, so much prettier than a phone, or mobile. It connected him to the fluttering angel woman in the white dress. What he'd seen, it wasn't right. But it wasn't his business, whatever went on. It didn't concern him. No one noticed him, no one would believe him.

They'd look at him that particular way. There'd be trouble.

No. Best to stay out of it all.

He tucked the phone back into the left pocket of his suit jacket; in truth it was of no use to him. There was no one left for him to call, apart from Rita, or Gus. He'd call either of them if he could.

Or he could just go and visit.

That was easier.

It chirruped in his pocket, like a trapped insect.

He pulled it out but as usual he was at a complete loss. This one was black now. No lights. No nothing. The glass screen was cracked where it had hit the side of the skip.

Mad-Dog didn't like talking to people, so he put it straight back in his pocket. Most people used phones – he saw them on the street talking into them, making arrangements, showing friends things on the small screen.

It still surprised him that people had such busy lives and lived them on their phones.

'How's it going?'

'Darren, hi. It's Scott.'

'You busy tonight?'

'No, she didn't, she didn't, you're joking.'

'What a cow.'

'You wanna hang?'

'Yep, I'm just at the bus stop.'

None of what he heard was necessary, none of it important. All of the things he gleaned and overheard on the street were inconsequential, but people still did it, they talked and laughed into their own fallen stars. Plastic and ether and wires tenuously holding lives together.

He would visit Gus, he would know what to do.

12

HUMAN TOUCH CAN BE quite magical, thought Stella. This, however, wasn't. Her tormentor's name was Corrine.

'I am Corrine,' she'd said in a deep accented voice. They'd shaken hands and that was the sum total of the conversation. Stella didn't mind, she didn't have the energy for small talk. She lay face down on the massage table and, with her head though the small hole, stared at Corrine's feet. They were bare, strong, planted on the wooden floorboards, like piles driven into the ground.

Stella felt the strong Eastern European hands kneading her like tough dough. Each vein stood out on those hands and roped their way up her arms. Pulling, stretching, Corrine ground into all the tight places along Stella's shoulders and back. She tried not to groan with the pain. It wasn't supposed to hurt like this, was it?

Corrine seemed to know what she was doing. She managed to get into all the right spots. The oil she was using smelt of fresh mown grass with a hint of something medicinal, but good grief it was painful. Stella relished it in a masochistic way. Feeling something was better than the numbness that had taken hold.

Oh fuck, Stella could feel herself starting to cry. She sniffed, loudly.

At one stage the door opened and, mercifully, briefly, Corrine stopped. Stella took some deep breaths in preparation for the next bout of pain.

A small voice said, 'More towels for you.'

'Thank you, you can put them over there,' Corrine said.

Gentle footsteps crossed the room.

Stella struggled to sit up and cover herself.

'Lie down,' said Corrine, 'you must stay lying down.'

'No, no, just hang on a minute, I need a tissue.'

Corrine whisked a couple of tissues out of a box and handed them to Stella.

'Thanks,' she said and blew her nose.

Corrine settled her down on the table again. 'You mustn't sit up so quickly, you'll feel sick,' she said, her tone almost sympathetic.

The pain started again with the heel of Corrine's hand just below the small of her back. Stella groaned. She tried thinking about something else, anything else to take her mind off the kneading and pressing. What about Charlotte, asking her how she felt about kids. Shit. I don't know. But maybe? Why not? But who with? Fuck, she thought. I'd probably be a useless mother.

Corrine had finished and left the room.

Checking her phone Stella saw she had a bit of time before meeting up with Charlotte for hummus, sprouts and perky little carrot sticks. She dressed, perched her sunglasses on her nose and let herself out of the room.

The spa complex was built in a U shape. A Shinto-inspired garden filled the central courtyard with rocks, and groomed stone gardens with artfully placed moss. Clipped, twisted trees dotted the scene, ancient art brought into the new world. A covered porch wrapped around three sides, with steps at various intervals leading into the serene garden. Stella closed the door behind her, stretched her arms above her head, marvelling at the way Corrine had managed to find every sore, tight muscle in her body; that's the art of a good masseuse, she thought. She hated to admit it, but Charlotte had been right, this had been a great idea. It was good to have a change of scene, given that Teri's funeral was going to be difficult for all of them.

Stella smiled to herself; this was truly one of those places that preyed upon middle-class affluence and anxiety. It felt refreshing to be outside. The massage room had been warm, verging on stuffy. She closed her eyes and turned her face towards the sun and the late summer warmth, the last of the season before things started to change. Stepping off the deck she strolled around the back of the main building. There was a pathway winding through some large shrubs, old camellia bushes with the remnants of their flowers turning rotten brown in the dirt.

At the end of the path were a series of out-buildings. The first one was obviously the laundry – there must be a shitload of washing that needed to be done each day, thought Stella. The second was gardening equipment, a lean-to attached to a regular two-car garage. It was empty, large patches of dry oil singed the concrete floor.

A girl was standing on the steps leading up to the main building. Her shiny black hair was cut in a bob. She was petite and very pretty. Was this the wee girl who had come into Corrine's room? Behind her, partly hiding was another younger girl.

Stella smiled over at them. The one behind ducked her head, but the girl at the front stared straight at her.

'Hi there,' said Stella, waving her hand.

The girl looked down at her feet, then back up, a small smile playing on her face.

'That's pretty,' Stella said, pointing to the silver chain around the ankle of the older girl. 'What's your name?'

'My name is Fern,' came the small voice. The girl hiding behind stayed silent. 'This is Sia.'

'Such pretty names. I'm Stella. Is this your sister?'

A door slammed. A voice demanded, 'Why are you here, are you lost?'

She spun around and found herself face to face with a

fierce-looking Asian woman. She was shorter than Stella with bony hands and high, sharp cheekbones. Her hair, streaked with grey, was tied up in a rough ponytail.

'This area isn't for clients, you must go around to the garden, around to the front.' She waved her hands in front of her as if shooing away errant chickens.

'Sorry. I was just stretching my legs,' Stella said. 'Are these your daughters?'

'Yes, yes. They are my daughters. Now you must go to the front garden.'

'They're very pretty, your daughters.'

'Yes, thank you.'

'Why aren't they in school today?'

'They are both unwell today. I keep them home.'

'Well, I hope you're feeling better soon,' said Stella to the girls.

Stella walked back towards the front of the building. There was no way she'd ever be able to afford to visit an equivalent place in London, she thought. Those kinds of establishments required a membership, or at least the donation of a kidney.

They drove back to Wellington in comfortable silence, the kind of silence that can be broken any time, with any topic. Stella would bridge the difficult stuff with Charlotte another time. All she could see in her head was those two wee girls, so pretty, so alive. Their image pushed against the one of Teri's death, of her falling. Stella opened the glove compartment for the mints. She offered one to Charlotte.

'Not for me thanks.'

'I believe they're sugar-free, Lottie.'

'Who'd have thought,' she said, as dry as a stony riverbed.

'Go on, you know you want to,' said Stella wiggling the packet at her.

'Cut it out, Stell, I'm driving,' said Charlotte, laughing at her sister.

'The weird thing is I actually enjoyed myself today. That masseuse I had was something else.'

'Corrine, right?'

'Yeah.'

'I had her once, she was amazing,' said Charlotte.

'How often did you go to that spa with Teri?'

'Just a couple of times, why?'

'I don't know, it's just something that's rattling around my head. Did she ever mention Ravosky to you?'

'Maurice? Why do you ask? I mean, I spoke to him at the party,' said Charlotte. 'He seemed harmless enough, but I just about choked on the aftershave. I wanted to tell Teri to give him a nudge to tone it down. It didn't seem to bother her, but yeah, now that I think about it, she did mention him.'

'Really?' Stella turned to face her sister, her eyes narrowed. 'What did she say?'

'Specifically? Is it important?'

'How would I know, you haven't told me yet.'

'Yeah okay, Constable Weston, keep your knickers on.'

'Sorry, it's just something doesn't feel right.'

'You know, I worry about you, Stell. I know that might seem a bit strange with you being older and having been in the police, but not everything is bad. There are some good things in the world you know, you just have to find them.'

'You're quite right, Lottie, because what I need is a good swig of whisky to chase down some painkillers.'

'Check my bag. You won't find any whisky, but I'm not so far up my arse that I don't have some painkillers floating around. Is your tooth still playing up?'

'Yeah, it is.' Stella swung around to the back seat reaching for Charlotte's bag, plumping it on her knee she felt around inside for a pill-sized packet. She pulled out Charlotte's phone.

'Nice. That's a fancy new one you've got there – when did you get that?'

'That was something,' said Charlotte. 'Teri mentioned that she'd got some sensitive information on her phone.'

'Sensitive? What does that mean?'

'I don't know, she didn't say.'

They were both quiet as Charlotte navigated around an articulated truck and numerous cars in the fast lane that insisted on dawdling at ninety-four kilometres an hour.

'So, was it just a business arrangement, do you think, you know, between Teri and Ravosky?'

'What? You think that Teri and Ravosky were having some kind of affair?'

'I don't know, the older I get I find things don't surprise me like they might have. What do you think?'

'Hold up, Stell, you're beginning to sound like Dad.' Charlotte laughed.

'Oh, thanks for that, but it's true. Maybe they were having an affair, maybe it went wrong, who knows. Maybe she had some compromising photos on her phone,' said Stella, half to herself, 'or photos of business papers, something that could harm him.'

'What I do know,' said Charlotte, 'was that Teri was doing some work for him, something to do with his business concerns. She never mentioned him to you?'

'No, not that I remember.'

'Well, maybe they were having a bit on the side – he's probably married. Maybe she thought you wouldn't approve … sorry, Stell, I know it's a raw spot.'

13

MAD-DOG STOPPED outside Gus's place to catch his breath.

The last few days he'd noticed a distinct wheezing feel in his chest. He found even the simplest of walks made him breathless. A young man sat on the pavement outside. He was there on a piece of folded cardboard with another piece of card resting in front of his crossed knees. *No job, money for food would be appreciated, thanks.* A few coins sat in a hat he'd placed upturned in front of him. Mad-Dog watched him for a while – he'd never done that, never just sat there and begged. He gave people something in return for their generosity; he gave them music. The weekday strollers wove around the young man, some glanced, some pursed their lips in his direction, some just shook their heads.

Most kept walking.

Mad-Dog knew why he was in the situation he was in. The trajectory of his decline was what he deserved after what happened, what he'd done. It was enough to be alive without them, enough punishment to live. But there was no law or reason that said he had to live 'well'. He walked over to the young man sitting on the cardboard, took off his glove and extended his hand. The young man looked up. Like recognised like, they shook hands. The man's was cool to the touch. Mad-Dog caught sight of bitten fingernails, nicotine-stained fingers. He couldn't have been much out of his teens and looked too young to have such stains.

'Good luck,' said Mad-Dog.

'Thanks,' the young man said. 'Any coins?'

'Sorry, not today.'

Mad-Dog started up the stairs to Gus's workroom. He could have taken the ancient lift but he didn't like the small space. He held on to the curved wooden banister, his right hand still tingling from the touch of another human. Stopping at the first landing he leaned forward again to catch his breath. Then started up the second lot of stairs. He pushed open the door to the corridor. All the other doors were closed, the iridologist, the forensic accountant, the dietician. Quiet enveloped him, no noise from the street reached here. The faint sound of music came from Gus's room further down the corridor, Beethoven's Sonata No. 5 – *Spring*. The violin soaring over and under the piano. The carpet underfoot silenced his feet. He stood outside the door, the music louder now.

'Christophe,' exclaimed Gus when he opened the door. 'Come in, how lovely to see you. Are you busking today, or here for the tea?'

'Tea would be lovely, thank you.'

Occasionally, when he was feeling chirpy, Mad-Dog would open the door with a little flourish and say in his quiet voice, 'Augustus, how fare thee?' Gus would reply with, 'I fare thee well, Christophe, I fare thee well and you?' and Mad-Dog would say, 'I can't complain.'

Today was different. Gus set about making his visitor some food as well as tea.

Mad-Dog sat back on the couch and took the mug Gus offered, placing it on the wide armrest. He balanced a plate with croissant and cheese on his knees. Gus sat on a low chair and busied himself with polishing the back of a cello, small, circular movements. The earthy nut smell of wax mingled with warm pastry. Occasionally he stopped to sip his tea.

'It's getting colder, my friend,' said Gus.

'Yes.'

'You'll need to go indoors soon, you don't want to end up like last winter.'

'No, I'll be more careful,' replied Mad-Dog.

'You're not getting any younger.'

Mad-Dog smiled. 'None of us are, none of us are. But thank you for your concern and for the tea.'

'Any time,' said Gus.

Mad-Dog finished his food, stood up and took his plate and cup to the curtained kitchenette. When he turned back to the workroom he fished in his pocket and pulled out the phone, laying it across the palm of his hand.

'I found this,' he said.

Gus peered over the rim of his glasses. 'Well, that's seen better days. Where did you find it?'

'In a skip.'

'Some things are treasures, some are not.'

'True,' replied Mad-Dog.

'We live in a throw-away world, everything these days has a shelf life.'

'True again. What should I do with it? Should I hand it in to the police station?'

Gus wiped his rag in a tin of polish and started the circular motion again. 'You could, I guess, but as it was thrown away, you're most likely wasting your time.'

'You're probably right.' Mad-Dog wondered about saying more, describing the angel, the scream, the sound her body made as it hit the pavement. A sheet of tiredness hung over him; he rubbed his eyes.

'I'm heading home soon, my friend,' said Gus. 'Can I give you a lift?'

'Thank you, but no. There's some things I need to do and I'm happy to walk. It isn't far.'

'She wouldn't want this for you, you know,' said Gus as he handed him some food in a bag.

Mad-Dog lifted his head and stared at him for a while, then his eyes dropped to the floor.

He took a minute to pick up the bags and rope.

'Thank you for the tea,' he said, his hand on the door knob. 'It will be fourteen years this week,' Mad-Dog said, as much to himself as to Gus, and he closed the door behind him.

14

She waved Charlotte off at the supermarket and flicked Lassie a quick text while waiting in the queue: *I have wine, cheese, questions, you at home?*

His reply zinged back: *Sure, come over.*

Stella started up Majoribanks Street. An older couple walked down the street towards her, arm in arm, heads close together in conversation. She couldn't hear the words but she heard them laugh. The man lifted his hand to catch the end of his companion's floating silk scarf. He caught it and tucked it back into the front of her jacket, then brushed a wisp of hair behind her ear. An intimate moment Stella felt she shouldn't be seeing. They passed by her, heads still close together – arm still in arm.

Turning into Austin Street, Stella stopped and stood on the opposite side of the road from Lassie's apartment. It was the top left in a block of four. A generous bay window faced out onto the street, its shape softening the hard line of the concrete building.

Plonking her bag of groceries on the pavement she looked up – the light was on in the lounge, the curtains still open. What was it he'd said at her parents' party when he was quizzing her? Something about his love life, that he'd tell her another time. Shit, what say he had someone up there with him? Stella wasn't in the right frame of mind for polite conversation with a girlfriend of Lassie's.

She chewed the nail of her right index finger and briefly contemplated bailing on him.

Rubbing her hand across her eyes – it's now or never, she thought – she crossed the road and climbed the few steps to the front door. Stella rang the bell and rummaged in her bag for more painkillers. Her tooth was definitely starting up again. Pulling out the packet she'd found in Charlotte's bag she punched out the last two into her hand and waited for the door to open.

Mitchell Lassiter, like Teri, was one of those people who was supremely unaware of their own attraction. Yes, he dressed well. Yes, he had regular haircuts and shaved and all those kinds of things, but there was another element. He stood there in rumpled jeans and an old T-shirt that he'd probably had since uni. His feet were bare. Stella knew then she'd made a mistake.

'You were quick,' he said. 'Do you want coffee?'

'Just hand me a glass,' she said, opening her hand. 'I need to swill these.'

She smiled at him, her best 'everything's okay' smile and walked past, shrugging out of her jacket. Lassie closed the door and headed up the stairs behind her. Stella was already in the kitchen expertly spinning the top off the bottle and pouring a couple of glasses.

'Cheers,' she said.

'I thought you were off the booze,' he said.

'I have my moments.'

They clinked their glasses together; she threw the pills into her mouth, took a large swallow of wine and leaned against the bench.

'How have you been?' he asked.

'I've got toothache,' she said.

'That's not what I meant.'

Stella swilled the liquid around in the glass. 'Up and down,' she said. 'But that's to be expected. What about you?'

'I dunno, it still seems so unreal.'

'I know. I haven't even been to see her parents yet. I'm dreading it actually. Do you ever get the feeling that you think you know someone, but you really don't?'

'All the time, why?'

'I went for a drive up the coast with Charlotte today. She wanted to spend some "quality time" together. She organised a spa day. Not really my thing, but a nice thought.'

'Yeah, I can just picture you getting your nails done.' He laughed.

'Ha, ha, fuck you. Apparently she's been working in the antiques shop along from Mum's. The owner travels a lot, so she's been training Charlotte to deal with the business when she's away.'

'I know the place, it's been there forever.'

'She also told me that for the last couple of years she's been trying to get pregnant but it's not happening.'

'That's got to be difficult.'

'Yeah, I should have known these things, shouldn't I? I just feel that I'm out of the loop.'

'You are,' he said. She stared at him. 'You've been away for a few years now. Things change. As difficult as this may sound, we're all still getting on with our lives. We're not hanging out at the school gate waiting for you to finish your class. We miss you, of course but …' he tailed off. 'Have you thought about coming home?'

All the time, she thought, all the time. 'I've had a shitty couple of days,' she said. 'But it doesn't make me want to de-camp back here.' As with Charlotte she had no desire to hash over what she'd seen at the wharf and she'd never admit to anyone, let alone Lassie, that her London life was less than perfect. Loneliness comes in all shapes and sizes; it wraps itself around the unsuspecting, a slow choking. Stella kept busy, that was her MO. Away from the business life slowed down too much. There was space and time to fill, memories to evade, people and places to avoid. Teri's death forced her to stay here awhile. That much, at least, she owed her friend.

Stella took another large gulp of wine and looked around the kitchen. There was an impressive bunch of purple hydrangeas in a vase on the bench; a pale green tea towel hung over the oven door railing. A large stainless-steel container sat on the bench next to the oven, full of those awkward cooking implements Lassie used to have in a jumble in a drawer. A designer clock dominated another wall. Either he was becoming interested in interior design, or he'd had help. The clock was showing 8.40 – Jesus, thought Stella, it had taken an age to get back from up the coast.

Lassie was busy sorting out the plate of cheese and crackers; she finished her first glass and poured a second.

'Let's head into the lounge, if you're going to drink like that you'll need some food in you.'

It was a large room with an ancient leather couch and a couple of low armchairs. The coffee table was covered in magazines and a badly folded weekend newspaper, copies of the *Listener* stacked underneath. There was some art on the wall, something abstract and colourful. The bay window was a feature on one side of the room with a massive bookshelf on the other, floor to ceiling. In front of the bookcase, piles of books grew out of the carpet like a rare and haphazard mould. Lassie may have a brilliant legal mind but thank goodness it stopped at cataloguing his home bookcase. Stella wandered over, tilted her head sideways to look at the titles.

'Still into those unfathomable Russians?' she asked.

'Not so much, I've graduated to the unfathomable Chinese.'

'In the original language, I presume.'

'Absolutely. I've been learning Mandarin for that reason,' he deadpanned.

'Sure you have.'

'What about you, Stella. Have you learnt anything new lately?'

'Me? Not likely, I'm a one-trick pony.'

Stella ran her hand along the spines of the books. All those words, all those ideas, all in one place. Of course it was all on the internet now, the death of the book and all of that. She pulled one off the shelf: *Suite Française* by Irène Némirovsky.

Stella wiggled it at him. 'Any good?'

'You'd like it. Amongst other things it's about a woman who's having a difficult time of it.'

'Oh, thanks. Subtle as ever I see.' Stella finished her wine and held out her glass. 'Can we squeeze the bottle? Charlotte dropped me off, I'll Uber home.'

Alcohol made her at once sleepy and desperately awake; her head was in danger of floating away entirely. The pills were working. She crunched on some crackers to try and calm her insides, which were a hot mess of not enough breakfast, a strange vegetarian concoction for lunch, no dinner and too much coffee, liberally sprinkled with pain-killers. Charlotte was right. She absolutely needed to take better care of herself, but kindness was the one thing that Stella didn't deal well with. It unnerved her.

'So, this spa that Charlotte took me to, apparently she and Teri went there a couple of times,' Stella began. 'Ravosky's name was in the visitors book.' She waited for a reaction.

'Where?'

'At the day spa, it was there right under Teri's.'

Stella plonked herself on the couch next to Lassie, kicked her shoes off and tucked her left foot under her right knee.

'So what? He was probably having a relaxing massage just like you were. Or maybe, god forbid, he was having a facial.'

'He doesn't strike me as the relaxing massage type,' Stella replied.

'And you know this how?'

'I don't know. I don't trust him. There was something about him, at the party, he just seemed …' She fiddled with her glass. 'I stalked him,' she said.

'You what?'

'I stalked him,' she repeated. 'Not literally. Online. I spent most of last night checking him out.'

'What did you find, Detective Weston?'

'Not a lot. He has no social media presence, no Facebook, Instagram or Twitter.'

'Yeah, I can't imagine Ravosky regularly updates his Instagram feed.'

'Fuck you. There's a brief LinkedIn mention – so I checked all the business registers, the Companies Register, the Trusts Register, anything and everything.'

'Let me guess – you found nothing.'

'Yep, well, he's on a couple of trusts and mentioned in a few board papers. He owns some properties, or his companies do, there's some kind of trawling business he's named as being part of, as well as a couple of humanitarian NGOs. He's mentioned on a couple of military memorabilia collecting sites. Nothing else. But, he could be hiding behind shell companies, any number of convoluted hidey-holes.'

'Hiding what, exactly,' said Lassie. 'You've judged him guilty but I'm not sure of the crime.'

'You're kidding, right? Teri is dead. She did not commit suicide. She was helped over that railing.'

'Wow, that's a pretty long bow, don't you think?'

'No, I don't. If it wasn't accidental and it wasn't suicide – it *wasn't*,' she said firmly, 'it has to be murder. That's it. There had to be someone else in that room. Final.'

'And you think Ravosky did it?'

'I'm not saying he was the one who pushed her, but he's

involved somehow. I just feel it.'

'Okay, for the sake of argument, let's say you're right – why? Why would Maurice Ravosky, upstanding Wellington businessman and antique collector, want Teri dead?'

'I don't know,' said Stella through gritted teeth. 'That's what I'm trying to find out. Maybe she had some dirt on him – she did work for him after all. Maybe they'd had an affair and she wanted to end it, but he didn't want to, a lover's rage. Charlotte said that Teri mentioned she had something on her phone.'

'There you have it. Whatever it is will be backed up somewhere in the cloud,' replied Lassie, piling cheese on a cracker. They were both quiet for a moment; the only sound was Lassie munching.

'Maybe, maybe not,' said Stella. 'Only if she set it like that.'

'Synching things is pretty automatic these days, isn't it? But then again she might have been cagey about where and how she stored things.'

'Good point, so what's on her phone?'

'God knows. The police will have it. Have you spoken to McCarthy?' Lassie asked.

'Not yet. He'll want to talk to you as well.'

'Most likely.'

Stella stood up. She paced over to the window. The glass in her hand was empty, she could feel her fingers tighten around the stem. She wanted to throw it. She wanted to hurl it against the wall and watch it shatter.

'Do you think he'll be at the funeral?' she asked.

'McCarthy?'

'No, Ravosky.'

'I imagine so,' said Lassie. He leaned forward and poured himself a half glass of wine. Swirling it, he took a sip, sank back into the couch and rested his feet on the table.

She waited.

She needed a smoke.

Lassie was one of the few people that could do this to her, infuriate her beyond rational thought. She wondered if he did it on purpose, the lawyerly thing. Giving the impression he was deep in thought.

'So,' she demanded, 'what do you think?'

'What do I think?' he said. 'I think your reasoning is off. So, the man has various business interests and fingers in companies – he's a businessman, that's to be expected. He has shares in a fishing vessel, so what? Are you going to tell me you think he's doing the dirty on the crew? Maybe he's one of those chaps that keeps them out on the high seas for months at a time, pays them a pittance then throws them overboard when they've outlived their usefulness.'

Stella glared at him. 'I get the impression you're not taking this seriously.'

'No shit, Sherlock, taking what seriously? Firstly, you seem to have the impression that Ravosky and Teri had a thing going on. They didn't, well, not that we know of. Secondly, you've had a huge shock. We all have. This sort of event could make any one of us go a little bonkers.'

'I'm not bonkers, I'm frustrated that I can't make any sense of it all.'

There it was again, her radar wasn't working. Her intelligence-receiving antenna was on the blink. She'd had no idea about Charlotte's job, or pregnancy desires. She'd been convinced that Ravosky and Teri were an item and here was Lassie telling her otherwise.

'So, if they weren't an item, what were they doing together at the party?'

'As I said, Teri was doing some PA work for him. He has several businesses. I told you, he has an office in the same building as me on The Terrace. She popped into my office and told me we were going to be neighbours. That was about nine or ten months ago.'

Stella stared at the lights over the city, each one a life. Then half to herself, 'But why be a plus-one at someone else's party? That doesn't make sense.'

'If there's one thing I know about Ravosky, he's a champion in the schmoozing department,' he said. 'If he thought there'd be someone there he needed to talk to, he'd find a way in. His way in, on Saturday night, was as Teri's plus-one. End of story, those are the facts.'

'God, do you have to be a lawyer all the time? Facts and proof, like with Teri. You're so convinced that she committed suicide, where are your facts and proof there?'

'That's not fair, Weston. None of us knows what goes on inside people's heads. You of all people should know that.'

For a moment they were both quiet. She sat back on the couch. The only sound was a clock ticking, then a motorbike backfired up the street like a Guy Fawkes firecracker.

'Bugger it, you're right. She mentioned Ravosky wanted her to meet someone,' said Stella. 'Even so, I just don't believe she did it. I don't believe she pulled up a chair, took off her shoes, climbed up and jumped from four floors. That's some serious shit, Lassie – it would take a huge amount of pain and anger. I really don't believe she had it in her. I'd just seen her that night, at the party, she was radiant.'

She leaned forward and put her head in her hands. She was loath to admit she'd forgotten that Teri had told her about the job with Ravosky. There'd been a long email about it – she'd sounded excited at the thought of starting something new. The painkillers with that last glass of wine had well and truly kicked in – Stella was feeling lightheaded and a bit sick. It had made much better sense in the car on the way home from the spa.

'I don't know, I don't know,' she said. 'I just know there's something going on.'

'You're trying for answers that aren't there, Stell. We all are. Okay, there's been the terrible, incomprehensible death of our friend, but trying to tie Ravosky into it doesn't make sense and you need a dentist.'

Stella stared down at his bare feet. He was right, she was off kilter. 'I have toothache, but it will go,' she said.

'Really? If you think about something hard enough it comes to pass? I wish I had that superpower.' He laughed gently.

'Don't fuck with me, Lassie.'

'You need a dentist, that's what you need.'

'You're beginning to sound like my parents.'

'I always did like them.'

He put his hand on her neck, massaging gently. She leaned into his hand and closed her eyes. She needed to feel, she needed her body and mind to fall down the rabbit hole. She chewed the inside of her mouth. The sharp metallic taste of blood mixed with the remnants of wine.

Finally, she faced him. 'I don't know what to do,' she said. 'I don't know …'

For what seemed the longest time they stared at each other, then with one smooth movement, she swivelled her body around and sat astride him, her face in his neck. She could smell him. His face had the bristle of late evening, his hands were on her back, under her shirt, on her skin.

Her head turned, her mouth found his. Their kisses were hungry. Biting. This was what she needed, to feel something, the warmth of another human being. To have her mind and body taken somewhere else, even if only for a night. She needed to feel skin. It felt familiar, the need she had for him. His hands were on her hips pulling her towards him … but no, he was pushing her back.

'Um … Stell, sorry, this isn't a good idea.'

'Shit, yes, of course. I'm sorry.'

She swung her leg off him and sat back on the couch. Shit. She felt her face heat up, grateful for the low light in the room. How embarrassing.

'It's late, you can stay here if you like.' He gave her hand a quick squeeze. 'I'll get you a duvet.'

Stella slunk down and closed her eyes. She had no idea what was in those painkillers, but fuck they were good. Her head was spinning. A car drove past with a woosh that sounded like the road was wet. She tried to listen for the rain, but all she could hear was the blood pounding in her head.

15

MAD-DOG WAITED. The light had faded, it would be safer for him now.

After he'd visited Gus, he'd gone around the corner to the skip. The police tape had all gone, except for one shred left fluttering around the bottom of a post – the only evidence that anything had happened. He was happy to see his skip was still there along with his cardboard. Clambering over the cold metal side and ignoring the twinge in his knee, he looked at all the potential treasure that would help keep him warmer at night. Tying the rope securely around the flattened cardboard boxes, he dragged them over to the side. From there he would be able to heave them out onto the street.

Mad-Dog froze.

There was someone on the side of his skip looking at him. They stared at each other, like dogs sniffing out the enemy, growling low and mean.

'This is my skip,' Mad-Dog muttered.

He stared at the stranger out of the corner of his eye and shook his head slightly. The eyes of the stranger were cold, pale ice-blue ringed with dark lashes. Mad-Dog thought he looked quite young, maybe early twenties. Mind you it was difficult to tell these days, especially in this light.

He was clean-shaven, even his head. There were three silver rings in his left ear, one on top of the other climbing up the outer rim. His lips were too fleshy for a man. They were soft pillows, women's lips. Just underneath his bottom lip was a tuft of hair growing, a deliberate fungal sprouting. His hands gripping the sides of the skip were in gloves, close-fitting black leather. Mad-Dog waited.

He held his body close, keeping himself turned away, but still able to watch as the interloper stared into his skip, stared at him. Mad-Dog felt his eyes. He felt the air change around him. Maybe if he kept very still the man would give up and leave him alone. He wasn't one of the freegans, Mad-Dog thought, he was too smartly dressed in a leather jacket, a dark scarf at his neck. He shivered. If he wasn't the police and he wasn't a freegan, what did he want?

'Were you here a couple of nights ago?' the man with the three earrings asked.

Mad-Dog stared at the side of the skip. 'I'm doing nothing wrong. I'm searching for cardboard.' His hand went up to touch the breast pocket that held the fallen star.

The man's voice was smooth and surprisingly high for such a mean face. 'Listen, mate, I just wanna know if you were here a couple of nights ago?'

'I'm just here for cardboard,' he said again. 'I need the cardboard.' Mad-Dog was frozen in place, his right knee was aching, he needed to move.

'What's your name?' asked the mean face.

My name, thought Mad-Dog, why does he want my name? Peace and quiet and cardboard is all I want. He doesn't need my name. If I don't tell him, maybe he'll be angry. If I tell him, I have nothing left to give.

Mad-Dog pulled his hat off his head and rubbed the thick mat of hair hiding underneath. Quickly he shoved the hat back onto his head. He didn't like questions. They made his head hurt. He vacillated between the possible answers. His knee creaked. Soon it would give way and he'd be unable to get out of the skip. Still not looking at the man, he turned slightly.

'Christophe,' he said finally. 'What's your name?' he fired back surprising himself.

The man laughed, an unhappy sound.

'James,' he said, his mouth smiling but not his eyes. 'You remember that, won't you?'

'I'm just wanting cardboard.'

'Course you are, mate. Find anything else interesting?'

'Like what?' asked Mad-Dog.

'I dunno, just anything out of the ordinary, or maybe you've seen something?'

'Like what?' Mad-Dog asked again. 'What could I see from here, from the inside of a skip? I've done nothing wrong.'

'Never said you did, mate, never said you did.'

James jumped down off the skip. He looked up at Mad-Dog, raised his gloved hand and gave him a salute before sauntering off towards the lights of Tory Street.

Mad-Dog sat down heavily and rubbed his knee. Quickly, fumbling, he hoisted his cardboard stack over the side of the skip. It flumped onto the ground. Climbing out of the skip breathing heavily, he waited for a minute. Positioning the cardboard on his back, he began to make his way up to Mount Victoria. These boxes, along with a major piece of tarpaulin he'd scored a while back, would help keep him dry.

He trudged along. He didn't like that man. Didn't like him calling him 'mate'. There was something about him, something that made him nervous. Maybe Rita would help him. She was nice, she liked him, gave him food. Sometimes she would give him money for the night shelter. Rita was in the library, that's where he always found her. Sometimes she wasn't there, but most times he went she was. She would take him into the café and buy him a nice drink; he liked that. Gus had his idea about the star, but maybe Rita would have a better idea.

Yes, he would go tomorrow and ask her.

He beetled around through some of the side streets and ended up on Courtenay Place, a friendly enough spot during the day or even early evening, but late at night it was best avoided. He paused outside the Embassy Theatre to catch his breath, then started up Majoribanks Street. Maybe he was getting older, maybe he just needed some decent food, but Mad-Dog was finding the hills took more and more out of him. Ah well, at least it wasn't raining.

He stopped at the top of the street where the town belt started. He looked behind him. For a minute he wondered if there had been someone there, following.

But not this time. He had successfully become one of the invisible people.

16

THE RECYCLING TRUCK WOKE STELLA. The screeching noise sliced through her head like a knife through soft organ meat. The clock read 8.36. Lassie would have left for the office a while ago.

She groaned.

She wasn't sure which hurt more – her body courtesy of Corrine, her head, her tooth or her pride. Her body would sort itself out in time, her tooth and her head she could fix with the same painkillers, but her pride? That would take a little more effort. Lassie had covered her with a duvet after she'd flaked out. The room was dim, everything was in shadow; the books on the shelves, the table, the modern angled lamp in the corner all looked different in the morning.

There was a small gap in the curtain; a sliver of cool light was sneaking through. She wanted to wind time back. She laughed. Fuck, how many times had she had that exact thought.

Pushing the duvet off, she swung her legs around and looked down. Her jeans were still on but her sweatshirt had been removed. She sat there for a minute and tried to remember if she'd done it. Nope, I've lost that brain cell, she thought, followed quickly with, I have to get my shit sorted. Stella looked over: her phone was on the table, a recharging cord snaking down to the wall socket. There was a missed call from Charlotte and a text from Kate: *I'm back tomorrow, call me, not sure I can cope with Friday.*

Shit, she'd completely forgotten Kate was arriving back from her gig in Auckland. Jesus, she was a hopeless friend. Kate would be feeling it just as much as any one of them.

Stella replied: *So, so sorry not to be in touch hon, will call soon, we'll get shitfaced!*

Then she fired off a quick text to her dad: *Can you recommend a dentist?*

A fresh towel was on the chair. Stella grabbed it and padded off to the bathroom. She filled herself a large glass of water and opened one side of the bathroom cabinet above the sink in search of Panadol. There was half a box left. She downed a couple and checked out the rest of the cabinet. Curiosity never really killed anything, she thought, it just helped to answer some questions. There were the usual antacids, some Dior aftershave, Band-Aids, nail scissors. Then her eye caught sight of the stick of men's deodorant sitting uncomfortably close to a bottle of women's deodorant. She pulled open the other side and stared. Nail polish remover, some cotton pads, a tube of mascara, a half-empty box of tampons. There was no doubting it, there was definitely someone of the female persuasion in his life. Jesus, fuck. It made last night all the more excruciating.

Stella turned on the shower and waited for the hot water to come through, leaning her forehead against the cool glass. She stepped in and, with one hand on the wall to steady herself, let the water wash over her and pool at her feet. That poor child in the sea, what a terrible, senseless death. Then Teri's smile appeared in front of her – her beautiful face, the sound of her laugh, both images threatening to unhinge Stella.

Finally the tears started.

In time she needed to be strong, not only for herself but for Kate and for Teri's family. For now she bowed her head and let them flow.

Oh god, she should visit Teri's parents before the funeral.

She switched thoughts. Of course he'd have someone. Why wouldn't he? He's a nice enough sort of chap, not a psycho-killer. Why in god's name hadn't he said anything though? She let the water run over her face, washed her hair with his suspiciously female shampoo then rinsed off. Everyone around her seemed to be managing. Lassie had his career, his apartment and clearly a woman waiting for him. Kate had her creativity and a gorgeous girlfriend. There were people who adored her. She had a creative life and a decent income. Charlotte had some difficulties to deal with, but she still seemed to be on top of things. They all seemed to have grown up. Stella wondered if she'd missed that bus, if that email or memo had been deleted, the one that read *Instructions on how to be a grown-up*. As for Teri, she'd had her job, her life, people that loved her.

Why the fuck had she jumped?

Maybe Ravosky had some connection to the spa. Maybe he owned it as part of his business portfolio. So what? That still didn't equate to murder. Was he using the business to launder money and Teri found out? That could be enough to make anyone act crazy. He was a businessman, maybe she told him she was going to get him where it would hurt. Maybe he threatened her, she threatened him, then it was all over.

That was a lot of maybes.

She needed to access Teri's phone. Clearly she had something on there, otherwise why mention it to Charlotte? The police would have her devices. Shit, the police. Stella turned off the water and grabbed the towel. The police would mean McCarthy. DI Meathead McCarthy. Frank to his friends. He'd need to question her further about what she'd seen at the wharf as well as about Teri, he'd sure as hell get his jollies by doing that. It'd be Dee and William all over again. Christ, this was morphing into a sadistic nightmare.

I've been here less than a week and already I'm waist deep in past shit, thought Stella. As soon as this is over, as soon as the funeral happens, I'm out of here. I don't care what people think. I just need to get as far away as possible.

Hang on, Lassie said he'd been phoned by a mate in the force about Teri's death. Maybe he would let her bypass McCarthy and give her some kind of starting point. She needed do some more online stalking. She needed to visit Teri's parents.

But what she really needed was proof. Good, solid proof. Her phone pinged with a text from her dad: *Dentist apt made, Gerry, 103 Lambton Q, level 4, Wed. 11.15 am*

Then it rang.

'Hi, Mum.'

'Darling, I'm just checking you're okay. We didn't see you last night.'

'No, I stopped off at Lassie's and before you say anything, it was purely platonic.'

'Of course it was, sweetheart, you don't need to explain. How was the spa?'

'Great, really.'

'Now listen, I have two messages for you, the first is from Rita,' she said, 'she wants you to visit her at work, and could you come and give me hand in the shop? I'm snowed under today, besides you need a job. I'd also like you to drop off some flowers to Teri's parents.'

'Thanks, Mum, but I'm not …'

'Stella, I won't take no for an answer, you're going to be here for a while you've got to do something, keep busy, take your mind off things.'

'I hope you have this kind of conversation with Charlotte.'

'Touché, my darling, I'm never quite sure how your father and I managed such different offspring – it's a mystery.'

'Yeah, well, it's a mystery to us, too, and yeah I'll go see Rita. You said there were two messages?'

'Oh yes,' said Peace. 'A journalist called and wants to talk to you. She left a number, I'll text it to you.'

'Nah, don't worry about it, Mum, it's something I can sort out later.' Fucking journos, thought Stella, doesn't take them long to sniff out the dirt, they just don't know when to give up.

Finishing the call with Peace, Stella stared at her phone. She scrolled through her contacts and settled on Teri's number. It rang then went straight to voice mail. Her voice was a happy sing-song: *Leave a message and I'll get right back to you.*

Lassie was wrong. They were all wrong.

17

SHE PULLED THE FRONT DOOR closed behind her, pausing on the steps to enjoy the late morning sun. After the shower, coffee and muesli, she'd started to feel a version of normal. Later in the day she'd stop by her parents' house for a change of clothes, more likely to pinch something out of her mum's wardrobe.

Wellington was a city of movement. It was full of changing light, littered with gems of stillness. Light breezes played along the streets, lifting leaves and debris in continual motion. Clouds scuttled crablike across the sky. The sooner she could tick visiting Aunt Rita off the list, she thought, the sooner she could focus on Teri.

Stella cut through Civic Square, past the gallery. The place was mostly empty at this hour, just the occasional tourist, or a mum with a buggy. A man was sitting on one of the benches with a violin case resting next to him; from the pocket of his rumpled suit jacket he pulled out a few last crumbs for the pigeons.

The elegant silver fern ball that hung suspended over the square glinted in the morning sun. A sculpture of simple beauty held by wires that, in certain light, remained invisible. In a flash, the ball was replaced by Dee at the end of the rope. Oh shit, thought Stella. She's following me, like a Shakespearian ghost, she's there. She's always going to be there. I am never ever going to get away from that image.

The pigeons had huddled in a group at the violinist's feet, pecking at whatever they thought might be food; a ragged orchestra of cooing and warbling, strutting, fluffed-out feathers. London pigeons, Wellington pigeons or the pigeons in Rome, they're all flying rats, she thought, and shuddered. He shouldn't be feeding them; they're a bloody nuisance. She walked past, close enough to momentarily unsettle the flock. He didn't look up but waited for the birds to settle again before sprinkling a few more crumbs on the ground.

She carried on around the boarded-up old library, through the alley past Unity, and along Customhouse Quay to the new library hub on Panama Street. Through the doors, the smell of coffee hit her first, then the noise. Air-conditioning, computers, the hiss of steam, the clatter of cups in the café, all added to the ambient sound. Café tables were dotted with open laptops, their owners pecking away at the keyboards in-between sips of strong coffee. A brace of mums towing toddlers and bags of books made their way to the kids' section. Almost every available armchair was taken already by magazine readers there for the duration. A couple of tables over by the windows were home to students, and the sound of children playing came from the other end. Stella looked around in case she could spot her aunt.

'Hi, I'm after Rita Stewart,' Stella said to the young chap at the information desk, trying to look at his eyes rather than the spectacular handlebar moustache he wore.

'Sure, I'll just go and get her.' He made a quick phone call. 'She won't be a minute.'

'Thanks.'

Even though this hub was new, the familiarity of the place hit her – this was her city, her streets and it had been her home once. She wasn't even sure what, or where, home was anymore. London, or here – wasn't it meant to be where the heart is? She closed her eyes. Her shoulders were stiffening up. That massage had helped but it also stirred up a whole load of crap, a bit like being back here. The past doesn't leave you, she thought, it just sometimes takes a while to catch up. It might take a longer route, it might even stop off for a while somewhere sunny, but it still arrives at the door, puffing slightly, holding on to an overstuffed suitcase, saying *remember me?*

Stella remembered every detail of exactly why she'd left the country. But the one thing she'd learnt was that shit always follows you. She'd been in London for a couple of months when it hit her, when the insomnia started, when the drinking started as well. She'd get to sleep all right, but it was waking each morning at 3 AM that threw her. Those nights when the same reel played over in her head. Worse still, it played as a constant dreamscape even when she did manage to sleep. She'd known he was married, but what was his response? Leaning on the counter she closed her eyes and tried to picture him. He'd said he was separated, that his wife was 'unbalanced'. Yeah that's right, that was the word he'd used, *unbalanced*. Stella was hooked. She had a thing for complicated situations. She'd tried telling Teri about him.

'Crazy, I know, but I think I may be in love.'

'Stella Weston *in love?*' said Teri. 'Wow, that's really cool, when do I get to meet him? He's got to pass the Teri Test, don't forget.'

They were sitting in the Fig Café, each with a glass of red wine. Stella was picking at the bowl of fries the waiter had placed in front of them.

'Don't mock me.'

'I'm not mocking, Stell. It's just a bit of a surprise. Does the lovely Lassie know about this?'

'It's none of his business really, we were a fling. It's under wraps, but it's true – I never thought I'd actually fall for someone.' She paused and fiddled with her glass. 'He's married but they're …'

'Oh, Stellanova, not the married man thing. That's way

more trouble than it's worth, you know that. If he's capable of doing this to his wife, what's to say he won't do the same to you? Let me guess,' said Teri. 'They're separated, she doesn't understand him, it's all very amicable. Stell, *tell* me you're joking. This one is as old as an old thing can be.' She grabbed Stella's hand, almost knocking over her glass. 'Please, please tell me you're not falling for it,' she said. 'Oh shit, sweetie, you've got it bad.'

Rita was coming towards her. I will not talk about Teri, thought Stella, if I do I will truly lose it. This has to be light, fast, easy. She pasted on a smile. Rita was dressed head to knee in a flowing electric-blue ensemble, finished with a pair of tartan tights and black boots with industrial soles. Her glasses hung from a chain around her neck.

'Hi, Rita, lovely to see you,' she said.

Her aunt gave her a warm hug. 'You're too thin, and lovely to see you too.' She swung her arm out expansively. 'What do you think of our latest library hub?' she said. 'Not quite what we had but it will have to do in the meantime.'

'It's not bad,' said Stella. 'I like that there's still a café. Does the library go through to Brandon Street?'

'Yeah, it does, but enough of the tour guiding, I didn't get a chance to talk to you properly the other night.'

'Sorry about that,' said Stella. 'I left on the early side, I was totally whacked.'

'Travel will do that,' said Rita. 'Oh ... it's so good to see you, lovely.' Rita hugged her again, longer this time. 'Peace told me about your friend. I'm so sorry.' She finally let Stella go. 'Let's get that coffee, and a scone?' she said, and picked up a couple of carry bags that had been sitting at her feet. 'They do fabulous cheese scones here, my shout.'

'What have you got there?' Stella asked.

'Just a few bits and pieces for someone.'

They settled into one of the café tables. Stella put her coat over the back of the chair – if she was in for a speech, better to get on with it.

'How long are you back for, Stella?'

'Not sure. Look, I know the deal. I know my parents are worried and all of that – you don't need to go over it. I'm *okay*, really I am, and besides, they've got Charlotte here, she keeps an eye on them.'

'You can't leave it all to Charlotte,' said Rita.

'They're not at death's door … and they're not exactly in the "ageing parents" category just yet.'

'Listen, Stella, I don't want to alarm you or anything, but after your mum's health scare …'

'Her what?'

'Damn,' said Rita. 'She hasn't told you, has she? She told me she would.'

'What – health – scare?' said Stella, very slowly. She'd put a rocket up Charlotte later for not letting on.

Rita sighed. 'I'm sorry,' she said. 'But you need to talk to Peace.' Two cups of coffee and plates with scones were placed in front of them. 'Your parents really worry about you, they worry that you're, I don't know … adrift.'

'Adrift?' How poetic, a lifeboat on a raging sea, thought Stella.

'Maybe it's time you came home. I'm worried about you,' said Rita. 'You can't keep hiding out in London.'

'Who says I'm hiding?' Stella took a sip. 'I miss Wellington coffee though,' she said.

'There's nothing quite like it,' said Rita. They were both quiet for a moment. Rita buttered her scone. The doors out to Panama Street swooshed open, a young woman walked in, a violin strapped to her back, earbuds firmly in place.

Rita broke the silence. 'Your parents won't ever say

anything. They don't want to pressure you at all. They love you and they fear for you.'

'They always have, Rita, that won't stop no matter what I do,' said Stella. 'But they've clearly had more to worry about than me ... besides, isn't it the prerogative of parents to worry?'

'True.'

'But now you've told me I need to worry about them,' she said.

'I'm sorry, me and my big mouth.'

Stella shook her head. She closed her eyes and picked the skin around the index finger on her right hand.

'I keep seeing her,' she said finally. 'In the garage. Dee, she phoned me. She must have known I was on duty, she wanted me to be the one to find her and I did. I don't know if she actually wanted to die, or for me to get there in time. But I didn't get there until it was too late. Maybe it was meant to be different. I just ... I just, I'll never know. Fuck.'

She'd said too much. A pearl of blood formed around the nail on her finger. She jammed a hand in her jacket pocket in the hope of finding an old tissue. Rita whisked one out of a packet.

'Here,' she said. 'Wrap this around it. Have you been to a counsellor?'

Stella sat back in her chair, a smirk on her face. 'You're joking, right? I went to several in the early stages; all of them had pretty much said the same things. It will pass. It's not your fault. She did this to herself, it's a personal decision, yadda, yadda, yadda.' She pulled the tissue away, blood still oozed. 'But you know what really, really made me puke was that he blamed me entirely. He got kindness and understanding, people were terrific. But for me, oh no, it didn't take long for the word to get out that we'd been having an affair.' Stella was on a roll. 'The mood changed.

Don't screw the crew, certainly not your married superior. Talk about a pack mentality. I became the punching bag, the person to hate. That's why I quit. I couldn't face it day in, day out.'

Stella pulled the tissue away again. Her finger was white where she had been squeezing it. Folding it over to hide the smear of blood, she blew her nose, then crumpled it into a tight, hard ball. She kept her eyes on her hands. 'After the funeral, after the inquest, I handed in my resignation. They didn't try to stop me, said a lot really. I had some savings, my British passport courtesy of Dad and I got on a plane. That was pretty much where it ended.' She lifted her head up and stared at Rita. 'I was on the detective ladder, I'd been shoulder-tapped. I was thrilled at the time, it was what I'd been working for, it was the whole reason I was there. Walking away was ...' What happened to keeping it *light*? 'So, no thank you on the counselling front, it won't change a bloody thing.'

'You let them win,' said Rita.

'Ouch.'

'Maybe, but tell me I'm not right,' said Rita. 'London may have given you anonymity, the ability to start over. But you'll never shake what happened. So what are you going to do? Spend the rest of your life running?'

'Yep, that's the plan. I have work in a private detective agency – it's donkey work really, but it keeps me busy. That's all I want. To keep busy, to try and forget.'

'How's that working out for you?'

Stella needed to change the conversation. It was difficult enough cramming all this stuff at the base of her memory. She didn't need Rita's bluntness bringing it into daylight.

'I'm not sure if you've noticed or not,' Stella said, 'but a man over there keeps staring at you. I saw him in Civic Square feeding those bloody pigeons.'

Rita swivelled in her chair then stood up from the table. 'It's okay. I know him. Wait here. I'll be back in a minute.'

He was taller than Rita, and wearing a blue suit jacket that looked a little too big for him. His beard was flecked with grey and not that tidy, the same with his hair. It looked as though he may have tried to make an effort. He placed the violin case on the floor and leaned in towards Rita, bending like an apologetic performer. His hands fidgeted, fluttered, as if wanting to escape from his wrists. He was trying to keep them under control but they started up again. Stella couldn't see his shoes. You can tell a great deal about someone by the state of their shoes.

He fished something out of his jacket pocket and handed it over to Rita. A wallet, maybe. Rita smiled at him. Her hand lightly touched his, soothing the flutters. He put whatever it was back in his pocket – she handed him the carry bags she'd been holding. He took them and nodded his head, bowing like a Japanese gentleman. He ducked down again and picked the violin case off the floor.

Then he was gone through the library towards the Brandon Street entrance.

'Who was that?' asked Stella.

'Bit of a sad case really,' Rita said, sitting back at the table. 'No deflecting, I want to finish talking about you first. Your friend's death must have been an incredible shock, especially with …'

'Thank you, yes, it was. Actually, maybe you could help. I know for a fact that librarians know everything.'

Rita laughed. 'We try, what do you need?'

'I'm trying to find out about a guy called Maurice Ravosky. Teri worked for him and I just want to rule him out.'

'Rule him out of what?'

'Being a suspect.'

'Sorry, Stella,' Rita said. 'I thought it was a suicide. Are you involved in the investigation?'

'No, I'm not involved, not officially anyway. Let's just say I have my suspicions, plus I don't want to go to the police until I have evidence.'

'Why don't you ask your dad to help? Maybe he could check financial dealings.'

'I'm not sure that an accountant is what I need right now, but I will check with him.'

'So what do you need from me?' said Rita with a smile. 'You can get most stuff online.'

'Yeah, but what I'm interested in is articles, business dealings, real estate ownership. Anything that's not online, anything that could help with who he is and what he's into.'

'Okay, will do, but have a think about what I said earlier.'

Stella finished her coffee, placing the cup carefully on the saucer. 'It's not as easy as that,' she said. 'But I promise I'll give it some thought. Now, tell me, who was that man you were talking to.'

'Ah yes,' Rita said. 'I came across him a couple of years ago. I was coming back from lunch and I saw him rummaging in one of the bins outside the old Civic Square library. I know it happens, but I was still shocked. I handed him a sandwich I hadn't eaten. He looked so pathetically grateful it was heartbreaking.'

'So, does he actually play the violin?' Stella asked.

'Yeah, he does. I've heard him. He's not bad, in fact I was surprised at how good he was. He busks to make a bit of cash.'

'Does he have a name?'

'He told me his name is Christophe, Christophe Janvier. But other than that, I don't know him at all.' She finished the last of her coffee. 'He comes in almost every week now, so I try to have some food for him. I don't know how he eats most of the time. He probably visits the soup kitchen.'

'Why is he on the street?'

'I haven't asked, he hasn't said. He's so quiet and polite.'

'He looked a bit ragged,' said Stella.

'Well, in the summer he pretty much lives outside. In the winter he told me he heads for the night shelter. He gets food there as well, but even so, it's a tough existence.'

'Can't be good for his violin, being outside all the time.'

'I asked about that, I thought he might like to leave it here with me, but he said that he stores it somewhere.'

'Where abouts?'

'It was odd, he just kind of mumbled something about someone called Luther.'

'Luther? God, what kind of name is that?'

'I don't know. I didn't like to pry.'

They were both quiet for a moment. 'It's been lovely seeing you,' said Rita. She stood up. 'But I need to get back to work.'

'Yeah, no rest for the wicked and thanks for the coffee,' said Stella. 'What was he showing you?'

'He does a lot of dumpster diving around the city, and was in a skip near Tory Street on Saturday night when some woman threw a phone in. What a waste. It hit the side and the glass shattered. The battery is dead, it's probably junk.'

'On Tory or near Tory?'

'Ummm, Tory Street, no, hang on … it was a side street off Tory.'

'You're kidding.'

'Sometimes he rambles,' said Rita. 'He reckoned a woman threw the phone from a balcony. Actually, he called it a *star*.'

'Shit, I have to find him. I have to go.' Giving Rita a quick hug, Stella dodged around a couple of library-goers and raced out the Brandon Street entrance. Damn it.

Damn it. He could have gone either way along Brandon, to Lambton Quay or Featherston Street, even back up towards the police station and Civic Square, or in an entirely different direction. He might have cut through any of the side streets. She did a perfunctory look along Lambton Quay, then jogged towards Civic Square. He could have been over the bridge and around the lagoon by now.

Nothing.

No sign at all. No sign of the tired blue suit jacket. No sign of the salt and pepper hair, of the straggly bearded man who may have witnessed what happened and be in possession of Teri's phone.

How on earth was she going to track down a bloody homeless man? God knows where he dossed down at night. She'd need to check the night shelter, have a chat with them. There was always a layer in the city, in any city, of the dispossessed. The ones that politicians wrung their hands over but ultimately did nothing about. They weren't voters, so who gave a crap?

Christophe was clearly one of the dispossessed. An older person, fallen through, or maybe not. She'd seen it plenty of times in London. So many times in fact that she'd stopped seeing it. The young guys sitting on a piece of cardboard in the Tube station, wearing oversized jackets, hats pulled down almost over their eyes. Some with a scrawny dog beside them. They'd have a hat out in front begging for a few coins. Now it was here too, she thought, visible, inescapable poverty. Sure, some of them might be doing it as a 'lifestyle', but really? Kid yourself all you like, she thought, that's not living.

The freezing cold nights, when she'd tumbled out from a bar or club in London, drunk, alive. An arm through an arm, the promise of crisp white sheets, a shag and a decent sleep. She'd passed the soup caravans, the lines snaking away from the holes in the sides where they served food. Shuffling bodies, heads bowed. Dickensian life in the twenty-first century.

18

MAD-DOG KEPT TO THE FAR LEFT of the pavement. He carried his violin in his left hand, the bags Rita had given him were in the right. He liked Rita. She was kind to him, like he was to the pigeons. They weren't songbirds, apart from the cooing, but they made him smile. They were tough, resilient: they stuck together; they survived.

He liked the birds on Mount Vic, where he slept. There would be darkness, then slowly the quiet would be punctuated with two or three notes, bell-like, pure and clear. The tūī would introduce him to the day, tell him he was still alive, then the tūī would be joined by a chorus of starlings. They made him laugh, they strutted and preened, they were the bullies of the greenery. He liked their bolshie attitude. Like him, they were imported.

Mad-Dog's bones ached, especially his hip, but now he had food he wouldn't need the shelter for a couple more nights. Stooped over, he coughed, unable to stop. It happened last winter as well, but this year it was starting a whole lot sooner. He'd have to watch that. He straightened up, the coughing stopped. He continued on, the sole on his shoe still loose, step, flap, step, flap.

For the last few nights, the sky had been clear, the breeze light. Perhaps he could last a few more nights out here before going inside. Winter was always a difficult time. He needed warmer clothes, which meant seeing people. He needed more food, which meant seeing people. He needed better shelter, which definitely meant seeing people. It wasn't that he minded the people who ran the shelter, the other men were the problem. They frightened him. They seemed like versions of people he used to know, but more unkempt.

The nights were noisy as well. Coughing, lots of coughing, loud snoring, the flush of toilets, the early morning wake-up. Still, it was good to know it was there if needed.

Mad-Dog had been coughing quite a bit himself lately. Last winter he'd had pneumonia and ended up in hospital for a couple of nights. People came to talk to him, serious young things with clipboards and forms for him to fill out. Too many questions, too many words.

He went through Manners Street and towards Cuba Mall; there were benches there – he sat down. Today there was sun, warmth seeped into his bones, interesting people swirled around him. Maybe today he would play a bit. If he put the case out in front of him, he could earn a little money. Standing up, Mad-Dog put the case on the seat.

He opened it and took out the bow.

He turned the knob to tighten the hair. Then he removed the little box of rosin from the front cubicle. He swiped it up and down the hair of the bow a couple of times and placed the rosin and bow back in the case. He unwrapped the violin from its silk scarf, and picked up the shoulder rest. Carefully he attached them together, picked up the bow and stood there. He then put the open case on the pavement in front of him. Eyes closed. Mad-Dog placed the violin on his shoulder, made sure his strings were tuned to each other, then lightly rested the bow on the strings.

He played Bach, a slow movement from one of the unaccompanied sonatas he dug from his memory. His fingers didn't manage the fast passages too well these days. They were stiff and he was still a little cold, but the slow movements gave him time. Eyes still closed he played into the notes, a stream of sound that washed him far away. A gentle clinking sound meant that someone had tossed coins into his case. Mad-Dog didn't open his eyes – the rush of the street would spoil the illusion. He finished the final note with a deep sigh. He wouldn't manage any more today.

Opening his eyes, there were a few coins nestled into the velvet. He scooped them up, put them in his pocket. He reversed the procedure, wrapping his violin in the silk scarf, gently placing it in the case. He loosened the bow and tucked it into the lid, securing it with the little knob. The lid clicked shut; he bent to pick up the bags that Rita had given him.

When Mad-Dog had his violin case in his left hand, shopping bags in his right, he looked up. Across the mall a man was leaning against one of the lampposts. It was the man with the ice-blue eyes, from the skip, James. Mad-Dog swallowed. He felt a cough starting in his chest. His right hand, with the bags, instinctively patted his breast pocket. James straightened himself up. He jutted his chin in Mad-Dog's direction, then made a gun shape with his hand, pointing it at Mad-Dog's head.

19

STELLA SLEPT BADLY, her dreams full of half-formed images, lights and voices she didn't quite recognise. When she woke it took her a minute or two to remember everything, then like a swollen river it flooded back. Sleep, even filled with crazy dreams, was better than this. Her friend was dead. Even saying it in her head felt unreal.

Her brain filtered through it was a week day. Suburban quiet blanketed the house; her parents would be at work. The bed was warm and the room smelt of home. Peace had put flowers in a vase for her; the sheets were brushed cotton. They were the things she remembered Stella loved. Being back was like diving headfirst down a rabbit hole, you knew instinctively that it was a bad idea, but compulsion overtook good sense.

Maybe she shouldn't have come back.

Maybe Teri would still be alive.

Leaning over, she flicked on the radio, hoping the chat of the early-morning announcer would take her mind off things. She needed to understand what had happened. She didn't believe her friend had committed suicide. Charlotte, her parents, Lassie could all think what they liked. Especially Lassie. At times he was a sphinx, that exterior of calm, the way he had of talking as though trying to hypnotise a dangerous animal drove her crazy. She wanted him to rail against it all, to show something, anything. What she needed was to find Christophe and see if it was Teri's phone he'd shown to Rita.

Stella felt the pull of nicotine. Her parents hated her smoking and would be annoyed if she smoked inside. Suddenly she was wide awake, listening. The 8 AM news bulletin still had the drowned girl as the lead story, but with absolutely no new information, no identification, no next of kin, no one coming forward. An underage Jane Doe. The next item was the report of a homeless man found in a central Wellington alleyway, bashed unconscious, further details would be released soon, if anyone saw or heard anything to contact the police.

Shit. She grabbed her phone, hurriedly flicking through her contacts.

'Rita, hi, sorry to phone so early, but did you hear the news on the radio?'

'Yeah, I've just been listening.'

'Could it be your friend?' asked Stella.

'I've no idea. You didn't find him yesterday then?'

'No luck.'

'There's lots of rough sleepers in the city these days – you could phone the hospital.'

'I'm not next of kin. They won't tell me anything.'

'Why are you so interested in him?' asked Rita. 'What's he to you?'

'I know it sounds crazy but that phone that he showed you ...' Stella took a deep breath. 'It may be Teri's.'

'You're kidding? How would he ...?'

'Look it's a long story, but I'm serious.'

'I'm sure you are, but shouldn't you go to the police with that information?'

'Nah, that won't work.'

'Well, if you're sure,' said Rita. 'I'll give you a call if he comes in today. I don't usually see him two days in a row, but you never know.'

Pacing round in the courtyard outside the kitchen, puffing on a cigarette, Stella knew she should contact McCarthy, but her skin prickled at the thought. Fuck it, who else was there who could help? Evidence and leads can go cold fast, so how exactly would that conversation go? *Hi, it's Stella Weston here, the one who stuffed up her life and career by fucking a colleague and driving his wife to suicide. I have some intel you might be interested in.*

She blew out a thin stream of smoke, then ground the butt into the tin Peace had provided. Nah, she was on her own for now. She had to keep her dental appointment this morning, deliver some flowers to Teri's parents and – crap – there was the formal statement with McCarthy lined up for the afternoon.

Fuck this tooth. It was all just wasted time.

20

Lambton Quay was busy with mid-morning shoppers.

The busker juggling coloured tennis balls was in his usual place. Hole-in-the-wall coffee bars were doing a brisk trade. Stella hurried past a couple of young men in dark government suits, white shirts, nondescript ties.

The dental surgery was on the fourth floor. She walked into the lift, stood there eyeing the bank of lights. There was a faint whiff of body odour and takeaways. It was airless, painted an industrial maroon colour. Scrape marks lined the lower wall section. She pressed four.

Nothing happened.

She pressed again. Eventually the doors creaked shut and shuddered upwards. The lift bell dinged, doors opened; Stella stepped into the corridor. Pushing open the frosted glass door she found herself in a bright airy reception.

'Stella?' said the woman behind the desk with the name tag that said *Grace*.

'Yep, that's me.'

'Hi, we've been expecting you,' she stood up. 'Are you all right? You look a bit … um …'

'I'm fine, thanks.'

'Okay, you can fill these in while you wait,' said Grace, handing her a clipboard with a sheet of questions. 'They're our new patient forms.'

Stella sat on the plump couch, balanced the clipboard on her knee and filled out all the sections she could. The table was full of the usual magazines. A modern, standard lamp was in the corner. Hushed lift music, piped from another dimension, was shattered by her phone beeping, a text from Kate: *Drinks this avo? At club before riff-raff arrive.*

Yep been a shit morning. At dentist, will need pain relief.

Kate came straight back: *Yuck. I'll make sure there's a full bottle of the hard stuff.*

Thanks. I owe you.

Eventually a patient came out, stood at the counter to sort out their bill with Grace. When she said the amount, Stella raised her eyebrows. Shit, she'd need to put that on her card, she certainly wasn't going to have her parents pay for it.

'Hi, Stella?' said a voice.

She tilted her head and found herself staring into the face of the dentist who looked like a nineteen-year-old playing dress-ups. His hand was extended towards her.

She shook it. 'Sorry,' she said. 'I thought I was seeing Gerry?'

'No, he's only part-time now, trying to retire. I'm his son, Peter. In the footsteps of the father and all of that.'

He was too cheerful. Stella intrinsically distrusted anyone who could cause pain and be jolly in the face of it. He took the clipboard off her, handed it to Grace and nodded his head in the direction of the surgery.

'Shall we get started?'

She stared at his receding back and debated whether to make a run for it. She didn't want some fresh-faced dentist poking around in her mouth. However, she also knew that she was between the proverbial and the whatever and needed like fuck to get this pain sorted.

'Okay, so here's how it's going to work,' said Peter after she'd sat in the chair. 'I'll have a quick look, take some X-rays, then we'll get you out of pain before we start anything.'

'Sure, just do what you've got to do,' said Stella.

The room smelt of fear and antiseptic mouthwash. She glanced up at the assistant. It was Grace. Clearly she was multi-talented and doubled as the receptionist; at least she looked older than nineteen. Peter clipped a stiff blue paper towel around Stella's neck with a silver chain. She tried her best to relax her back and neck. Not an easy thing to do when you're stretched out, mouth open with a very recent-looking graduate puffing cold air onto your tooth. She winced, trying not to swear.

'Sorry about that, we've got to do the painful stuff so we know what we're dealing with.'

He stopped, sat back and looked at her for a moment. Then proceeded to ask a mass of questions about the pain, when, where, how, why? It took all her willpower to answer as honestly as she was able without resorting to saying, 'Just pull the fucker out, why don't you?'

'Good thing I've had a cancellation this morning. You're up for an emergency root canal,' he finally said. 'I'll take some more X-rays just to be sure, but from what you're telling me we need to deal with it sooner rather than later. We should do it now, otherwise you risk a more serious infection.'

The pain relief was pain in itself. The needle was the size of something that looked like it could fell a horse. Stella decided there was nothing else she could do except ride this particular wave until it was over. As the injections went in, all she could see was the body in the water, her tiny hands, the open mouth. There must be a family somewhere, wondering, grieving. Like a piece of gristle stuck between teeth, there were parts of the image that refused to budge.

Eventually Peter smiled at her. 'You can sit up and rinse,' he said. 'I'm going to see to some other things – that'll give the pain relief time to work, before we get to the main event.'

'Will I end up drooling out the side of my mouth?' she asked, spitting into the swirling water.

'Not too much,' he said with a grin.

Oh great, she thought, not only do I get the kid, but I get the kid with the dodgy sense of humour.

Stella got off the chair and walked over to the window. The surgery looked out over Lambton Quay. In a strange optical illusion it felt as though the room was cantilevered over the street. She'd never seen this view before – you can live in a place for years, yet still be surprised by its ability to confuse. People scurried along below, some carried large bags, others waited to cross at the lights. The roof of a bus cruised past, followed in quick succession by another, then another. She put her hand on the cool glass then transferred it to her cheek.

It offered precious little relief.

Four floors up. This was how high Teri was, before she fell. Stella looked down to the pavement. Something or someone, some event, had propelled Teri over the edge. She tried to imagine it. The act of pulling up a chair to the glass balcony, kicking off shoes, standing on the chair. No. She didn't do it. She was helped, there were no two ways about it. There was someone else in that room with her, someone willing to kill for something.

Fuck, that was too many questions, too many unknowns. There was no entry for Stella into the investigation, no say in events. She was powerless and she knew it, so did McCarthy and he would love every bloody second of it. What she did know, what she could be sure of, was that here was another family, another set of parents questioning, grieving. Closing her eyes she leaned her head against the window. There was Charlotte, her mother's health, Teri, the girl in the water. Stella felt herself crying, shit.

Wiping her eyes, she prodded her cheek and lips, they were going numb. Grace came into the surgery.

'Are you okay?' she asked, handing her a box of tissues. 'It's not that bad really. We can give you more pain relief and Pete is very good at this sort of procedure. We can put a DVD on for you. See, there's a screen on the ceiling.'

Stella blew her nose. 'Thanks, but I'm fine, really.'

'Okay, but we're used to people being a bit nervous, so you're in good company. How's that lip feeling now, good and numb?'

'Yeah, it's getting there.'

'I'll be in the room, assisting, so you let me know if there's anything that I can do for you.'

Stella smiled at her; her face only partially moved. Great, she thought, here comes the drooling. Grace fussed with dental instruments at the other end of the room and Stella turned back to the window. She stared down at the street. He was down there on Lambton Quay, by the lights at the pedestrian crossing. It was him. Christophe. Complete with the dark suit and carrying the violin case. Thank Christ he hadn't been beaten up.

'Listen, Grace, I have to dash out for a minute,' she said.

'Do you need the loo?'

'Yeah, I need the loo, I'll be back in half a tick.'

She started out the door but ran smack into Dentist Pete. 'You're not doing a runner, are you?' he said, trying not to laugh. 'That'd be a first for me.'

'No, I just need to …' She was trying to sidestep him in the narrow corridor.

'Pete, she needs the loo,' said Grace from behind them.

'Oh sorry,' he stepped aside. 'It's just through that door, round the corner, you can't miss it.'

'Thanks, I'll be back in a minute.'

Stella raced for the door, out to the lift. Pushing the buttons on the wall, she heard it creaking from a distant floor in the building. Shit, shit, shit, this was going to take forever. She wrenched open the door to the stairwell and started down two at a time, holding on for dear life to the railing. Out on the street she stood scanning the crowd. A bus whooshed past. The lights were just changing to red. The crossing beep sounded that it was okay to safely cross.

She started to make her way up the street. He was out here, he had to be, she just had to spot him. There were too many dark suits. Too many people carrying bags of stuff.

She caught sight of his back, past a group of tourists. Stella pushed through them, calling a hasty 'sorry', caught him up and made a grab for his arm. He swung around and stared at her.

'Can I help you?' he asked, transferring the box he was carrying to the other hand. They stood there in a strange stand off. Stella looked down at her own hand still on his arm, then back up to his face.

'I'm so sorry,' she said. 'I thought you were someone else. I'm so sorry.'

She started to back away from him; the unknown man kept his eyes on her.

A woman came towards her. 'Are you all right, dear?'

'Yeah, I'm fine, thanks.'

'Okay, it's just …' The woman pointed to Stella's chest.

It was then she realised she still had the blue paper napkin clipped around her neck. Shit, she must look like some kind of deranged escapee. She wrenched it off.

'You're back?' said Peter when the lift doors opened. 'I was getting a little worried. I've never actually had anyone do a runner before. How about we get on with it?'

Stella followed him into the surgery and lay back on the chair. The next fifty-eight minutes were grindingly hideous. Scraping, pushing, more pain relief, wads of cotton wool and some kind of latex dam stretched over her mouth. She'd opted out of the DVD and was pleased they'd given her a pair of oversized dark glasses to wear. Fuck it, she'd been convinced it was Christophe she'd seen out the window. Now what? That poor guy she'd grabbed – she'd scared the shit out of him. She could only hope that it wasn't Christophe who'd been beaten. She needed to find him before some thug of Ravosky's did.

Stella closed her eyes, trying unsuccessfully to relax.

21

BOREDOM WAS THE WORST THING.

The days, stretching like pizza cheese in front of him. Bending, never ending, a droop, then break. Then the next day, much like the one before and the one that would follow.

Mad-Dog had walking loops and if he walked a certain route, it would take him a particular amount of time. He would see the same shop people, or charity workers, or other rough sleepers. Sometimes, his first stop was the soup kitchen on upper Tory Street. Trouble was, he had to cross the duel horror of Cambridge and Kent terraces, at the busiest hour of the morning, to get there on time. He might visit Rita at the library again. He especially liked the upstairs space; it was much quieter and well stocked with newspapers. Occasionally he visited the drop-in centre, just down from the Majestic on Willis Street. But these places he reserved for the bad weather. When it was okay outside, he preferred to keep walking.

Moving, always moving.

Walking gave his day structure, gave it reason. It made him tired. It filled in the time before heading up the hill to his tarp. The sleeping bags. The cardboard. He'd checked the calendar. He kept it in a plastic bag so as not to get wet, even so it was limp from the damp. Tomorrow was the day, fourteen years ago. Today he would walk, tomorrow he would take the bus over to Makara, over to the cemetery.

Walking helped him forget.

He started early. Rita had made him a pile of sandwiches and muffins. He divided up what was left, put some in his pocket for later and wrapped the rest in another carry bag.

If he looked, there might be a late apple on one of the fruit trees in the communal garden.

No matter what the season, the days on the street were long. If you had a job, a family, a life, there were any number of things to fill your time. In fact the days could seem too short. Out here is a void, hour upon hour, day upon day of time. Time equals thinking, thinking equals memory. Mad-Dog needed to steer clear of all that, except for tomorrow. He allowed himself one day. Gus had offered to drive him out there, but the answer was still the same: 'I'm fine with the bus.'

It was a straightforward loop. Courtenay Place, then on to The Terrace, left into Salamanca Road and on up to the Botanic Gardens. He never stopped in this first part. The roads were busy, cars and buses, motorbikes and courier vans, all rushing somewhere. Students from the uni patrolled these pavements in singles and hordes. Their hair bright colours, their clothes dull and grey, ears plugged with headphones attached to more noise.

Mad-Dog kept his head down, leaning forward. Kept moving, slow steps one in front of the other. There was no need to rush, the sky was clear with a few low clouds. It may rain, but that wouldn't be until later. Occasionally he stopped to blow his nose. The wind would, no doubt, pick up, but he had his coat and hat. And besides, walking helped keep him warm.

He kept his hands in his jacket pockets. His right hand found the phone he had there. He liked the feel of its smooth corners, the rough cracked glass on one side – it helped him to remember the angel before she fell. It bothered him, niggled at him. Had she thrown the phone because it was useless, or because it wasn't? Had she wanted him to find it, or not? Was it his now, or should he hand it in?

He waited until he was right inside the grounds of the gardens before he stopped for a proper rest. Leaning against a tree by the side of the path, Mad-Dog tried to catch his breath. He also tried to ignore the pain radiating out of his left hip. He lifted his head and watched a young woman with a child. The girl wobbled along on a little wooden balance bike, then stopped and raised her hand to wave in his direction.

'Come along, Molly.' The mother glanced over to him and placed a protective hand on her child, steering her in a large circle, away.

Mad-Dog sighed.

He took off a glove and rubbed his eyes, trying to loosen the tight band that had crossed his forehead. Straightening up, his hip protested. He couldn't afford painkillers. How strange, he thought, to take something to kill pain. Pain was what kept him alive. He continued towards the rose gardens. Today they were busy, the café humming. A few brave souls sat outside, but the rest were at tables behind the massive glass windows, ordering their lattes, frilled cupcakes and posh sandwiches.

On the steps down to Tinakori Road, Mad-Dog held tightly onto the railing. Several early lunchtime joggers whooshed past him, a cloud of sweat and strong laundry detergent catching them up. He liked Tinakori Road. He could look in the windows and take his time. There was a nice flower shop, Bloomin Gorgeous. If she was outside, she often stopped for a chat. She'd made him a cup of tea once.

'I'm just about to have one,' she'd said.

Mad-Dog tried to remember their conversation. Scents and colours. She asked if he had a favourite flower.

'Lisianthus,' he said, without hesitation.

She raised an eyebrow. 'That's an unusual one,' she said.

'But they are uncommonly beautiful, good choice.'

Today she was busy inside.

He didn't stop but kept on to the park just by the motorway. He liked this park; it was small and narrow but well designed. The noise from the motorway a low hum at his back. The Lady McKenzie Garden for the Blind. He had no idea who she was, or what she'd done to have a garden named after her, but he was grateful nonetheless. Much of the foliage had been cut back for the autumn. He ran his hand over the trimmed lavender and sage. He picked a small sprig of thyme, rubbing it between his fingers to release its heady scent. He sat eating a sandwich. It was quiet, peaceful. In the CBD the streets would be busy with lunchtime shoppers. Office worker bees swarming for their food. Wallets flipped open, cards swiped, plastic and paper stuffed in bins after food was stuffed into mouths.

He's watched them. They didn't see him.

Mad-Dog could feel himself cooling off. He knew if he got too cold, it could be difficult to warm up. Pulling an apple from his pocket, he rubbed it against his jacket lapel. It was small and tart; he finished it quickly and hid the core in the foliage of the garden.

Earth to earth. It would rot. It would be useful.

Now he needed to choose. He could go down Molesworth, past Parliament and on to Lambton Quay, or turn left into Pipitea, then Mulgrave and stop at Old St Paul's. He opted for the latter. He was tired today, more so than usual. Sleep was always intermittent, even at the shelter. But when he was outside it was worse. Yes, he had sleeping bags and an old pillow and now more cardboard. The tarp helped keep the rain and dew off him. But the ground was unforgiving. That'd be why his hip was playing up. And he was worried about the phone in his pocket. It was an itch he couldn't quite scratch.

The angel, the phone, James, they all appeared in his sleep as he drifted off. Maybe he should go to the police. His mind was a pendulum – each time a thought swung past, he'd counter it with another of equal weight. He didn't know how much longer he'd got out here.

The church was quiet apart from the music being piped through a speaker. Bach, a piano concerto, one of the doubles in C minor. Beautiful, especially so in this building. He nodded to the woman in the small office and sat in a pew. The bench was hard, even with the thin red cushion. He didn't mind. He just sat and listened. At one point Mad-Dog felt himself nodding off, his head jerked, a grunt sounded from his mouth. He jiggled a piece of apple from between his teeth then stood to leave; one hand on the back of the pew in front, he hoisted himself upright. His hip, a sharp pain in protest.

Out in the courtyard the wind had arrived; leaves were jolting along the cobblestones; the air felt damp. When he got there, Lambton Quay was particularly busy. The fountain in the park was all shining silver, gurgling water all over the tiles. Smart young women walked briskly along the pavement in the office uniform of black on black. The machinations of bureaucracy and business swirled around him – soon the streets would quieten again as the worker bees buzzed back to their high-rise boxes.

Even before this, even before being out here, Mad-Dog had never understood the need for money. They'd had each other, a home, a child. That seemed enough. He bowed his head and moved on.

That was it. He'd made a decision. I'll go to the police, he thought. I will hand in the phone to them and that will be the end of it.

At the end of Lambton Quay a crowd gathered at the pedestrian crossing, forcing him to wait. He could push through, but he was in no hurry. Several buses lumbered past. The buzzer at the lights sang like a kookaburra, flat and tuneless. The crowd surged forward. He stayed behind. It took him three light changes before he managed to cross. He muttered to the cars and the buses that were stopped, 'Go slow, keep watching.'

Outside the police station he was overcome by a wave of tiredness and started to cough again, a deep rattling sound that doubled him over and eventuated in a thick gob of mucus inside his mouth. Two steps to the gutter, he leaned over and spat it out.

'Ya filthy bastard,' came a voice behind him. 'Get a job why don't ya.'

Mad-Dog didn't bother to look.

The walk and the coughing fit had drained him.

What he needed was sleep and some food. The steps up to the station were too much for him today. He would come sometime tomorrow and hand in the phone.

\

22

STELLA PAID THE EYE-WATERING dental bill and took an Uber home.

Peter had advised her to take things easy that afternoon – like hell she could do that. She touched a hand to her face; her lip was fat and unresponsive. Her tongue, like an inexperienced kisser, felt alien in her mouth. She needed to get the police interview with Meathead McCarthy over, then try to meet Ravosky, followed closely by Lassiter, with another phone call to Rita thrown in. She couldn't shake the image of the man in the suit she'd accosted on Lambton Quay, how convinced she'd been it was Christophe.

Back at her parents' place, she changed her clothes, charged her phone, pocketed a couple of Panadol for later. She was filling a glass with water when her phone rang. She looked at the screen, took a deep breath then answered.

'Hi, Mum.'

'Sorry I didn't see you this morning,' said Peace. 'How was the dentist?'

'Okay, I'm just pleased it's over,' said Stella. 'I saw Aunty Rita earlier ...' She was buzzing – every fibre wanted to shout at her mother, but instead she kept her voice as calm as she was able. 'You *wanted* Rita to tell me, didn't you? What the bloody hell's been going on, Mum? She said you'd had a health scare.' So much for keeping calm.

'Darling ...'

'Don't I have a right to know?'

'Darling, please ...' Her mum's voice sounded small down the phone. 'It was nothing, really. My blood pressure went a little high, then it wouldn't settle. I had a night in hospital while they sorted it out, that's all. There was mention of an irregular heartbeat, but I'm being monitored,' said Peace. 'For now it's under control.'

'You know I'll grill Charlotte and Dad about it, so you'd better be straight with me.'

'Please don't go on at your dad or Charlotte. He found the whole thing difficult. They both wanted to tell you,' said Peace. 'I told them not to. There was nothing you could have done at a distance and coming back wouldn't have changed anything.'

'What about Tim? Does he know?' Stella leaned against the bench swishing the last of her water around the glass.

'Tim does his own thing,' said Peace. There was a long silence from her end of the phone. 'I am sorry we didn't tell you about the hospital thing,' she paused, 'and I'm so sorry for your loss, Stella. I know how much Teri meant to you and losing a friend in these circumstances …'

'Let's just be clear about this, Mum. She didn't jump, okay?' said Stella. 'Let's also be clear about something else. I am part of this family – you will not keep things from me, no matter where I am.'

'I'm sorry, sweetheart. Are you okay?'

'Absolutely,' Stella said a little too firmly. 'Honestly, I'm fine, it's all fine. I'm going to try and catch up with Kate at the club.'

'Did you take the flowers to Teri's parents?'

'Yeah, they weren't home, so I left them at the door.'

'Can you help tomorrow morning with some deliveries?' asked Peace. 'I'm a bit snowed under.'

'Sure, Mum, will do. I'll be there bright and early.'

Walking up the steps to the central police station, Stella had an overwhelming sense of déjà vu. She'd been good at police work. It was why she was put forward for detective training – but she'd lost it all over a stupid affair that ended badly.

Very badly. She stood in the foyer, same carpet, same smell. She dreaded bumping into an old colleague. That would be beyond excruciating. Meathead McCarthy was going to make her wait, that was a definite for sure. He'd been the one assigned to Dee's suicide …

'Did you know the victim, Denise Porter, otherwise known as Dee?' That had been his opening question.

'Yes.'

'How did you know the victim?'

'I knew her husband, William.'

'How did you know the husband?'

She stared at him, willing him to break eye contact first. 'We worked together,' she said, slowly, deliberately.

'Were you,' he paused, 'sleeping with him?'

'You know all of this – you know I was.'

'I know, but I still have to ask.'

'No, you don't.'

'Why should I treat you any differently?'

'Because I'm a colleague,' she said.

'Do you think I'm enjoying this?'

'I don't know. Are you?'

'Weston, you found the body of Dee Porter, an apparent suicide. I'm trying to figure out what your involvement in all this is. Why did she place a call to you before killing herself?'

'My involvement,' she spat the word out. 'Fuck you, McCarthy, you know full well.'

'Yes, but I need to hear it from you.'

Now she had to talk to him again.

Stella sat and waited. The images went in rotation, first Dee, then Teri, now the body of the girl. She understood the reality of what she'd seen in the water, but not the significance, if there was any at all. She scrolled through the event minute by minute, reminding herself of the details. That's what he'd want. That's what he'd use to try and trip her. Time of day, temperature, what the tiny body looked like, was she on her front or back, details, details. Stella couldn't shake it.

Eventually McCarthy turned up with a junior in tow. Good grief, she thought, don't tell me he's actually mentoring someone. The interview room McCarthy took her to was the exact replica of every single small airless room she'd ever been in. There was a table and a couple of utilitarian chairs, and machinery for recording the events waited on one end of the table. McCarthy slapped a brown folder onto the table then sat and motioned her to do the same. The junior stood, observing. Stella took off her jacket, placed it over the back of the chair and sat down.

'So, Stella,' said McCarthy, rummaging in his jacket pocket for a pen. 'This is a little awkward.'

'Only if you make it.'

The junior sniffed.

'Can I get you a glass of water, coffee?' he asked.

'Let's just get this over with, shall we?'

'Switch on the recording,' he told the junior, and to Stella: 'I'd hate for there to be any misunderstandings.'

'Does that happen often, misunderstandings?'

The junior sniffed again and switched on the machine. 'You're good to go,' he said.

DI McCarthy shuffled some papers then went through the preliminaries of introductions, time, date, then the first question. 'You found the body of the girl?'

'Yes,' she said.

'Was anyone with you?'

'No.'

'You said you'd been at the pool?'

'Yes.'

'You live in London?'

'Yes.'

'So …' He stopped to excavate something out of a molar with his tongue. Eventually he gave up and used the nail of his pinkie finger to do the job. Sucking sounds ensued. 'So, you're just gracing us with a visit?'

'Yes, I suppose so. Have you found her next of kin?'

'We're working on that.'

'What about a name, anything?'

His eyes flicked over her face. 'That doesn't concern you.'

'Other than drowning, do you have a cause of death?' she asked.

'You know I can't discuss that with you. We won't know for sure anyway until after the autopsy.'

'Well, the media are all over it. I've had a journo try and contact me but they've got nothing,' she said.

'The media couldn't organise a piss-up in the proverbial.'

Stella leaned forward and tried again. 'But does it look suspicious to you?'

'Ms Weston,' said McCarthy, 'you are a member of the public who alerted us to the unfortunate finding of the body of a young Asian girl. You are not the police, you are not investigating, you are here to help us with our enquiry and give us a statement. You are simply a member of the public.' Staring directly at her. 'Do you understand?'

She sat back in her chair. Christ, he was loving this. 'Yes, I understand,' she said.

'Now, with regard to the *other* unfortunate death. You were a friend of Teri Mossburn?'

'Yes.'

'When did you last talk to her?'

'Saturday night at my parents' party.'

'How did she seem to you?'

'She was great, really great. Happy, vibrant. There was no hint of anything darker.'

'So, you knew her well?' he asked.

'Yes.'

'Did you happen to notice if she had a phone with her on Saturday night?'

'Yes she did.'

'You can be certain of that?'

'Absolutely,' said Stella. 'She showed me how she carried it under the strap of her dress.'

'Right,' said McCarthy, 'interesting.'

'You haven't found it? What about a computer, have you got that, at least?'

'I'm not at liberty to say.'

'Of course not,' said Stella, 'I'm told you believe Teri was a suicide.'

'I'm not sure who your source is, but it seems that way.'

'So, you're not trying to find anything or anyone else?'

'Should we be?'

'You're the police here, remember.' Stella crossed her arms. 'I'm not doing your job for you.'

'If there's something you're not telling us, we can have you for obstruction.'

The pain relief, from Pete the dentist, was beginning to wear thin, as was her patience. He was winding her up, she could feel it. Like some kind of deranged chess match, it had to end eventually.

'That'll be all for now,' said McCarthy. 'Don't disappear anytime soon.'

'I've no reason to.'

23

Stella stood outside the door of the club and lit a cigarette. She'd stop soon, she'd have to, they were getting too bloody expensive.

The Chandelier Club where Kate had her next gig was in the back of a building that fronted Cuba Street. The street itself was a strange mix. There were tattoo parlours up stairways, alternative-looking shops that may, or may not, sell dope-smoking paraphernalia, ethnic clothing stores and the ubiquitous Indian restaurant with the two-for-one-on-Mondays deal. Closed doors, with numbers and names written on, indicated there were flats upstairs, most likely many flats squeezed into the available space. All these jostled alongside a couple of decent cafés, several high-end restaurants and the Bristol pub, which Stella noticed had been newly gentrified. It was the street where new money, old money and no money rubbed together in a functional kind of way.

She scanned the crowd in the hope of seeing Christophe. It seemed extraordinary to Stella, the idea that he might have been in the area at the time of Teri's death. Why hadn't the police cottoned on to him? A man sat down heavily on one of the benches. A soft sports bag was slung over his shoulder, a greasy cap low on his forehead. An equally dirty sweatshirt sat under an oversized jacket. His sneakers were clearly a size too big, and neither shoe had laces. He was unshaven. Dark hair poked out from under his cap, his hands blue from tattoos. The wind was in the wrong direction and Stella caught a whiff of old smoke and unwashed body. Eventually he looked around.

'What do ya want?' he said.

'Do you want a smoke?' She held the packet out.

'Sure.'

He took two, putting them in his pocket. Reached for another, which he put in his mouth. She flicked the lighter for him and waited as he inhaled deeply, not looking at her.

'What do you want?' he asked again.

'I just want to talk.'

'Okay.'

'You're out on the street a lot?' She sat down next to him.

'Yeah, so what?'

'Do you know who was bashed the other night?'

'Yeah, are you police?'

'No. I'm just trying to contact someone. Do you have any idea who might have done it?'

'Nah, bloody arsehole. If I find out I'll bash the bastard myself so he knows what it feels like. I was the one who found him.'

'The guy that was beaten up?'

'Yeah, fucking awful. It was Warren – he's a mate,' he said. 'Haven't seen anything like it for a long time. They smashed his head, blood everywhere, even tried to dislocate his fingers.' He dragged deeply on the cigarette, held the smoke in his lungs before exhaling loudly.

'What did they want?'

'Fuck knows. It's not like he had anything worth stealing. He's just an old fella, wouldn't hurt anyone.' He flicked the ash from the end of his cigarette, a sharp twitching movement. 'They trashed his trolley.'

'His what?'

'His trolley,' he said it slower, drawing out each sound. 'His supermarket trolley. He nicked one ages ago. Used it for his stuff. He collects things, sees things, tries to flog them off. He's pretty useless at it, poor bastard. That's what I saw first, the overturned trolley. There was stuff everywhere.'

He flicked the butt onto the ground and smashed it with the toe of his sneaker. 'I saw him. He just kinda groaned. He kept saying, *I haven't got it, I haven't got a phone.* Don't know what shit he was on about. Delusional, I reckon. Why would they beat him up for a phone?'

They were both quiet for moment.

'Do you know anyone called Luther?' Stella asked.

'Nope.'

'What about Christophe?' Stella tried again. 'He's on the street like you. I'm trying to find him, you heard of him?'

'Nah. I don't know anyone called Christophe. What do you want him for?'

'He's not in any trouble or anything. I just need to talk to him, he may have seen something,' she said. 'So, do you know him?'

'Is that his street name?'

'His what?'

'His street name. The guys out here, I don't know all their real names,' he said. 'I'm Beanie. There's Gutter and Digby. Georgie-Pie got the bashing, his name's Warren, and there's Mad-Dog, and Postman. So, what's his street name?'

'I've no idea,' she said. 'I just know he's called Christophe.'

'Can't help you then, can I?' Still no eye contact. 'Have you tried the night shelter – they know most of the guys on the street.'

'Not yet,' she said. 'Thanks anyway, Beanie.' She stood up and turned to leave then stopped and spun around. 'He plays the violin, does that help?'

Beanie lifted his head and looked her in the eye.

'That's Mad-Dog you're after,' he said slowly. 'Mad-Dog. What's he done? Is he in trouble?'

'Mad-Dog?' said Stella. 'No, he's not in any trouble. I need to talk to him, that's all.'

'I don't know who that Christophe guy is though.'

She smiled. 'Listen, Beanie, if you see him, could you tell him that Rita in the library needs to talk to him. It's important.'

'Okay.'

'Here, have the packet,' she said, handing it to him. 'I appreciate your help.'

Grinding the butt of her cigarette into the pavement, Stella typed a text to Rita: *If Christophe comes in get phone from him – v important.*

She hit send, then pushed open the door to the club. Mad-Dog, she thought, how on earth does someone end up with a name like that? It was good information; anything that would help her to locate him was a step forward. McCarthy was going with suicide, but there was no way Stella was going to let it end with that. She stared down the long dimly lit corridor. Her eyes followed a string of coloured lights that were conveniently switched off. Painted on the walls in Day-Glo green were some well-positioned arrows directing her up the stairs. Stella wrinkled her nose slightly. It wasn't a boiled cabbage smell, just the regular combination of old smoke, damp mould, drying piss from the street and stale perfume. She'd encountered worse in her time. She was grateful there wasn't the added 'dead body' smell.

At the top of the stairs, on the first floor, she opened the door. The corridor was well lit, but it seemed to lead to a series of apartment doors. Back on the landing, she took the stairs to the second floor. She pushed through heavy swinging doors and found herself in another dimly lit hallway. The walls were draped in black. Strings of tiny fairy lights trailed along the ceiling but had been turned off. At the far end was a drape of red velvet curtain.

This kind of place was made for night-time. It would come alive with the music, the chatter of voices, clinking glasses. The sound of fun and sex and entertainment, people out to have a good time.

During the day they reverted to their true selves, the makeup came off, the peeling paint became visible.

Fumbling through the curtain, Stella found herself in the club. The only sounds were the dishwasher going full tilt in the kitchen and someone cursing because the coriander hadn't come in with the grocery order. Her eyes took a minute to adjust to the bright light. It was smaller than she expected but it wasn't meant for a large crowd. The idea was exclusivity. The patrons enjoyed knowing that it was somehow a private arrangement; it made them feel like they had something the general public didn't. She'd been to enough of these kinds of places in London. Her boyfriend at the time liked to frequent them. It gave him the thrill of acting like he was some kind of gangster, an offshoot of the Kray twins in a sharp suit with a moll on his arm. It took him out of his married-with-toddlers, suburban nightmare. He was wealthy, with the house in Kent and an upmarket apartment in central London. She played along because it was entertaining. He'd paid for the drinks, the sex was fun and there were no strings attached. The perfect arrangement for both of them.

She walked across the partly carpeted floor of the bar. A raised stage jutted out, poles attached from the ceiling to the floor. One of the staff was pushing a vacuum cleaner around like taking a reluctant elderly dog for a walk. Behind the bar a young barista flicked a tea towel around the glassware before placing them on a shelf. Every inch of her arms was inked. A piece of bone pierced through one ear, a gigantic tube in the other. Her nails were painted black, her lips bright red to match her hair. Good god, you're someone's daughter, thought Stella. Followed with, Good god, I sound like my mother.

Kate was chaperoning the baby grand piano onto the stage. The chairs were stacked on the tables, while the vacuum cleaner droned. The lights were too bright. There was the continuation of the unidentifiable smell that may have been food mixed with flat beer, or whisky. It was difficult to tell.

'Hiya,' said Stella.

Kate looked up, a huge smile playing across her face. She flung her arms wide open, hopped off the stage. 'Stella, oh my god lovie, it's been too long.'

Kate was tall, taller than Teri even. Stella often wondered why all the people in her life seemed to be so much taller than her. She had a tangle of very black, very dyed hair all piled up and fastened with a massive fork-like arrangement. Even at this hour of the day her eyes were ringed with kohl, her lips painted a glossy red. Kate jangled. Every move she made was accompanied by the sound of bracelets, necklaces and interesting rings. A vibrant green silk kimono was thrown artfully over a completely black ensemble. Kate was as adorned as much as Stella wasn't. She found herself being enveloped by this woman, her massive chest, the wonderfully hippy scent of patchouli.

'So, you found us all right?' Kate said, finally letting her go. 'My god, I'm going to start blubbing. It's so fantastic to see you.'

'You too, it's been a shitty few days. I almost didn't find you. Talk about a rabbit warren back there.'

'Welcome to Wonderland, Alice. You'll be happy to know we haven't lost anyone yet, that I know about,' Kate laughed. 'Do you want a coffee?'

'I'd love one,' said Stella.

Kate wandered over and had a quick chat with tattoo girl.

'Let's talk over here,' said Kate.

Guiding Stella around the stage and over to a plush, upholstered booth, she slid in around the back of the table and patted the seat beside her. 'I hope you're going to come Friday evening. It should be a good show,' said Kate. 'I'm still trying to get my head around Teri's funeral. It seems indecently sudden to be getting back to performing. Getting up on a stage, entertaining the great unwashed.'

'I know what you mean,' said Stella.

'It's just that if I don't go on, they'll can me and get someone else. I can't afford to lose this gig.'

'I understand. No one will think the worse of you,' said Stella. 'We're all in shock, Kate, all of us. The funeral will be shit, but we know that already. We've just got to get through it.' She picked at her nail.

'Mitchell will be coming,' said Kate.

'And I wouldn't miss it either. I can't remember the last time I saw you perform.'

'You've been away a long time – the show's changed.'

Stella leaned back into the booth and closed her eyes. She realised just how easy it would be for her to go to sleep. 'I can't imagine Lassie in a place like this.'

'You'd be surprised who turns up. There's a huge number of people who love to be titillated.'

'Titillated being the operative, eh?' Stella laughed. 'So, do you get your tits out in this show?'

'Not anymore, darling. I'm just the singer. It's the others that do the burlesque stuff. They're quite stunning.'

'I'm sure.'

'Although, I do display an indecent amount of cleavage and quite a bit of leg at times – don't worry, I still bat for the other team.'

Stella thanked the tattooed barista for the coffee and the two tumblers of whisky she placed in front of them. One of the things about London she didn't miss was the inability to get a decent cup of coffee from pretty much anywhere. Not sure it was worth moving back to Wellington for though. She stirred the cup and took a sip.

The tattooed barista was still standing there. 'Kate said you were friends with Teri,' she said.

'Stella, Birdie, Birdie, Stella.' Kate jangled her hand as she did quick introductions.

'Birdie?' said Stella.

'Yeah, short for Bronwyn.'

'How did you know Teri?'

'She worked here for a while, moonlighting, she told me she needed the extra money. I didn't know her well, but she seemed really nice,' said Birdie. 'I was sorry to hear what happened.'

Stella stared at her coffee. 'Yeah, thanks.'

Birdie picked up the tray and headed back to the bar.

Kate took one of the whisky glasses and pushed the other one towards Stella. She raised the glass towards her. 'To Teri,' she said.

'To Teri.'

They clinked their glasses together. Stella coughed as she felt it burn all the way down. It slammed into her like a fully loaded van, then shot into her brain. She coughed again and took another sip of coffee.

'Did you know Teri worked here?' Stella asked.

'Yeah. It was a while ago though and we were never here at the same time. I think she was planning on an overseas trip and needed the extra money. She said something about wanting to surprise you in London.'

'Well, I am surprised. I knew nothing about that, but I'm finding out there was a whole lot about Teri I didn't know,' said Stella. They sipped their drinks. The cleaner had finally finished and was clearing up. 'How are you holding up, Kate?'

'Oh, you know … what about you?' Kate asked.

'Yeah, about the same as you I reckon,' she said. 'There's good moments and bad. I started today with a visit to the dentist and a root canal – don't get me started on yesterday's events. Let's say I've had better weeks.'

'Why? What happened?'

How do you tell someone about a body? How do you convey the horror of what you feel, what you've seen? The girl under the wharf, young, precious. Or the pregnant wife of your lover at the end of a rope. Once the image was in your head, you couldn't erase it like a blackboard, or wiping a computer clean. No amount of alcohol, or sex, or drugs will smooth those edges. She relayed it anyway, she needed to tell someone – her voice sounded flat, unemotional, official.

Kate leaned over and gave her a long hug. 'You poor thing. What an awful thing to come across. I can't imagine …'

'It's been a shit week, Kate. As an added bonus I've just come from a police interview with Frank McCarthy. You remember him – Meathead McCarthy. That was a bloody riot.' Stella sat back in the padded seat of the club. She lifted the glass to her mouth and drained the last of the whisky. 'Now with this on board – who knows what I might do.'

'I'm serious, sweetie. Mitchell is worried about you. I'm worried about you.'

'Well, that's very kind of both you and Lassie, but really, I'm okay.' Friends or no friends, the idea they'd been discussing her, prickled her skin.

'You don't have to do this tough-guy thing – Teri's death has hit all of us.'

The mention of Teri silenced both of them. Kate, Lassie, Teri, they'd been together, all the way through uni. Kate had been a good friend to them all. She'd be feeling like shit as well.

'And what about you?' said Stella.

'It gets harder and harder to deal with. One minute I'm crying, the next I'm furious as hell at her for doing this. I'm meant to be performing this weekend. I'm not sure I can,' said Kate in a fresh flood of tears. 'I'm so angry she didn't talk to me, or anyone.' She blew her nose on a tissue.

'She didn't do it and it's sure as hell not your fault. I'm angry that someone did it to her.'

'You don't think Teri's death was suicide?'

'It wasn't. I mean, do you believe she jumped? Like you said, why didn't she come and talk to you? You knew her for as long as me.' Stella willed that someone would hand her another shot of whisky. She looked at her friend. Her *friend*, one of the few, besides Teri, who still stood by her.

'I don't know, hon. I wasn't at the party that night and, to be honest, I feel awful. I've been so busy with gigs I hadn't seen much of her in the last few months.' Kate drained the last of her drink. 'Mitch told me the preliminary police report came through – they're going with suicide. Do we know if there was there a note?'

'Dunno,' Stella said. 'Our charming meathead detective may know something, but he sure as hell wouldn't tell me. And yes, I know, the chair was up by the balcony.'

'What more do you need?' said Kate.

What I need is to find Teri's phone, thought Stella. That's the missing piece of evidence.

'What I need is the bathroom.' Stella pushed her way out of the booth and Kate pointed her in the right direction.

Stella's head was pounding. The door swung closed behind her with a soft thud. Finding herself in a corridor with a number of other doors she sighed, bloody Alice in Wonderland again. She checked both ways – none of the doors declared themselves to be the women's loo, or a loo of any kind. Fuck it. She opened the nearest one and flicked on the light. It was a utilities kind of arrangement, shelves of cleaning fluid complete with antiseptic smell. Stella flicked the light off. Behind her another one was opening. Perhaps that was the loo.

She was dying for a pee.

She heard a voice, an angry voice.

A young girl stood there. She looked around six or seven, maybe even younger, Stella couldn't tell. Her arm was being held tight by the man standing over her. The girl was crying. Her little body strained away from her captor. Her head bowed, eyes to the floor. Stella couldn't make out what she was saying. But she could sure hear what he was saying.

'Do as you're told, you little bitch.'

He shook her arm. She nodded her head, wiping her eyes with her free hand. He looked up.

Stella walked towards him. 'What are you doing? Let her go – you're hurting her.'

His head moved slowly, like a coiled snake ready to lash out. He was small, compact, muscle on bone.

'Let her go,' she said again.

He loosened his grip, but still held the girl tight.

'There's no need to yell at her,' she continued.

'What do you want?' he asked.

'I'm trying to find the loo.'

'Well, it isn't down this end.'

'Are you okay?' said Stella to the girl.

'Fuck off,' he said.

He opened the door behind him and pushed the girl back through it. The corridor was quiet. Stella blinked a couple of times.

That didn't make sense.

She began to wonder if her mind was playing tricks. She'd only had one glass of whisky, admittedly on a totally empty stomach, but still. The door closed behind them.

Back in the club Stella eased herself into the booth next to Kate. She was quiet for a moment.

'There's a brothel attached to the club, isn't there?' she asked.

'Yeah, it's all legit,' said Kate.

'I know it's legal, but have you ever seen any kids here?'

'Kids? No. Oh, hang on, yeah. I have actually. A couple of times. I think there were child-minding issues, so one of the workers bought her kid here. Trevor wasn't thrilled.'

'Who's Trevor?'

'Trevor manages the club. I'm not sure who's exactly in charge of the working girls, or what they make.'

'What about the building, who owns that?'

'Oh, Stella honey, I've no idea. I get contacted by the managers of these places, we work out a contract, we sign the deal and that's that. Why are you asking?'

'Humour me,' said Stella. 'Do you have anything to do with the working girls?

'Not particularly,' Kate said.

'What about a guy who works here. A little taller than me, shaved head, he's got one of those clit ticklers on his lower lip, silver rings in his ear?'

'That'd be James, and I hate that term *clit tickler.*'

Stella laughed. 'So do I. I just ran into him. Nasty piece of work. What do you know about him?'

'Not much, bit of a wanker,' said Kate. 'Struts around like he owns the place.'

'But he doesn't own the place, does he?'

'Shit no. He's just one of the heavies employed to keep things under control.'

'So, you don't see the working girls back there?'

'Sometimes I do. It's not an *us and them* situation, I'm here for the performances. We have a backstage area the size of a chicken coop. There's a separate entrance for the brothel – such an old-fashioned term, *brothel*.'

'Yeah, but what else are you going to call it?' said Stella. 'Are there many Asian working girls?'

Kate sat back. 'A few, I guess. There are all makes and models, some of them are quite delicious. Some are really smart and savvy, others are just strung out. The need to make money doesn't discriminate.'

Stella's phone beeped with a text from Rita: *Christophe just left won't give me phone. V suspicious, said someone else wants it.*

'Damn it,' said Stella. Who the fuck else knows he's got the phone, she thought.

'What's going on?'

'To tell you the truth, Kate, I don't know. All I have are suspicions and not much else. Teri was tied up in something, but I've no idea what.'

The episode in the corridor had been no more than fifteen seconds, twenty tops. But for that entire twenty seconds, Stella had tried not to stare at the slim silver chain which the girl wore around her left ankle.

Stella left the club. Cuba Street was in late afternoon shadow, pigeons pecked around the vacant outside tables for their dinner. Sun umbrellas flapped and rattled in the wind. Beanie was no longer sitting on the bench. The Bucket Fountain tipped and sloshed drunkenly. She looked around, no Christophe either. Talk about a needle in a haystack.

'Stella,' a voice called from behind her. 'Wait up.' It was Birdie. 'You forgot your jacket.'

'Thanks, I think that whisky went straight to my head.'

'Have you got a minute?'

'Sure, what's up?' Stella asked.

'Look, I don't want you to think that I'm being nosey or anything. I really liked Teri.'

'You're not being nosey.'

'It's really nothing I suppose,' said Birdie. 'It's just that, well, Teri asked a lot of questions.'

'Yeah, what kind of questions?'

'She wanted to know about the prostitute side of the business.'

'She wasn't doing that was she, being a working girl?'

'Oh god, no,' said Birdie. 'She was squeaky clean. She was always amazed how much she made in tips working the tables. The men loved her. But no, she wasn't working the other side.'

'So, what was she trying to find out?' Stella asked.

'She asked how much money they made,' said Birdie. 'How often they worked, if any of the women bought their kids in, things like that. I think she wanted to start up some kind of child-minding business for them.'

Yeah, that'd be Teri, Stella thought. Always thinking about how she could help.

'Do any of the women bring their kids in?'

'Yeah, they do, occasionally. Management doesn't like it. They don't want to be liable for any accidents or anything.'

'What can you tell me about James?'

'James? He's a fuckwit. I'd steer clear of him.'

'Why's that?

'He can be …' she said. 'I've heard he can be violent.'

'Listen,' said Stella. 'If you think of anything else can you let me know? Ask Kate – she's got my number.'

'Sure thing.'

'I've gotta go. Thanks for my jacket.'

24

WALKING TOWARDS COURTENAY PLACE, Stella came across a couple of guys sitting cross-legged on pieces of cardboard. Both were holding up *I'm homeless, can you spare change* signs. Neither of them had heard of Christophe or Mad-Dog.

Stella felt irritable. Her jacket wasn't warm enough and her feet were starting to hurt. The pain relief from the dentist had worn off a long time ago. She ducked into a chemist, bought some painkillers and downed a couple with gulps from a takeaway coffee. Crossing the road at the Embassy Theatre she started down the other side. She went into a couple of the shops and cafés to ask about Christophe. Older man, violin case, sometimes busks? Same thing. No one knew anything. How can one man be so invisible, she thought. He's out here, he has a name, he has a life of sorts, he earns money. Where is his family? Where are his people?

Standing outside a tatty gift shop Stella looked at the marble steps of the building next door. They looked out of place along this stretch of the street. They were polished and shiny. Brass plates were screwed into the wall by the large double doors. One advertised the services of a *Forensic Accountant,* another was *Iridology and Dietician.*

It was the one underneath that caught her eye.

She went in, and up two flights of stairs. These buildings were all remarkably similar. Polished wooden railings, marble stairs, a rickety lift that you used in fear of your life. In the corridor she could hear classical music coming from one of the rooms. She found the door and knocked.

'It's open,' a deep voice boomed.

She pushed open the door, a little breathless from the stairs, and was engulfed in the sound of an opera being played at volume. The room had a high ceiling and was full of light from a single large window. A comfy sofa sat along one wall, another wall hung with all manner of stringed instruments.

'Sorry,' called out the voice. 'I'll just turn that down a bit.'

A large man, with an equally large beard, appeared from behind a curtain. A gold ring hung in one ear. He had a head full of thick wavy hair. The intricately embroidered waistcoat stretched across his ample tummy was a riot of texture and colour. The opera fell quieter.

'How may I help?' he asked.

'My name is Stella Weston—' she began.

He thrust his hand out. 'Augustus V Schmidt, pleased to meet you.'

She shook his large warm hand and smiled at him. 'I understand you're a luthier.'

'I most certainly am,' he said.

'What is that exactly?'

'Excuse me?'

'What do you do?'

'You walked up two flights of stairs to find out what I do?' He smiled back at her.

'Well, I wasn't about to risk my life in that lift,' said Stella. 'I guess I'm just curious.'

'Well, Ms Weston,' he began, 'sometimes we get mistaken for someone involved in the dark arts, or someone who is of a religious nature, a Lutheran.' He smiled to himself and stroked his lush beard. 'However, a luthier is someone trained in the fine art of string instrument care and restoration.' His voice was lightly accented. European. Possibly French, Stella thought.

'That's really specialist,' she said. 'So, you'd know most of the string players around?'

'Most of the ones who need their instruments looked at, yes.'

'Have you ever come across a guy called Christophe?'

His eyes narrowed slightly. 'I may have. Why do you ask?'

'He's not in trouble or anything,' she said.

'That's good. Are you police?'

'No, well, I used to be, but not anymore. It's just that he may have seen something or found something,' she said. 'I know he's on the street. I know he's called Mad-Dog. That's about it really.'

Augustus V Schmidt laughed. A great booming sound bounced out from his chest. 'Mad-Dog, that's a good one. That's someone being ironic, I think. Couldn't be further from the truth.'

'You're probably right, Mr Schmidt. Either way, do you know him?'

'Call me Gus, and yes,' he said, 'I know Christophe Janvier. Would you like a cup of tea?'

'That would be lovely,' replied Stella, slightly surprised.

Gus busied himself behind a curtain. Stella heard the rumble of a boiling kettle, the clinking of china cups.

'It's just regular, if that's okay,' he called out.

'Anything is fine,' said Stella. She walked around the workshop, her hand trailing over the dips and curves of the instruments. It seemed extraordinary to her that these lifeless bits of wood, in the right hands, could produce any kind of sound. Let alone a good one. A cup and saucer was placed in her hands.

'Do you take sugar?' he asked.

'No, thanks.' She sipped the hot liquid.

'Please, have a seat,' said Gus, pointing to the couch.

'And tell me why you want to speak to Christophe.'

There was something about him, something about the room, the warmth, the quiet music, the smell of wax and polishing oil. She felt she could trust him – even so, she kept it light on details. Gus leaned against his workbench and listened.

'Interesting,' he said when she finished. They were both quiet for a while, sipping their tea. He stroked his beard. 'I don't wish to sound negative, but the chances of Christophe having that poor girl's phone are pretty slim, don't you think?'

'I don't know what to think anymore. But I have to keep trying. How often do you see him?'

'It's difficult to say,' said Gus. 'I see him more in winter. He comes in, I make him tea and some food. We chat, or not. Then he leaves.'

'So where does he live, where can I find him?'

'That's a tricky one. Christophe doesn't want to be found. He lives rough. The last time I checked, he had a camp somewhere up on Mount Vic. When the weather gets bad, he goes to the night shelter. Other times I've let him sleep on the couch. He's very tidy, very easy.' Gus paused. 'Not every homeless person is a drug-addled, alcoholic criminal. Sometimes events simply overwhelm and a downward spiral begins,' he said. 'With Christophe it was the death of his wife and child. He never recovered. He stopped working, teaching, playing. He lost his house. His friends tried to help, but …' He sighed. 'I do what I can, what he will allow, but I fear it's only a matter of time before the street catches up with him. He manages, mostly.'

They were both quiet, listening to the last phrase played through the speakers. Stella stood then and handed her cup and saucer to Gus. 'Thank you for your time and the tea. That music was beautiful. What was it?'

'"Je crois entendre encore" from Bizet's *The Pearl Fishers*, a story of love, betrayal and sacrifice. In other words, every opera that's ever been written.'

'Well, it's still beautiful,' said Stella.

'Yes, it truly is. I will try to speak to Christophe of your concerns, but I won't have him hurt, not again.'

It was late by the time she got back to her parents' house. There was a note on the bench: *Dinner in microwave xxx Mum*

Truly, there was no place like home. Stella pulled open the fridge. There was a half-full bottle of Sauvignon. She looked at it, closed the fridge door and poured herself a large glass of water.

'I see you found the food,' said her dad, coming over to give her a hug. 'How was the dentist?' He gently stroked her cheek.

'Crap, but at least it's done now.'

The microwave dinged. Stella pushed open the door. 'Is this bowl of total yumminess your effort?'

'No, that's your mum's doing.'

'Well, I definitely miss this, and you of course.' She smiled at him.

'Good to hear.' He sat at the table.

'So, were you ever going to tell me?'

'About what?'

'About Mum – were you ever going to say anything?'

'Ah, Stell. The tyranny of distance.'

'Bollocks and you know it,' she said.

He ran his fingers through his thinning hair and pulled his dressing gown around his neck. 'I wanted to tell you, but your mother said no. She didn't want you to worry. You know her, she wants calm. To her it wasn't a big deal.'

'And you?'

'Life seldom gives us what we think we want,' he said finally. 'There was no conspiracy, Stella. She just wanted to protect you, that's all.'

'I know, Dad, I understand, but another time ...'

'Another time I'll come over to London and tell you personally.'

'Where's Mum?'

'She's got her wall-climbing class tonight,' he said.

'Should she be doing that, with her heart and everything?'

'Try telling Peace to do anything, Stell. You know the plum doesn't fall far from the tree.' He stood up and kissed the top of her head. 'Night, I'm off to bed.'

Stella opened her laptop. She was searching for who owned the building that housed the Chandelier Club – maybe there was a connection there. It proved fruitless. It was owned by a company called Midpoint Holdings Limited, which, in turn, was owned by another company. Ravosky's name wasn't mentioned anywhere. He wouldn't be that stupid; he'd have someone else front it. It was all smoke and mirrors. Stella closed the computer. But now she'd found out – not only where Christophe stored his violin, but where she might find him.

25

THE NEXT DAY, after a quick swim, Stella helped Peace with deliveries. With her mum's small car full of brightly coloured and perfumed bouquets, Stella crisscrossed the streets of central Wellington running in and out of buildings like a floral superhero.

'It's a great help to me,' said Peace. 'The cost of couriers these days is astronomical.'

'Happy to,' said Stella. She knew her Mum wasn't being completely upfront. Peace had a good deal going with the couriers – she just wanted to give Stella something to do.

With one eye on the delivery list and one on the road, she kept a lookout at the pedestrians. There'd been another report of a homeless man being bashed. They hadn't said much, just that it was down the back of an alley off Courtenay Place. She hoped like hell it hadn't been Christophe. She'd tried to contact Gus, had left a message but he hadn't returned her call. The hospital staff wouldn't tell her a thing as she wasn't next of kin.

Waiting at the lights, on the corner of Manners and Victoria, Stella spied Beanie across the road. Bumping two wheels up onto the pavement, she pushed the hazard light button and jumped out of the car.

'Beanie,' she yelled.

He turned around to face her and ambled over. 'Got any smokes?' he asked.

'Sure,' said Stella, rummaging in her coat pocket. 'Here you go. I heard there was another bashing.'

'Yeah, last night.'

'You know who it was?'

'Nope.'

'Have you seen Mad-Dog?'

'Nah, maybe it was him that got bashed. Haven't seen him for a while.'

'Shit, I hope not. How about you come to the hospital with me. We could spin a yarn and get in to see who it was.'

'Sure.'

'Come on,' she said, jerking her head towards the car. 'Let's go.'

Beanie picked up his bag and followed her. 'What's with all the flowers?' he asked, pulling open the door.

'I'm doing deliveries for my mum,' said Stella, winding the window down for some fresh air.

'At the hospital?'

'No, I'll finish these later. We've got to get onto the ward and find out which poor bastard was beaten up last night. What's your real name, Beanie?'

'Steven,' he mumbled.

'You'll have to tell me the real names of any of the guys you know on the street, okay?'

'Okay.'

Wellington Hospital was bright and new. Wide steps led up to the automatic doors that swished open. At the front desk Stella smiled at the receptionist.

'Hi, I'm really hoping you can help me,' she said. 'My friend Steven here thinks that one of his friends may have been brought in last night. His friend lives rough, on the street, and was beaten up. Are you able to tell me what ward he'd be in?'

'I need a name,' said the receptionist.

'Of course. But the trouble is, we're not sure what name he might have given or even if he was in a state to give it. He goes by different names. How about Christophe Janvier?'

She looked at the screen. 'No, we don't have anyone with that name.'

Thank goodness, Stella thought. He might still be out there. 'What about David? Craig? Maybe Gerald, do you have a Gerald?'

'First or last name?'

Stella raised her eyebrow at Beanie. 'Any idea?' she asked.

'Nope.'

This was hopeless, Stella thought. Then she remembered. 'What about Gutter, or Digby, maybe Georgie or George?'

'We have a Digby Taylor who was brought in late last night,' said the receptionist.

'That's him,' said Beanie. 'Fuck, they got Digs – can we see him?'

Digby was sitting in bed propped up with several pillows. A large white bandage wound around his head covering one eye. His other eye was heavily bruised and bloodshot. His left hand was bandaged, leaving only a swollen thumb showing. He attempted a smile when Beanie and Stella came into the room, but ended up pointing to his throat. It was then Stella saw the massive bruising around his windpipe.

'Hey, Digby,' said Beanie. 'What the bloody hell happened to you?' Digby shrugged and winced. 'I've never seen you looking so clean. It suits you, man.' Digby made a strange gurgling sound that may have been laughing. It was hard to tell. 'This is Stella,' said Beanie. 'She's okay, she just wants to talk to you.'

Stella perched herself on the edge of the bed, while Beanie slumped into a chair. 'I'm sure the police have talked to you,' she said gently. 'But I'd just like to ask you some quick questions. Is that okay?'

Digby nodded to a pad and pen on the side table. Stella picked them up and handed them over.

'Did you see who did this to you?'

He shook his head, then started writing with his good hand. Stella steadied the pad for him. Reading upside down: *shaved head bastard had knife.*

That has to be James, thought Stella. 'Was there just the one person?'

He nodded.

'What did he want?' she asked.

Digby made a small shrug of his shoulders and started writing: *looked through pockets, kept saying phone.*

'It's not you he was after,' said Stella. 'He wants Christophe.'

'That's Mad-Dog's other name,' said Beanie.

Digby sighed and closed his good eye.

Back at the car Stella unlocked the doors and hopped in. Beanie got into the passenger seat. He looked glum.

'It's fucked,' he said.

'What is?'

'Beating up Digby like that. What shitty arsehole does that for entertainment?'

'It's not entertainment, Beanie. They wanted Christophe, Mad-Dog. They want something from him. Listen,' she said, 'if you see or hear anything you have to let me know. If he's done this to Digby and Warren, he'll do the same to Christophe if he finds him.'

Beanie turned to her and smiled, a wide grin that showed the number of teeth he was missing.

'Yeah,' he said. 'I'll just whip out my mobile phone and call you.'

'Okay, okay, point taken, but here …' she said, scribbling on a scrap of paper '… here's my phone number. Get to a payphone, anything, and call me. Or go to the library hub on Brandon Street and ask for Rita. She's a friend of Christophe's and mine, she'll help you.'

'Sure thing, Wonder Woman.' He laughed again.

'Hey, don't get mouthy on me,' she said. 'I'm the one who's been giving you free smokes.'

He took the piece of paper and shoved it in his pocket. 'Mad-Dog won't fight back, you know,' he said.

'How did he get that name?'

'Because he doesn't fight. He stood up to someone once. Just stared at them till they said, "You're just a fucking mad dog," and the name stuck. He didn't seem to mind. I never knew his name was Christophe.'

26

STELLA DROPPED BEANIE in town, finished the deliveries, then parked outside her mum's shop, the aptly named Bloomin Gorgeous, to refill the car with more flowers. It wasn't a bad job. Everything smelt nice and people were generally pleased to see her. The flowers reminded her of Digby lying in hospital. Christophe wasn't safe. She needed to find him.

'You seem distracted,' said Peace, handing Stella some of the smaller bouquets.

'I am a bit,' she said. 'Do you worry about Tim?'

'Of course, what parent wouldn't? But what I know about Tim is that he's had seasonal work up the Hawke's Bay area, now he's possibly in Nelson doing other work.'

'I don't know,' said Stella. 'Is it just me, or are there more homeless on the streets? Last time I was here, there was Blanket Man and maybe a couple of others. Now it seems that everywhere you look there's someone sitting on a piece of cardboard with their hand out.'

'You know Blanket Man had a name, Ben Hana, but you're right, things have definitely got worse here,' said Peace. 'There's more poverty and it's all over the news about the housing shortage. But what can you do? I give to charity, I help when and where I can. But honestly, it's a bottomless pit. What's that got to do with Tim?'

'I'm not sure,' said Stella. 'I just hope he's not doing the same somewhere.'

'Well, that's a charming thought.'

'Sorry, Mum, it's just that he's my brother and I don't know where he is.'

Stella took the last of the bouquets out to the car.

A homeless man holds the key to all of this, she thought. Someone without roots, without love, without the basic necessities of life, and I have to find him.

'Just before you go,' said Peace, 'could you run these over to Audrey in the antiques shop?'

'Yeah, I didn't know that Charlotte was working for her.'

'I'm sure I mentioned it in an email at some stage. It's very part-time, mainly when Audrey is travelling.' Her mother smiled. 'It's been very positive for Charlotte. It helps to keep her mind on the good things in life. Audrey's been lovely, we all try to help each other along this stretch of road. She helps me with props for my window, in return I give her a fresh bunch of flowers every week, regular as clockwork.'

'The green dollar is alive and well, I see.'

'It works for us. You notice the rise in street people, but some of the working poor are feeling it as well,' said Peace. 'I truly don't know how she keeps that business afloat; it never seems that busy, but Charlotte has a job she enjoys and she gets paid. That's all that matters. Mind you, I spied a lovely garnet pin in the cabinet. I might take a closer look next time I'm in.'

The shops along Tinakori Road weren't dealing with the working poor, thought Stella. They were all bijou places. Cafés, galleries and froufrou designer shops snuggled next to high-end pre-loved clothing stores. It was quaint and drafty. Rents were exorbitant. If you were a champion at spitting, you'd be able to spit and hit Parliament Buildings. High-maintenance sash windows, steep roofs and rickety wooden staircases were all part of the look.

The antiques shop was just the same: Antiques & Curios, not very original but it did the trick. Probably the same stuff in the window as when she last went in, Stella thought. She peered in. It was bursting with the usual collection of china, furniture, deceased estate belongings needing a new home. There was something quite fascinating about other people's things, especially jewellery. They'd been longed for once. Given as a gift, received and valued as a token of true love. Now they jostled each other for attention in a dusty antiques store.

The entrance was through a side door, down a short alleyway. It was all artful cobblestones, ye olde towne effect that only partially worked. Stella opened the door to the sound of a jingling bell overhead. Music was playing, something classical and easy. The early afternoon light played with the dust on the china, and glinted off one of the excessively framed mirrors on the wall. Easing her way around the piles of precariously placed items and past the narrow staircase, Stella saw that every available surface of the room was full. Even under the tables. Under every chair were heaps of bowls, cups, piles of books, stacks of dinner sets her grandmother might have owned. You'd need to spend the good part of a day just to find whatever it was you thought you wanted.

A faint cough sounded behind her.

Stella turned around slowly, careful not to knock anything over. She found herself face to face with Audrey. Her mother had been right, she didn't seem to have changed at all. Stella noticed her eyes first, they were large, a deep warm brown. She must be in her mid-sixties by now, but it was difficult to tell. Her face was unlined and very pale, the look of someone who spent too much time inside. A single strand of pearls lay around her neck, a dress ring on her left hand. She stood very straight, her hands held in front of her as though in prayer.

Nope, she hadn't changed.

'May I help you?' asked Audrey. 'Oh, I see you've brought my flowers. It's Stella, isn't it? Peace's daughter?'

'Yes, I'm just giving Mum a hand for a couple of days.'

'How lovely.' She smiled and her face lit up like a serene Madonna. 'You've been overseas – Charlotte mentioned it.'

'Yeah, I've been working in London. I came home for Mum and Dad's fortieth wedding anniversary.'

Stella handed over the flowers.

'They're beautiful, as always,' said Audrey. 'Peace is so talented. I think I'll use a different vase for these ones.' She looked around and spied what she wanted. 'This one is lovely. I'm always pleased when it doesn't sell – how silly is that. But it's one of my favourites.' Stella watched as Audrey stood on tiptoes, on a low stool, to lift it off a high shelf. She fussed with the flowers. 'Thank you for delivering them.'

'You're welcome.'

'Of course, you know Charlotte has been a most wonderful help to me. She's become my right hand when I'm travelling.' She looked at Stella, taking in the black jeans and boxy jacket with large silver buttons. 'You're not very alike, are you?'

'Nope, she's more like Peace, I'm more like Dad.'

'That's often the way. I always think it's important to find one's sense of style and self, then stick to it,' said Audrey. 'Be a leader, not a follower. Who was it who said: *Fashion fades, style is forever?*'

'Not sure, all I know is that I often feel like the poor cousin.'

'I know what you mean.' Audrey laughed. 'Money changes everything. So, are you home for good?'

'I'm not sure, I'm still trying to work out all that stuff.'

'You young things today have so much going for you – so many choices. You can pack up and go at any time. Such marvellous freedom.'

'You're not that old, Audrey,' said Stella. 'It sounds like you're travelling quite a bit.'

'Yes, for the business. I go on buying trips all over the place. But I find that I'm less romanced by travel. It's very hard on the body.'

'I couldn't agree with you more. Those long-haul flights are a bitch. I don't know how long I'll stay, but I have a funeral to go to as well.'

'I'm very sorry to hear that. Was it someone you were close to?'

It slammed into Stella. She felt tears pricking behind her eyes. 'Sorry, sorry about this. I'm not usually so …' she said and whipped out a tissue from the box sitting on the counter. That was all it took. One person's comment, one person's kindness, was enough to unhinge her, and the torrent of words started. Stella, slightly horrified, found she couldn't stop.

She unloaded. There was no guilt – there was no blame or comments from Audrey. Just the ear of someone prepared to listen as she unburdened herself.

'And it just keeps getting worse,' said Stella. Audrey stood there, her head to one side, a look of deep sympathy on her face as Stella told her about the wharf and the small body floating in the water, the bright silver chain around her ankle. The image, the shock of it. 'I'm so sorry to bang on like this. I really don't usually do this sort of thing,' said Stella, blowing her nose.

'Goodness,' said Audrey. 'It sounds like you've had quite a lot to contend with.'

'Yeah, I'm still trying to get my head around it. I didn't mean to take up so much of your time.'

'Not a problem. Really. Maybe I should change the sign outside to *Counsellor*.'

Stella smiled. 'It could add a new income stream for you.'

'Well, it might help pay for these,' she said pointing to her shoes.

'They're lovely.'

'They're my one vice, I find them hard to resist. Don't worry about your outburst,' said Audrey. 'It's often easier to let things go with someone you're not entirely close to.'

'Thank you,' said Stella.

Audrey fiddled with her necklace. 'So, the girl in the water, have you found where she was from?'

'No, the police won't tell me anything. I've had a journalist try contacting me,' said Stella. 'The media have been all over it but they've got no real details either.'

'And what about the missing phone?' asked Audrey. 'Have you found that?'

'Not yet, I'm still working on it. I just have to find that Christophe guy. He seems to be the key to it all.'

Audrey fussed with the flowers. 'Ravosky. I know him.'

'Really? How?' Stella asked.

'Well, you know Wellington, it's pretty much two degrees of separation in this city. I have a few regular customers and he's one of them. He has quite the eye for military memorabilia – I get the odd piece for him from time to time. Other than that, he has a general interest in diamonds and antique jewellery.'

'What do you think of him?'

'Personally? I don't know him. Professionally,' she paused, 'I'm not sure. He's very smooth. He glides in, has a look around, then he's gone – I can't add more than that. I looked him up online once; just his business concerns, you understand. He seemed to have quite a number of irons in the fire, as they say,' said Audrey. 'Well, I should get back to things.'

'Of course.'

'Good luck with it all, Stella.'

Stella checked her phone. 'I'd better get going, too,' she said. 'I've a heap more deliveries to do before the end of the day. Thanks again, Audrey, you've been great.'

'Pop in anytime, let me know how you're getting on.'

Stella's phone pinged a text – it was from Charlotte: *Still want a pick-up from Mum's?*

Sure do, I'll finish around 5, she fired back.

As she was leaving Stella looked down at the glass cabinet by the front counter. It was full of black velvet trays of rings and pins. Necklaces lay dormant, lockets closed on their secrets, beads and gems of every rainbow colour. On one side were silver chains, long, short and thick. Amongst them all Stella's eyes rested on the delicate one that was hung with small filigree bells.

'Is there something that interests you?' Audrey asked.

'Mum mentioned a garnet pin she liked the look of.'

'Oh, yes, that one there,' said Audrey. 'She admired it last time she was in.'

'I'll come back another time for a proper look. It's her birthday coming up, it could be just the thing.'

'I'll put it to one side for you, until you make up your mind.'

'Thanks, that'd be great.'

Across the road Stella saw the Fig Café was still there. Her mum needed her help, but Stella needed food. She hadn't eaten since breakfast several hours ago, now she felt drained and ragged after her outburst in front of Audrey.

'Excuse me,' came a voice from behind her. 'Are you going in, or just blocking the door?'

Stella swung around. 'Oh, sorry. I was just, you know, sorry.'

She stepped away from the door, letting the woman behind her go through. She hesitated then pushed the door open. An early Billy Joel album was playing on the sound system. Good grief, thought Stella, when did he become fashionable again? The coffee machine hissed and bubbled.

The barista was grinding enough beans to sink a ship. A few people were in for their afternoon fix, but the place wasn't crowded.

The barista looked up. 'What can I get you?' he asked.

Stella ordered a flat white and some food, then made her way over to the table by the window. Not much had changed in this place; it was the same café where she and Teri had hatched their travel plans for Thailand.

University was almost over. Teri hadn't been thrilled with her grades and was unsure of what to do next.

'Let's just do it,' Stella said. 'Let's just go somewhere, sit on a beach and sip those silly cocktails with umbrellas in them. Come on, Teri sweetie, it'll be fun.'

'It sounds like a good idea but …'

'But what? Kate's doing her thing. Lassie has his legal career on track. It's just you and me, kiddo.'

Teri laughed. 'You're a mad cow, you know that.'

'Yep.'

'Where are we going to get the cash?'

'I dunno, hon, but leave it to me – I'll sort it all.'

And she did, somehow. Stella had organised it. After they came back she'd have a job with the police, starting in the New Year, but Teri needed a jolt now. Maybe this would help her out of the funk she was in. Teri was not unhappy as much as unsettled. There was a restlessness about her that didn't seem to go away unless they'd had a number of drinks. It was probably just that time of their lives: uni finishing, people going off into jobs or overseas. A couple of their friends had even recently got engaged.

'They're far too young,' Teri said.

'You're not wrong there, sister.'

'What about you and Lassiter? Go on – I know you want to.'

'We already have,' said Stella with a wink.

They laughed. Phuket. What was not to love? It was hot and crowded, they ate at street markets and stayed in the cheapest accommodation Stella could find. At the beach they lay around on large towels and watched as Western men lolled about with Thai women they'd bought.

'Why do you think they do it?' Teri asked.

'Dunno, why does any man buy sex?' Stella replied, her arm draped over her eyes. 'It's easy, uncomplicated. It's a business transaction just like any other. They have their fun here, then go home to their dull lives and possibly dull wives.'

'That's pretty cold-blooded,' said Teri.

'It's commerce. The dictates of the market.'

'What happens to the women though?'

'What do you mean?'

'I mean, what happens when the bloke goes back to wherever he came from?'

'Who knows? She probably looks around for another source of cash,' said Stella. 'Don't let it spoil your holiday. I get what you're saying, hon, I do. But many of these women don't have choices – it's life or death for them.'

'Seems a pretty fucked up way to live, if you ask me.'

Stella and Teri drank way too much. They laughed and flirted shamelessly with a couple of older American tourists, Bob and Sean. On their last night, Stella, courtesy of an interesting food choice, was vomiting her guts out. It wasn't a good sound.

'I should stay,' said Teri to the closed toilet door.

'And do what, hold my hand?' Stella replied after another heave.

'But I feel awful leaving you.'

'I'll be fine, go have some chi-chi cocktails with the blokes.'

They'd argued a bit more, then Teri had gone out with the promise that she wouldn't be long.

Stella lay back on her bed. The mosquito net floated in the un-air-conditioned haze. Her mind leaned one way then the other, it mimicked her churning gut. Her father had warned her about this, about being careful where and what she ate. But what the heck, it was too late now.

She slowly sipped water from the bottle Teri had left. She was both sweating from the heat and from the intensity of the vomiting, cold and hot at the same time. She lay there shivering, a light cotton sarong wrapped around her shoulders. Occasionally she would pick up a corner of the brightly coloured fabric and wipe her face. Finally, Stella felt completely empty and the vomiting stopped.

She stretched out on the bed, then drew her knees up to her chest. Tightening the sarong around her shoulders she tried to sleep. She drifted in and out, worried about her stomach, worried about Teri.

Later that evening, Teri slipped back into their room and Stella woke from a restless sleep.

'Sorry, I didn't mean to wake you,' said Teri.

'I was only half asleep,' Stella muttered. 'What time is it?'

'It's after midnight.'

'How was your night?' she asked. No reply. 'Teri, you okay?'

'Yep, I'm fine,' she said. 'It turns out they weren't interested in Western women.' She dropped herself onto the end of Stella's bed and shut her eyes.

'Ah, shit,' Stella said, sitting up. 'Another couple of blokes wanting to buy a week's worth of fucking for the price of a meal. Hardly surprising I suppose.' Teri didn't reply. 'What, don't tell me, they wanted a threesome. No, hang on, they wanted a rent-boy?' She coughed. 'Wait, wait, don't tell me they wanted those men who look like women, but still have all their tackle.' Stella was on a roll. 'Oh god, they wanted to watch you with one of the …'

'Shut up, Stell, you're way off the mark.'

'What the fuck happened?'

Her friend bowed her head and rested it on her knees, her arms clasped tight around them. Stella waited. When Teri looked up again her face was flushed.

'Stell, I can't … I just don't understand …' she faltered. They were both quiet. 'Look,' Teri said at last, 'you go back to sleep. I need a shower.'

They'd left the next morning, her friend's face, her beautiful face, haggard from lack of sleep. She'd scraped her hair back in a rough ponytail, grey-cloud smudges under her eyes. On the plane home Teri seemed to fall asleep at last and Stella was loath to disturb her. But there were questions she'd never found the time to ask.

Stella closed her eyes for a moment. Teri's funeral would happen, she'd get through it, they'd all find a way through it. Her coffee and food arrived. Her mother was right – she needed to occupy herself. She also needed to make a little money and get her shit sorted.

It started to rain, a light, swirling mist that suited her mood.

27

STELLA PARKED IN A LOADING ZONE. The final delivery was to an office block on The Terrace. She grabbed the flowers, locked the car and crossed the road. Lassiter's and Ravosky's offices were in an old apartment building next to the church. She'd always loved this block. It reminded her of the movie *Blade Runner*, its dimensions small, but perfectly formed. There was a central lift. The old cage variety where you stepped in and pulled the concertina gates closed before the lift would work. The staircase wrapped around the lift well, the lift so slow you could chat to someone using the stairs on the way up.

The lift juddered and bounced to a stop. She pushed the gate open and stepped out. Lassiter's office was to the left. The door was closed; no doubt he was at a meeting somewhere else. Just to be sure, she got out her phone and called him. There was no ringing sound from his office. Keeping hold of the flowers she walked up the last flight of stairs to the floor that housed Ravosky's office.

The carpet was soft under foot. The carved wooden handrail curved around each bend in the stairwell. Up here there was little traffic noise from the street. Her ears attuned for any sound; there was nothing except airless calm. A door closed. She looked up. A woman in a red pencil skirt and striped shirt was coming down the stairs towards her.

'Can I help you?' she asked.

'I'm trying to find Maurice Ravosky's office,' said Stella. 'I think I got out on the wrong floor.'

'Oh, sure, just carry on up. He's just up there, top of the stairs and turn right.'

'Thanks, I appreciate it.'

'Beautiful flowers, he's a lucky man.'

Stella stopped at the top of the stairs and waited.

Nothing. No sound at all.

The lift started moving down to the ground floor. Quickly, quietly, she found his office. The door was closed. There was no sound from inside.

She tried the door. It opened. It wasn't his office but a large foyer room that acted as a reception area. There was a couch, a couple of chairs and a low table. In one corner a domestic coffee machine sat with a few cups on a tray. There was a desk to one side. Maybe that was where Teri worked, she thought. Stella put the flowers down and started opening desk drawers. Nothing. Just the usual admin bits and pieces: stapler, paperclips and a pad of yellow Post-it notes.

She checked the bookcase. It was filled with folders, none of them labelled. Quickly she flicked through them. Nothing, they were mostly empty. Just for show. Next to the desk was a two-drawer filing cabinet. Locked. She searched through the drawers again in case she could see any keys.

Shit. That was the lift.

It stopped on a lower floor. She heard the doors clang open and close.

Then she saw it. Leaning against the side of the filing cabinet. One of those large, hardback, page-a-day business diaries. She pulled it out. The lift started again, going up or down she couldn't tell. She quickly scanned the pages. It was the right year, but there was barely anything written down. One page caught her eye – it was Teri's handwriting. *Crossfield Holdings.* The lift door clanged. Shit, it's on this floor.

There were voices. She put the diary back. Grabbing the flowers, she stepped out from behind the desk.

'Stella, what a surprise,' Ravosky smiled at her. 'Are those for me?'

'Sorry, no. It turns out I'm in the wrong building.'

'Really?' He took his time removing his overcoat, hanging it on the wooden stand behind the door. He wore a darker suit this time, still bespoke, and the same diamond pinkie ring. He turned to face her; the cool blue eyes held her gaze. She willed him to blink first.

'I'm helping my mother with some floral deliveries,' she finally said.

'Ah, yes. She has that place up on Tinakori Road,' he said. 'You needn't look surprised. Like you, I make it my business to know all sorts of things about all kinds of people. My manner is slightly more, how should one say, "orthodox". Well,' his mouth turned up in a slight smile, 'so, here we are.'

'Yes,' said Stella. Her phone started ringing in her back pocket.

'Feel free to take your call.'

She looked at the screen, it was Lassie. He could wait.

'I wanted to see where Teri ... I'd better go,' she said. 'I need to get these to the right person before they wilt, the flowers that is, not the person.'

He walked towards her and stood barring her way out the door. His voice was smooth, in command. The kind of voice that got things done. The geriatric rattle of the lift moving again cut into the quiet.

'I admire your chutzpah, Stella, but you are treading on things you know nothing about.' The small room was filled with two more men in suits, with another one out in the corridor talking animatedly on his phone. 'We will talk soon, you and I, but as you can see, I have a meeting to attend to.'

'Yeah.'

'You will, of course, be at the funeral?' he said.

'Yes. She was my oldest and dearest friend.' She looked

directly at him. 'And I will find out what happened.'

'Meaning?'

How much should she say? She wanted to bait him, tell him anything that would get him talking. Anything that would get him to make a mistake. Her teeth found the loose piece of skin on her bottom lip. She worried at it. *He'll keep.*

'Nothing,' she said.

'I doubt that. Here's my card. Call me. Clearly there are things you'd like to discuss. We'll set up a proper time.' He stepped lightly to one side to let her pass.

She looked at the card. It was framed in gold. The lettering was simple, just his name and mobile number. No address. He lived in Oriental Bay – she'd at least managed to find that out, but not much else.

Out on The Terrace the late-afternoon traffic was lumbering up and down.

That was too close, she thought. What the fuck. I don't care if he knows I'm onto him. It might make him scared enough to make a mistake. She looked at her watch. I need to deliver these flowers and get the car back. Charlotte will be picking me up soon.

28

CHARLOTTE WAITED FOR THE LIGHTS to turn green, then turned left into Majoribanks Street.

'You realise this is bonkers,' said Charlotte. 'That you're bonkers – you know that, don't you?'

'Think of it as payback for that spa session,' replied Stella.

'But you enjoyed that trip. This, I'm not sure about.' Charlotte waited while a taxi driver did a dodgy three-point turn in front of them.

'You speak too soon. You never know, you might have fun.'

'You're kidding, right?'

Stella didn't want to sound like the 'older sister', but what the fuck.

'So, Lottie, were you ever going to tell me about Mum?'

Charlotte, eyes forward, carried on up the hill past Brougham and Austin streets. She said nothing, turned right at the top and parked the car.

'I wanted to,' said Charlotte. 'But Mum was adamant. Really fierce. Dad just wanted to keep things as stress free as possible. He was pretty freaked out by it all. He was lost. And honestly, it wasn't that big a deal in the end. Routine, the doctors kept saying. I'm sorry. I should have let you know, even after the fact.'

'I don't know where I'm going to end up living,' Stella said. 'But I can't be somewhere else and worried that you're keeping stuff from me.'

'Okay,' said Charlotte. 'I pinkie-promise to keep you informed.' She held out her hand. Stella smiled as they linked their smallest fingers together.

'If I get a parking ticket ...' said Charlotte.

'I'll pay for it.'

Charlotte laughed. 'With what? You're broke.'

'Okay, no need to rub it in. Listen, I just wanted another pair of eyes, some company …'

'And the use of my car.'

'Yep, that too. Mum needed hers, but hey, at least I'm honest.'

'I don't get it,' said Charlotte. 'If this guy is so important, why aren't the police searching for him?'

Stella knew it was crazy. She was well aware she should tell McCarthy about Christophe and the skip and Teri's phone. But she couldn't face him, couldn't face his patronising her.

'The police don't know what I know,' said Stella.

'Shouldn't you tell them? Oh, let me guess, it's a "hunch", one of those detective kinds of things?'

'Probably. But I have it on good authority that he has a camp somewhere up here. I'll let the police know if anything comes of this, I promise,' she said. 'Just let me see if I can find this guy myself. I wouldn't want to be accused of wasting police time, sending them on a wild goose chase over Mount Vic.'

'Has this got something to do with those attacks? I read about it online the other night.'

'It might do. Let's say that I'm hoping to find this guy before someone else does.'

'How do you know he's up here?'

'A friend of his told me. Rita knows him as well.'

Charlotte looked puzzled. 'He works in the library?'

'No, course not. She met him there one time and ended up giving him some food. He's been going back ever since. He doesn't say much, but I do know that he's not some drugged-out psycho. He's just fallen through the cracks – it's not uncommon, Lottie.'

'That sounds like Rita. She always did have a soft spot for the lame ducks.'

Stella was careful not to mention Christophe's street name – she didn't want her completely freaking out.

'So, it's a wild-goose chase,' said Charlotte.

'Ducks, geese, I think you're getting your birds mixed up. Come on, it'll be fun to hang out and have a walk together, get some of that fresh air and other healthful stuff.'

'It's freezing, Stell. Hang on, isn't that Mum's jacket … and gloves?'

'And hat,' said Stella. 'I did say to wrap up warm.'

Charlotte was in matching lycra yoga pants, fitted zippered jacket and shoes that looked way too clean. She opened the boot and fished out a large orange fluoro vest.

'Good grief, Lottie, I'm not sure we want to advertise our presence that much.'

'You never said anything about camo gear.'

Stella grabbed a water bottle from between the front seats of the car, twisted off the cap and took a drink.

'Good to see you're drinking something other than coffee and alcohol,' said Charlotte. 'Your liver will thank you.'

Stella smiled, twisted the cap back on the bottle and threw it on the front seat. Slamming the door shut, she pulled on her mother's gloves. 'Come on, fluoro-blimp,' she said, 'let's find this guy.'

It had rained on and off last night and again through the afternoon. The air smelt damp and earthy. The sky was shot with grey and heavy with another impending rainfall. The ground was wet underfoot. Stella could hear a dull thud, thud, thud from a distance. Around the corner a charge of runners pounded down the path. She and Charlotte stepped off the track to let them sweat their way past. Stella felt the push of air that changed with the pumping of their arms. They couldn't even manage a 'thanks', just a jut of the chin. That was one pursuit that she couldn't figure out. Running. From *what* was always her question. But then again, she'd had plenty of arguments with people about swimming. 'The one exercise you do where you don't get anywhere,' Teri had once said. She squeezed her eyes shut for a second.

'So, how's this going to work?' said Charlotte.

'I'm not entirely sure,' said Stella. 'How about you look one side and I'll keep an eye on the other. Look for anything that feels out of place. A colour, a piece of litter, broken branches that may indicate a track, anything at all. Just look.'

It was darker in the trees. The light was fading faster than Stella realised. The track itself was clear, but on both sides it was a tangle of undergrowth, matted branches caught up with vines that were mostly dead or dying. Pōhutukawa and macrocarpa sat comfortably next to massive eucalypts, their ghostly peeling branches reaching up to the darkening sky. A tūī sang a few notes, silence, then streamed out a few more. A starling replied.

They kept walking, not saying much. It was a well-formed and well-used track. Stella tried to think where she might hide if she ever needed to. What part of this hillside would be able to offer good camouflage, the ability to be unseen. It was hard to imagine being out here at night, at three in the morning when a mist would rise. Who in their right mind would choose this? That was the thing though, people who would choose this were seldom in their right mind. She wasn't even sure what that was – a 'right mind'.

They reached the ridgeline.

'This is actually really nice, Stell. I sometimes forget that charging up a hill can be properly invigorating, and it's cool just to hang out.'

Stella stopped and leaned forward to catch her breath.

They'd seen nothing on the way up, not even the hint of a campsite. She wasn't surprised at how unfit she felt. She was thirty-three with the energy levels of an eighty-two-year-old. Charlotte had hardly broken a sweat.

Charlotte, hands on hips, was doing deep side lunges. 'This is real needle-in-a-haystack stuff, though. I mean you realise how big Mount Vic actually is.'

'I know,' said Stella, adding, 'Ms Show-off. Come on, let's head back, but keep your eyes open – we might see something on the way down.'

Stella patted the pockets of her jacket. She was dying for a smoke but remembered she'd given the packet to Beanie. Besides she'd be better to wait until she was by herself – she couldn't face the reprimands of her younger sister. Part way down the track Stella stopped. The downhill bank was steep and overgrown, but there was a gap in the trees. She walked back a few steps, crouched down and stared. It may have been the light, but there was definitely an odd shape down there.

'Wait up, where are you going?' Charlotte called. 'Have you seen something?'

Charlotte caught her up and they followed what looked like a bit of track down through the trees. There were clumps of leaves, rotten and slippery, which slowed them a bit. Up ahead branches tumbled together, creating what might be a shelter.

'There's nothing there, Stell,' said Charlotte.

Stella kicked a couple of the branches away.

'No, you're right. But it might have been something once.'

Charlotte's phone pinged. 'I have to go,' she said. 'It's Ben, he needs me to pick him up from work. Come on.'

'No, you go. Honestly, I'll be fine,' Stella said, grinning. 'Go and pick up the hubby.'

'You know I hate it when you call him that.'

'Sorry, I know you do. Go and pick up Ben. Thanks for the lift and the company and say hi to Ben from me. I think I might spend a little more time around here. I can walk down to Lassie's, or Courtenay Place, and Uber home.'

Charlotte's fluorescent back disappeared up to the main path. Stella sat down on one of the fallen branches. Her sister was right – this was crazy. Mount Vic was bloody enormous. How on earth did she hope to find one man's hideaway? The very terminology told her he didn't want to be found. Stella shivered. She may be in borrowed clothes but she should have worn a thermal. Might as well carry on down the slope, she thought as she stood up.

It quickly became much steeper. She lost her footing on a muddy patch and slipped. 'Ah, shit,' she said as she landed on her arse. Mud smeared one hand, along the sleeve of her jacket and down her leg. She carried on down the slope. Branches grabbed at her hat. One pinged back and slapped her across the face. Ouch, shit, that hurt. Bramble – that hadn't been poisoned by the council – hooked into her sleeve. Her shoes were caked with mud and leaves.

Ahead was a clearing. More than a clearing, really. It was a park at the back of an apartment block, dedicated to small gardening plots. Each one was built up with railway sleepers or stacks of branches; it was easy to see some plots were better tended than others. Mind you, it was getting late in the season, so it was hardly surprising one or two might have looked a little ragged. Wooden frames held the last tendrils of dry and browning bean plants. Stakes propped up ageing tomatoes, rows of autumn silver beet, rampant mint and parsley. Fruit trees, lemon bushes, even a daphne had been added. Just like the allotments in London, gardens, a patch of earth jealously guarded by their owners that provided food, solace, the ability to get hands dirty.

29

CRASHING THROUGH THE LAST BIT of undergrowth Stella stumbled out to the clearing. She scraped as much of the mud off her shoes as she could and wiped her hands on the grass. How on earth was she ever going to find Christophe, Mad-Dog? Those two bashings were no coincidence. Someone else was after him.

Her phone rang. An unknown number. Shit, it was on twelve per cent battery; she swiped the screen and slumped onto a bench.

'Hello,' she said.

'Stella Weston?'

'Yes, who is this?'

'McCarthy,' came the voice. 'DI McCarthy.'

'McCarthy! What a pleasant surprise. What can I do for you on this cold, late afternoon?'

'Don't fuck with me, Weston.'

'I'm not. That's your prerogative. What do you want?'

'You visited a man in hospital?'

'Yes, last time I checked it wasn't illegal.' She flicked a couple of leaves off her boots.

'Why were you there?'

'None of your business, but since you ask so nicely, I took a friend of his to visit him.'

'You were questioning him.'

Fuck. He must have seen the piece of paper that Digby had written on.

'What do you want, McCarthy? My phone is about to run out of battery.'

'I want you to maintain your position as a civilian and keep your fucking nose out of police business.'

'That's not very polite of you. What makes you think it was me?'

'My colleague gave me a pretty clear description.'

'Hearsay.'

'Back off, Weston.'

'Yes, sir. I read you loud and clear,' she said. 'Hang on. Before you go – what about the girl in the water, anything more about her?'

'No.'

'Look, McCarthy,' she said. 'There's been fuck-all new media information. The journos haven't got anything, they're just going over the same old shit. One of them is trying to get hold of me for a story – so, what's going on?'

'That case doesn't concern you, and stay the fuck away from any journalist.'

'I found her, so vested interest,' said Stella. 'Do you at least have a name? Have her family been found?'

'All you need to know is that this is an ongoing investigation,' he said. 'It's bigger than you know and you mucking around in it could jeopardise the whole damn thing, Weston.'

The line went dead and Stella looked at her phone. It was well and truly drained now. There was no point checking her wallet. She didn't have any cash and she daren't put any more on her credit card. She'd have to call in at Lassie's place and use his phone or, god forbid, loan a few bucks so she could bus home.

The light was fading, the sky streaked with silken colours. A well-dressed older woman came out the back of the apartment block. She had a fluffy house dog on a little chain leash. In her other hand she carried a small bucket. Good grief, thought Stella. How much shit did she think that tiny thing was going to produce? She laughed when the woman tipped the bucket, and empty fruit skins and potato peelings tumbled into one of the communal compost bins.

Pulling her hat off, Stella ran her hands through her hair. She had an elastic band around her wrist and proceeded to gather her hair up in a loose ponytail, then shove the whole lot back under her hat. She hadn't seen Lassie since she crashed there the other night. Facing him wasn't high on her list of priorities. Maybe she should just suck it up and walk home to her parents' place, it wasn't that far.

A large well-fed cat ambled over and jumped onto her knee. Stroking the soft fur she felt tired, beyond tired. The last few days were catching up on her. So much was flooding back into her head. Teri, Lassie, Kate, her parents. Even the cathartic cry she'd had at Audrey's. She felt as though she were unravelling. A knitted jumper with a loose thread that she didn't know how to darn. Yeah, Charlotte was right, this was a stupid idea. Did she really think she would stumble across the hideout of some homeless chap who would benignly hand over Teri's phone? She'd made a few stupid decisions lately. What was one more to add to it?

She tried the buzzer.

Nothing. Stella turned to leave but stopped as she heard the faint thumping of someone coming down the stairs. Thank goodness Lassie was home. She'd worked up a suitable story, walking on the hill, lost track of time, no battery on her phone etc, etc. There was no way she was going to tell him what she'd actually been doing. He'd hit the roof and go all 'due process' on her. She hated doing this. Hated being the one that needed help, especially from him. She also needed a plaster for her heel.

The door opened. 'Hi, can I help?'

Shit, this was *her*. The owner of the deodorant. The one who had put the 'feminine' touch around his apartment. She was short like Stella, with long red hair out of a bottle.

Her eyes were lined with black that flicked up in the corners to make perfect Cleopatra eyes. She wore a slouchy T-shirt over leggings and legwarmers that were beyond fashionable. A pair of designer-framed reading glasses perched artfully atop her head. Her fingernails were painted black. She was young. No more than twenty-two. Fuck, he'd got himself some kind of groovy, flexible dancer type.

'Yeah,' said Stella. 'I'm after Lassie, Mitchell, is he home?'

'Not yet. I'm not sure when he will be.'

They stared at each other. Stella glanced down. Jesus, I look a fright, she thought. Her hand went to her hat and picked out a couple of small twigs. She could feel a scratch down one side of her face.

'Would you like me to leave a message for him?' said the dancer.

'No, it's all good. I'll text him.'

'Okay,' she said and closed the door.

Stella walked down the steps to the street.

30

H<small>E WAS A PATIENT MAN.</small>

He hadn't always been, but the last few years had taught him that patience, sitting back and waiting, was the key to survival. He'd taken a longer, more circuitous route to get to his place on the hill, deciding on Pirie Street rather than the usual Majoribanks. He'd kept glancing over his shoulder, still shaken from the other day when he'd been busking. What did that James want from him? His mind hurt, his brain hurt, he didn't know what to do.

It was the phone. It had to be.

Rita had asked him for it as well. 'My friend Stella would like to have a look at it,' she'd said to him. 'It could be important.'

They didn't know each other, did they? James and this Stella? But Stella was such a pretty name, and she was a friend of Rita's, so she had to be okay. He didn't like to think he was in trouble. It wasn't safe on the streets, that's why Mad-Dog hid out in the bush. He'd heard from Beanie that Warren and Digby had been beaten up in the alley behind that club. 'Beaten nearly to death,' Beanie had said. 'No idea who's done it, or why.' Digby was in hospital. Beanie had been to see him. Gone with that Stella woman. At least it would be warm there for him and he'd get fed, Mad-Dog thought.

He was tired, very tired.

He felt it in his feet, his back, in his bones.

Today it was fourteen years since his world imploded. He'd taken the tortuously long bus ride over to Makara Cemetery with other mourners. It was a service provided free by one of the funeral homes. He went once a year, just the once. He found their tree, the one he'd planted, the one that was growing over their bodies. He wasn't sure how long he stood there, but eventually it was time to leave. He boarded the bus last, sitting hunched in his seat all the way back to the central city.

Our reading of history is in a constant state of change, he thought. We move away from it, we move into something other, but it's always there. Draw a veil, erect curtains, a wall, alter the state of mind with substances legal and not.

It changes nothing.

It changes everything.

On his return Mad-Dog stopped over the road from the St James Theatre, still closed for renovations. There was a bench and he sat facing the tired façade. Old show posters were everywhere, ripped banners fluttering down the front of the theatre. A touring production of *Singin' in the Rain* had been advertised. 'Litres of real water on stage!' they trumpeted, as if that were some kind of drawcard. Try living outside sometime – you'll come across plenty of real water, he thought. He stood up and stabbed at the pedestrian button with an index finger, watching as the figure of the little red man flashed on and off, on, off.

He waited.

The lights changed. To his right a car stopped. To his left, on the other side of the road, a bus lumbered to a halt. The green man made his appearance. Slowly Mad-Dog stepped out onto the road. The car to his right inched forward willing him to walk faster.

Mad-Dog stopped. He stared at the driver. A young man in a jacket and tie sat at the wheel. He motioned for Mad-Dog to get a move on, get out of the way. Mad-Dog didn't move. Out of the corner of his eye the lights changed. The man blasted the horn. Mad-Dog's fist came down on the bonnet of the car, then he turned away and walked to the centre strip in the road.

'Fuckwit,' the young man yelled as he drove past.

'Cars, vehicles, murderer,' Mad-Dog muttered under his breath as he waited for the light change to get him across the next part of the road.

He loved the St James; it was a proper theatre. Opening nights were always the best, openings and finales, you can't beat a good finale. Normally he didn't pass this way, but today he did. He stood outside the main doors; one was open to allow the workmen through. Mad-Dog peered inside. The marble floor looked faded and dusty and the ticket booth at the far end was shut up and barred with a metal grill. To his left, the heavy theatre doors were closed. He'd never gone in that way, had always taken the artists entrance around the back.

There was no one there, no one to notice him. He walked over to the doors and pulled. They gave way under his hand. Without hesitation he slipped in. The carpeted corridor muffled his steps. There were more doors leading into the actual theatre. They opened under his hands.

It was hushed quiet and only partly lit. The open curtains exposed the expanse of stage, like the mouth of a toothless whale. He stood by the orchestra pit and looked down into it, breathing in the familiar, then up to the stage. Mad-Dog went over and pulled down the seat of one of the chairs in the front row; he sat down heavily.

She's there, in the shadows, waiting for him. She smiles and gives a little wave; he gives a small wave back.

The proscenium arch glows. Resting his head on the back of the seat he looks up. Cherubs, little fat cherubs smile at him from a height. Little babies, soft hands, soft smiles. They become missiles so easily. He leans forward, his head in his hands.

In the silence of the theatre. The squeal of brakes. Breaking glass as she hurtles through the windscreen. The screams, the graunch of metal on metal. And the blood, so much blood.

He rocks back and forth. I'm sorry, I'm sorry, I'm sorry.

Hands to his head, rocking, rocking.

'What are you doing in here? You can't be in here!' A voice, strident and harsh came from behind him.

Mad-Dog turned. Blinking. The intrusion jolted him. 'Sorry, I just wanted to look.' He stood up, the seat bouncing back into the upright position. 'I'll go now,' he said.

'You'd better jolly well. I don't want to have to call security.'

At the start of the communal gardens Mad-Dog stopped. There was a woman on the bench. He'd only seen her once before but he still recognised her. She was Rita's friend Stella, the one who wanted the phone, the one that had been in the library with Rita. Now she was here – what had Rita told her? Was she just there, or was she waiting for him? She even had Thomson on her knee. She was stroking him, scratching him under the chin and around his ears. If Thomson liked her she must be okay – he was a very fussy cat.

He sidled into the shadows of some trees at the edge of the lawn and waited. He tried not to cough, he didn't want to make a sound. His cough had been getting worse the last couple of days; the damp weather didn't help. His knee and hip were beginning to ache from the longer walk home. He was pleased he'd had the foresight to stop off for a cup of tea with Gus.

He would wait.

The woman from the apartments arrived. She was taking her little dog out for a walk. In one hand she held the lead, in the other she carried a small bucket of compost. He'd seen her before, many times, and he waited while she emptied the bucket into the bins. He hoped she wouldn't cross the garden and pass him, because the dog would sniff him out. Eventually she took the track up the hill to walk the dog.

Mad-Dog had cultivated invisibility, turning it into an art form. The periphery was where he felt safe. He could join in if he wanted, like with Gus, or he could pass life in the world of his dreams. When he was alone he could still be with them both. He could hear their voices, he could hear her singing. He could conjure them up in his mind's eye and they would comfort him. He would talk to them and he did so, often. Yes, people stared at him, but they didn't know what he knew.

Now, it seemed, people were asking after him, wanting something of him that he wasn't able to give.

He stayed hidden behind the trees, waiting as she stroked the cat. Her hair was bundled up under a hat, her outsized jacket was too big for her small frame. She looked tired, a little sad. If Rita knew her and liked her, maybe she was okay, but why did she want the star as well? She stood up, gave Thomson one last rub under his chin, pulled on some gloves and walked out of the garden.

After he was sure she'd gone he moved out of the shadow, across the garden and into the bush at the far corner. She'd been very close to finding him. This last part of the climb was always difficult; he coughed, a rattling sound in his chest, then scrambled awkwardly up the bank. Eventually he settled himself into his makeshift home grateful for the tarpaulin overhead; it made a big difference. It was dark green, the fabric good and thick. He'd managed to score some fruit from the Sunday market people. If he went late, just as they were packing up, they often gave him a few bits and pieces. He bit into an apple. It was sweet and crunchy.

And he's in the apple tree in the back garden ... a boy, sitting up in the branches, hidden by the leaves, crunching on a small tart apple, throwing the core onto the grass ...

It was the simple things he remembered about his childhood these days, a smile, a shared joke, skating on the canals in winter, the taste of an apple in the warmer months. He threw the core into the dark undergrowth.

The sun had disappeared behind the buildings. Like the stage at the end of a play, soon it would be completely dark and soon it would be cold. He coughed a few more times; his chest hurt. Reaching into his pocket he counted the money he had made from busking, there was enough. Tomorrow night he'd go to the shelter, but for tonight he'd stay here.

There was little sound at this hour; he was far enough away from the track. A rustling in the undergrowth startled him. Mad-Dog stiffened, his ears keenly tuned for any shift in the sounds of the night. He waited, the image of James, his nasty face, floating in front of him. Mad-Dog shrank from people like that, people who used power to intimidate.

Voices. He lifted his hat off his ears.

The sound was coming from the path further up the slope. The voices faded. They weren't coming for him. The undergrowth rustled again. His eyes weren't so good in the dark, his torch was getting low on battery power and he didn't want to give his position away. Maybe he should call out. Maybe it was Beanie – sometimes he crashed here with him. But Beanie would call out it was him. He wouldn't fumble around in the dusk. That was one thing about Beanie – he was afraid of the dark.

He waited.

It was probably nothing, a bird maybe, having a last scratch in the undergrowth. This camp was well disguised, Mad-Dog had made sure of that. It was a hollow in the hillside. A tree had fallen and was leaning on one side, its dying branches creating a wall that he had interlaced with more branches, like weaving a basket. A collection of plastic containers sat along one side. Some with lids, some without. Most of them he'd found in the skips. He had a couple of cushions, as well as an old sleeping bag. That's where the cardboard was good, layering it on the ground stopped the damp cold from seeping into his bones.

Mad-Dog rustled through a few bags to find some more food, but there wasn't much left from what Rita had given him. Yes, tomorrow night he'd have to go to the shelter. He coughed again. Why would someone beat up Warren or Digby? They had nothing to steal, no valuables at all. They wouldn't have been rude to anyone. Well, Digby might, but not Warren, he only ever talked to a couple of people. Maybe he was just in the wrong place.

Warren was a bit like the brother he never had. They were a similar age and build. They often wore the same kinds of clothes. People sometimes mistook them for each other.

Mad-Dog took his hat off his head, massaging his scalp with fingertips. It helped him to think. So many of his thoughts were jumbled these days and it was getting worse. No, no, he thought. But yes, maybe, just maybe the beating was meant for him, not Warren. It's the star, it's something about the star. That James fellow, the look he'd given him. Warren got it instead of me.

Rita had been very kind when he'd shown her the star. She hadn't laughed at him or anything like that. She'd said that it was most likely past repair. But why did her friend want it, he wondered. Why was she wanting to talk to him? Maybe she wasn't after him, maybe she was just there on the seat resting. He closed his eyes and scrunched up his forehead. Nothing appeared. All he understood was that people got hurt because of him.

He jammed his hat back on his head.

There it was again. The rustling, closer this time.

All his senses were on alert. It had started raining. Rain,

rain, go away, said Mad-Dog under his breath. He was in for a cold wet night; it was too late for the shelter. Thomson appeared, swishing his tail, walking in as though he owned the place. No doubt he made himself at home when Mad-Dog was out. He put his hand out to stroke the soft, slightly damp fur. There had been times when Thomson had stayed with him the whole night. The presence of another warm body, even that of a cat, was a pleasure. Mad-Dog stroked Thomson's back and rubbed him under the chin and around his ears. Thomson purred loudly; his eyes closed.

At least I've dealt with the phone, thought Mad-Dog. That is now the end of the matter.

31

It was a cool Friday afternoon the day they held Teri's funeral. The sky was low and grey. The wind hustled the clouds out to sea like the broom of an irritated cleaner. It suited Stella's mood. Old St Paul's was a beautiful building, calm and traditional. The last time she'd been there was for Charlotte's wedding. It had been summer, blue sky and happiness wrapped up in pre-wedding stress.

Stella was pleased it was overcast. There was something indecent about attending a funeral under clear blue skies. Cold wind whipped along the pavement stirring up the leaves that had already fallen. The air threatened rain. When Stella arrived with her parents, there were groups of mourners huddled outside, their backs to the cold. No matter what the situation, humans always group. Lassiter was with Kate and a crowd of others she didn't recognise. He looked up and gave her a small smile. Charlotte was standing with Ben but came over to give her a big hug. Ben did his brother-in-law version of this: a quick arm around the shoulder.

Stella was desperate for a cigarette and wasn't sure she could wait. Her eyes felt gritty from lack of sleep. After her trip to the pool the day before, her shoulders were aching again.

'Come on, Stella, we'd better go in,' said her dad. 'I'm so sorry, love, this isn't what you came back for.'

'It's okay. I'm just pleased I could be here for Teri's parents.'

'Nothing makes this right,' he said. 'Nothing will ever make this right.'

'Listen,' she said, 'you and Mum take Charlotte in and

save me a seat. I'll join you in a minute.'

'Are you going for a smoke?'

'Don't go on at me, not today.'

'Course not, love. I was just thinking that if I still smoked, I'd probably come and join you.'

Stella knew she only had a minute. Walking around to the side of the building, she rummaged in her bag and pulled out a packet of cigarettes. Lighting one she inhaled deeply, blowing out the smoke in an irritated huff. Her feet were sore. She had a large blister on her right heel from yesterday's walk-about, all in the hope that she'd stumble across Christophe.

Stella pulled on her cigarette again.

'May I interrupt you?'

'Fuck, you gave me a fright.' She stared at Ravosky.

'Such an awful habit, but calming all the same,' he said.

'Yeah, it is.'

He stood close. She caught the whiff of aftershave, the same she had smelt at the party. The cold afternoon light showed up the lines at the corner of his eyes, light mauve shadows resting underneath. His skin was pale. When he spoke she caught a glimpse of a gold tooth towards the back of his mouth. This close she could see his coat was expensive, the scarf at his neck looked like soft cashmere. Waving the packet in his direction, she raised her eyebrows in a question.

'Thank you, but no, I stopped some years ago.'

He gave the air of being supremely comfortable in his skin, in any situation. Ravosky was the kind of man who eased into boardrooms, gave advice and people would listen. He was one of those men who was, in equal measure, respected and feared.

'Teri was very fond of you.' His voice caught a little.

'She never mentioned you.'

'As blunt as always, Stella. But there's a matter I would like to discuss before you head back to the UK.'

'What makes you think I'm returning?'

'What is there here for you?' he said.

Stella's eyes narrowed. Was that a faint smirk at his mouth?

He stared at her without missing a beat. But it was there, the flicker in his eye, the straightening of his back. She smiled at him, her eyes non-committal. They were dancing a dance and Stella was unsure of the moves.

'I wouldn't have thought there was anything we needed to talk about.' She took another deep pull on her cigarette and blew the smoke over her shoulder.

'Well not here, of course, another time. Perhaps we could meet up for a drink at some stage?'

'Oh, dear god, please tell me you're not hitting on me at my friend's funeral.'

Ravosky took a step back. He took his time. 'You have quite the opinion of yourself don't you?' he said at last.

'I try.'

'No, my dear. I'm not trying to hit on you, as you say. I simply want to talk about a few things, about Teri. No matter what you might think of me, I really was fond of her. This is all a dreadful tragedy that I, like all of us, am struggling to come to terms with.'

'I'll be here for a while.'

'Please,' he said. 'Give me a call sometime soon – you have my card.' He waited as she finished her cigarette. 'We should probably make our way in now.'

His tailored back receded along with the last of the people entering the church. Flicking the butt on the ground, she crushed it viciously with the ball of her shoe. She checked her phone was on silent, then made her way inside. Lassie was sitting next to her mum and dad. He turned around motioning for her to have a seat next to him. As she sat down he leaned over.

'What did Ravosky want?' he asked.

'He wanted to get together for drinks at some stage.'

Lassie raised his eyebrows. She shrugged.

'Family and friends, thank you all for coming today,' intoned the celebrant.

And so it began.

They stood as Teri's body was brought in, carried in a simple coffin covered in ferns, interlaced with flowers. She would have wanted wild lilies, Stella thought. They were Teri's favourite weed as she called them, but it was the wrong time of year. Stella looked around her, anywhere but the procession to the front of the church.

Everyone was silent. Mozart's *Serenade for Winds*, the slow movement, played out over the sound system. Stella wished she'd had something to drink before coming here, or that she'd thought to bring a hip flask.

Teri's sister, Imogen, spoke. Her voice was strong, only wavering towards the end. She talked of her younger sister being 'happy, full of life and fun, generous to a fault'. Stella couldn't help thinking that if Teri were so happy, why were people so willing to accept the idea she'd jumped? If only Teri had said something to her the night of the party instead of making feeble jokes about Lassie, for fuck's sake. For the last few days Stella had been trying to remember the details of their conversation, the tone, analysing for hints, scouring every comment for something, anything, that would offer up a clue.

She looked around her – her trained eye taking it all in. It was the only way she could deal with the situation. Think about something else, anything else. There were Teri's parents and her brother, Steve, sitting up the front. Imogen was sitting with her husband and a small baby. That bunch in the pew behind were most likely an aunt and uncle, with a couple of cousins. The much older man was her granddad; Stella recognised him.

From the speakers came the ethereal voice of Eva Cassidy singing 'Somewhere Over the Rainbow' and Kate lost it.

There was a large screen to the left of the pulpit, playing a continuous loop of images of Teri. Teri with her family, as a baby, with her friends. The trip to Thailand, their graduation. There was Stella standing beside her in her gown, grinning wildly into the future. She squeezed her eyes shut, felt her dad's hand on her arm.

She opened her eyes and looked steadily at the long piece of highly polished wood in front of her. It ran the length of the pew in front and was used to rest a hymn book on when not in use. It was worn through years of hands brushing it, fingers stroking the satin sheen of its age. It was etched in places with initials of bored parishioners, or more likely the bored children of the parishioners. Stella focused on the letters, tried to work out what the names might have been to match the initials. To one side was the delicate image of a bicycle, etched with a pen, perfectly drawn. It was a means of escape, jump on that bike and pedal away.

She looked up. The sun had managed to break through the clouds outside. Stella watched as the stained-glass windows became illuminated, pulsating with a life of their own.

She switched off the funeral happening around her and reviewed the case in her head. Teri worked at the club, maybe she witnessed something that had bothered her. There was Christophe, who may have her phone, but was that honestly likely? And Ravosky – he knows something I'm sure of it, she thought. What about the spa? It was just a spa where Teri went to unwind, who wouldn't? It was a beautiful spot. The girl under the wharf, with the silver chain around her ankle came into view. What did McCarthy know? Shit, she thought, there would be another funeral taking place somewhere.

The service sheet she had been handed at the door was now folded eight times. It was a tightly wound missile that Stella squeezed in her right hand like a misshapen worry ball. Her hands were alternately sweaty then cold.

Teri's father made his way to the front of the church. He stopped at the coffin, bowed his head and laid a single flower on top of the ferns. Stella looked at the windows to her right. She couldn't face listening to what was going to come next.

Underneath one of the triptych glass windows sat a man about the same age as Stella. He wasn't anyone familiar; mind you, there were a lot of people she didn't know. He had dark, curly hair that looked a little unruly, a checked shirt collar was poking out of a worn jacket. He sat on the seat right next to the aisle, his shoulders hunched into his knees, shaking. His hand came up to wipe his eyes with a scrap of tissue. He wasn't anyone she recognised from uni. Maybe he was a cousin, or a more recent friend of Teri's. But it was the level of distress that interested her. Here was someone who was unafraid to demonstrate, in public, the enormity of his loss.

We're all too fucking Anglo-Saxon, thought Stella. What we need is a good weep and wail, a Māori tangi, or like Jews we could all sit shivah and let the grief pour from us. We're all so afraid of the abyss of grief. We're terrified we won't resurface, that we'll remain trapped at the bottom gazing at the rest of our lives from a great distance. Teri's dad was followed by the celebrant.

So where was Ravosky?

Stella looked around. There he was, fourth row from the front. She spotted the dark coat. 'Never underestimate your gut' was one of the first things she learnt in her training years ago. Her gut was telling her something was out of whack with Ravosky. Officially this wasn't her case; it wasn't her business other than Teri had been her friend. Meathead McCarthy would investigate and anything odd or out of place would be noted. Ravosky pulled out a small white tissue and wiped his eyes.

Stella walked into the lounge at Teri's parents' place and Teri wasn't there. Everyone else was. The room was stuffy and polite, bouquets of flowers were on every available table alongside plates laden with food. Friends, family, colleagues were standing around chatting, drinking tea and coffee. She heard Teri's dad in the kitchen. Her mother, Jane, was seated on a modern but uncomfortable-looking couch by the window; she looked small and alone.

Stella hung her coat on the stand, went over and sat beside her. 'Jane, I don't know what to say,' she said and gave her a hug.

Jane took Stella's hand. 'It's okay, love, none of us knows what to say. Except that she didn't do it. I refuse to believe it. She didn't do it, she didn't jump.' Her voice was strong, certain.

'I agree,' said Stella quietly.

'Teri seemed more settled than I've ever known her to be. She enjoyed her job. I think she may have even been seeing someone. She phoned specially to tell me you were coming back for your parents' party,' said Jane. 'She was so excited to see you. All those things don't add up to what they say she did.'

'I know. Don't underestimate your intuition. There will have to be an inquest. They'll go through everything, but it isn't cut and dried,' said Stella. She looked around the room. 'There are other people who want to talk to you. I'll come and see you soon.'

She felt a weight on her neck and shoulders. The room was stuffy with everyone trying so hard to be what they thought they should be. It was a strange repeat of her parents' party at the Boat Shed. There were half-recognised faces from a time when Stella had been a different person.

Prickling sweat started to form on her neck and under her arms. She needed to get out before she said, or did, anything she'd later regret. Lassie was nowhere in sight and Kate was across the room. People were enveloping Teri's mum and dad. Stella made her way to the front door in time to see Maurice Ravosky heading up the stairs. Her hand went into her pocket and felt the card he'd given her earlier. Stella waited a moment then followed him. At the top of the stairs she could hear him on the phone.

'I shouldn't be the one doing this,' he said. 'No, I don't have her phone and the police have her computer.'

Stella opened a door to one of the bedrooms just as Lassiter was coming out of the bathroom. Ravosky turned around and, for a brief second, the three of them stared at each other.

'Thank you,' said Ravosky. 'I was trying to find the bathroom.'

'I'll use the downstairs one,' said Stella.

'Stell, wait,' said Lassiter. 'I need to talk to you.'

They waited for Ravosky to close the bathroom door, then moved away. 'There's something up with him,' she said.

'What do you mean?'

'I don't know. But there's something wrong. He was up here snooping.'

'Don't be ridiculous. What would Ravosky be snooping around here for? Teri didn't even live here.'

'Her phone, Lassie, her phone. That's what he was after.'

'Why on earth would he want her phone? And why on

earth would it be at her parents' place? You can't go around blaming Teri's suicide on him.'

'Why do you give me this crap,' she fired back. 'I just heard him on the phone talking about how he needed to get Teri's computer and shit. I know you don't believe me.'

The bathroom door rattled. Lassiter grabbed her arm and pulled her into another room, closing the door as quietly as he could.

'This is neither the time nor the place, Weston. What the fuck's got into you?'

'What do you mean – *what the fuck's got into me*? I don't understand why you're so accommodating over this. Teri did not, let me repeat, did *not* jump over that balcony.'

'Keep your voice down.'

'I heard him, just now, talking about Teri's phone. Where's her phone, Lassie? More to the point, what's on her phone that he's so desperate to get?'

He stood there, his arms folded across his chest. He looked ruffled. 'The last time I looked, talking about a deceased person's phone wasn't an indication of guilt.'

'Of course not, but why does he want it?'

'Maybe they had a threesome and Teri took photos. Lord knows – and while we're on the subject, what on earth possessed you to go snooping in his office?

'Who told you I was snooping?'

'Ravosky did. I met him in the foyer. He told me you'd been there with a decoy bunch of flowers.'

'For your information I was delivering them for my mother. I got the wrong building, that's all.'

'How convenient for you.'

'Don't be a shit, Lassie. We're meant to be on the same side.'

'Well if you didn't act like a loose cannon we would be on the same damn side. Either way the police will sort it out. I know this is hard for you but this isn't your patch anymore. You need to get that into your head.'

They were inches apart. Stella clenched and unclenched her fists. The desire to take a swing at him was overwhelming. What was only a few seconds felt an age. Taking a step back she said, in a deliberately measured voice, 'Not my patch. What the hell is that supposed to mean?'

'This isn't about taking sides, Stella, it's about following due process. We all know how that works, don't we?'

Stella looked up at him, her shoulders slumped. She laughed without any semblance of humour. 'I was wondering how long it would be before all that was brought up again. I'm only surprised it was you, Lassie.' She made for the door. 'Just remember, I may be here as a private citizen but I still have the right to find out what happened to my friend. Just make sure your cronies on the force do their job properly, or I will be all over them like a rash on your dick.'

'I see your time in the big cities of Europe hasn't improved your language any.'

'Fuck you.'

Stella made her way down the stairs, grabbed her coat off the stand. Later she would talk to Teri's parents, but for now she stood on the porch and took a lungful of fresh air. She could do with another cigarette. Stella started to walk down the hill towards her parents' house. Ravosky was in one part of her brain, Lassie in another. The image of the girl in the water was there, too. Kate and Teri occupied the remaining space. And Christophe, now he was in there as well.

The earlier clouds were gone and the bright New Zealand light seared through to the back of her eyeballs. The wind had blown most of the cloud away. Everything was in clear relief. Stark colours like a child's finger painting, without the London haze to soften or mute things.

*

Stella went straight to the kitchen, flung open the fridge, grabbed the bottle and poured a large glass of wine. *Why didn't you talk to me, Teri? What the fuck was going on?* What bothered her most wasn't what Lassie had said about due process. No, it was the day he'd told her about Teri and believed she could take her own life.

32

PUSHING ASIDE THE CURTAINS into the club, Stella was stopped short by a large meaty hand belonging to a bouncer so big he filled up most of the available space. She only reached halfway up his chest. Tilting her head, she looked at his face.

'Name?' he said.

'Excuse me?' said Stella, taking a step back.

'Your name, are you on the list?'

'I'm here to see a friend perform. I didn't know there was a list.'

'Name?' he said again, tapping a yellow highlighter pen on a clipboard.

'Stella Weston,' she said trying to keep her voice calm. 'I'm here to see Kate Allbury – Kitty La Foy. She's performing tonight.'

He chewed his fleshy bottom lip as he scanned the printed sheet. His head was shaven, with a faint sheen to it, the goatee beard carefully cultivated. On the pinkie finger of his right hand he wore a gold ring with a not insubstantial diamond. Faint etchings of youthful tattoos showed on the backs of both hands. 'You're not listed here,' he said at last with a faint curl of his lip. 'I'll have to call management. Friday night is invited guests and members only, that's how we keep the ...' he paused, '... undesirables out.'

'Oh, for Christ's sake,' said Stella, half under her breath.

He picked up a phone from the table and punched in a few numbers. Stella waited and stared into the haze of the club hoping to see Kate, or anyone that she might know.

'It's me. Yep, yeah ... yeah. I've got a Stella *Weston* here

… yeah. Okay.' He put the phone down. 'You can go in,' he said. 'But I have to stamp your hand.'

Stella dutifully held out her left hand feeling like a uni student at an orientation gig. She couldn't remember the last time she'd been stamped to get in anywhere. His hand was warm as he held hers, pressing the ink onto her skin. She looked at the word *chandelier* lightly smudged in black.

'Thanks,' she said.

'Have a great evening and enjoy the show.' He pulled aside the velvet curtain and let her pass.

Stella took a few steps into the club and looked around; it was obvious she was underdressed the minute she stepped through the curtain. The place was filling up. The piano was now to the left of the stage and the fairy lights, that in the daytime looked cold and sad, lit up the ceiling with a magical twinkle. Velvet curtains draping the walls were red and luscious. Wait staff, in high heels, short shorts and even smaller aprons, worked the tables. The whole room had the feel of a cross between the movie *Cabaret* and a prohibition-era club. They'd clearly been told that less is more in the clothing department. Horseshoe banquettes lined one wall, offering a small amount of privacy but with enough visibility to see and be seen.

The soundtrack was a heavy bass beat overlaid with something more modern. It was loud enough to cause people to lean in to be heard, which was also the best way to expose the most cleavage. Stella stood in her skinny black jeans and white shirt. She'd taken her jacket off and was scrunching it in one hand, while holding on to a scarf in the other. Her hair was loose, but at least she'd washed and brushed it. She didn't do makeup. Her phone was in one pocket, a credit card in the other, snuggled against a couple of 'just in case' Panadol. Birdie was behind the bar. Out of the corner of her eye she caught sight of a hand waving.

It was Lassie.

Shit. Of course he'd be here, but between the fumbling pass she'd made, the scene she'd made at Teri's parents and the accidental meeting of the girlfriend, she really didn't want to spend any more time with him. He waved again. If he's got the bimbo with him I'm outta here, she thought.

'Hi,' she said.

He had what looked like an expensive bottle on the table.

'Here, let me pour you a glass, then I'll introduce you around.'

Stella kept her eyes on his hand holding the glass. He had beautiful hands, strong fingers, wide palms. God, they looked good. He tipped the glass sideways so the bubbles didn't overflow. 'I thought at the very least we should have a decent wake for Teri, something that she'd enjoy, so …' he handed her the glass and picked up his own. 'Here's to Teri,' he said. They clinked their glasses and Stella took a sip.

'Good to see you can keep this lot down. I remember you not doing so well at your parents' gig.'

'Oh ha, ha. Thanks for the memory jolt, I really needed that,' she said with a smile. 'Lassie—'

'Forget it,' he said quickly. 'I think we were both on edge. Let's just enjoy the show, have a glass or two or three and remember our friend.'

The others at the table turned out to be more recent friends of Teri's. Stella didn't quite catch their names, but they might have been something like Brian and Fifi. A Clark Gable pencil moustache covered Brian's top lip, his hair gelled back in a high wave. Tortoiseshell glasses and a floral shirt completed the look. Stella didn't need to look under the table to know that he'd have on cord trousers and suede shoes. Fifi, if that was her name, was all large earrings, large hair, shimmering lipstick. Stella could never fathom that one. Why bother putting on lipstick when you're just going to smear it on the glass you're drinking out of?

The lights dimmed. The DJ turned up the volume and a single spotlight appeared on the stage. Stella watched as, with a flourish, the curtains parted and exposed Kate standing there in full glory acknowledging the applause. As Kitty La Foy she wore a silver-sequinned top hat. Her hair, done in extravagantly large ringlets, fell gently around her face and neck. Her lips were fire-engine red and the bustier she had on barely held her large breasts in place. She struck a pose, her right hand plumped on her hip, her left hand holding the microphone. The black satin knee-length skirt was slit from knee to hip showing an expanse of fishnet stocking and suspenders.

'Ladies and gentlemen, welcome to tonight's Burlesque Extraordinaire,' she purred in her warm contralto voice. 'I'm Kitty La Foy, your mistress of ceremonies. Prepare to be amazed, entertained, impressed and ...' she ran her tongue over her lips, '... titillated.'

Kate was in her element. She shimmered, she preened, she seduced with double entendres and jokes you'd never tell your mother. As Kitty La Foy, she sashayed into the audience. The women wanted to either be her, scratch her eyes out, or fuck her. The men just wanted to fuck her, hoping their wives or girlfriends didn't find out. At one table she ran her hand over the shoulder of a punter, then eased herself backwards onto his lap, pushing her lovely, rounded arse into his crotch. She wiggled, glanced coyly over her shoulder. He raised his hand to squeeze anything he could get a hold of.

'Naughty,' she said, slapping his hand away.

He pouted. She laughed and planted a kiss on his forehead, leaving a lipstick outline for his wife to find. Kate knew she was delicious and revelled in each salivating look she got. Stella watched one man licking his lips as though he'd just eaten a juicy oyster. Sex for sale, but not quite. Sex on show, yes, but it was a case of look don't touch. We'll get the juices flowing, what you choose to do with it is up to you. Of course there'd be a brothel to be made use of. It would be crazy for there not to be. You sting them in the front with overpriced alcohol, then fleece the rest out the back.

Half-naked girls in high heels and Hugh Hefner bunny-style costumes wound their way through groups of customers. They knew how to ply men with drinks, laugh at their jokes in the time-honoured tradition. Stella watched; she couldn't imagine Teri doing this kind of work. The lights were low. Banquettes offered a small amount of discretion, but in truth many punters wanted to be seen showing off their liberal credentials.

Soon Kate was at the piano. She began with a smoky rendition of 'Love for Sale' followed by 'New York, New York'. Platters of cheese and crackers appeared at their table. Thank the sweet baby Jesus, Stella thought. She was in desperate need of solid food to soak up the alcohol. Between the hula-hoop burlesque act and the dance of the seven veils pole dance, another bottle arrived at the table and was cracked open. Toasts were made. Stella looked at Lassie, over the other side of the table. She wondered if he heard she'd met his girlfriend. Come to think of it, why wasn't she here with him?

Fifi excused herself. 'I need the little girls room,' she said.

Lassiter got up, changed seats and sat down next to Stella. He raised his glass and said, in a voice only loud enough for her to hear, 'Here's to our friend.'

Stella looked at him, his face close to hers. She picked up her glass and gently clinked it against his.

'Yes,' she said. 'Here's to our friend.'

They took a sip, Stella looked away. This wasn't going to end well, she thought.

'So,' she said. 'I met your girlfriend the other day.'

'My what?'

'Your girlfriend, the redhead. I was at yours the other day, didn't she mention it?'

'Why were you at my place?'

Shit, how much should she tell him? 'I was walking on Mount Vic with Charlotte. She left early and took her car. My phone was flat and I was out of cash. I thought I could charge it at your place and get a loan,' she said. 'So, what's her name?'

Lassie laughed. 'Skylark, or Skyla for short.'

Of course it is, thought Stella. It wouldn't be Mary, or Sue, it would have to be something exotic like Skylark.

'She's very pretty,' said Stella.

'And young, you forgot to say that she's very young.'

He laughed again, took a swig of champagne and leaned close to her ear. 'She's my niece, Stella, my oldest sister's girl,' he said. 'She's studying at Vic and living in a pretty grotty student flat. She hates it. I've given her a key.'

'Your niece?'

'Yep.'

Fifi arrived back at the table, wobbled as she sat down. 'Bit of a rabbit warren back there,' she said. 'You two look cozy, is there something I should know?'

'Um …' said Stella. 'I think I need the loo as well.'

Lassiter stood up to let her out. As she walked across the room she tried to see if she could spot James. Even with the food, the alcohol had pretty much gone straight to her head. For a moment she admired the act on stage. A belly dancer was contorting her middle section. She rolled it in and out. It rippled, her hips swayed, little bells around her wrists and waist jangled in time with the movements. The woman's feet were firmly planted, but every other part of her shimmered with each movement. She arched backwards, her long hair touching the back of her knees.

'Mesmerising, isn't it?' said a voice at Stella's ear. 'I always find the abilities of the human form to be utterly fascinating.' Ravosky stared at the stage.

'Yes,' she said. 'I'd have to agree.'

'I hope you'll take up the offer I made earlier. It was quite sincere. And I hope it will be soon. You may find it to your benefit.'

She swallowed. 'I'll give it some thought.'

'That's all I ask,' he said.

He placed his hand gently on her arm, then moved on to rejoin his table. His powerful aftershave wafted after him like vapour from a genie. She looked over at his table. What was he playing at? It's cat and mouse, she thought, and I know which one I am. She turned and pushed open the door that led to a corridor and the bathrooms. *At least I've got the right door this time.*

The large bathroom was empty. She washed her hands and looked in the mirror. The light was fluorescent and harsh. The room was warm. Raising her hand to her face, Stella traced the dark rings underneath her eyes. His niece, she thought. God, how embarrassing.

Teri's face appeared in the mirror and for the smallest fraction of time Stella forgot. She smiled at her friend, then she was gone. Stella stood there, eyes closed. Like the motion of the belly dancer, her head rippled with the last few days. The image of the girl in the water. The tiny body being lifted out, dripping wet. Stella didn't even know her name; McCarthy was being his usual fuckwit self and not telling her anything.

There was still no solid information in the media. Had her family come forward to claim her? Were they, too, preparing funeral arrangements? There it was again, a hard ball of anger just below her breastbone. For Teri and the girl under the wharf. I will find who did this to you, thought Stella. I will make them accountable.

The door opened and two elegantly dressed women appeared. Stella moved to one side to let them in, then left the room. That guy James with the earrings and bit of fluff under his lip, he was the key to this place. She looked up and down the corridor and tried to draw a mental floor map. That's the door back to the club, she thought, but those two doors along there, where do they go?

She tried the handles.

Both were locked.

Right at the end of the corridor, around a corner, there were a couple of stairs down and a door lit with a green emergency exit sign. Nothing else. This wasn't the corridor she'd been in the other day. It was all dead ends. This is crazy, she thought, heading back towards the club. The emergency exit door behind her opened. She spun around.

'What the fuck,' he said.

James.

He came towards her.

She held her ground. He stood in front of her – his face close. He reeked of coffee.

'I see you're by yourself this time,' she said. 'No young girls to threaten?'

'Don't fuck with me.'

'Why not?'

'You don't know who you're dealing with.'

'No? So why don't you tell me.'

He held her stare. Unblinking. She swallowed. I will not let him see me scared, she thought.

His arm moved up. She flinched. He laughed – a flat, brutal sound – and slowly rubbed his index finger just below his ear.

'Go back and play with your friends,' he said.

The bathroom door opened; the two women appeared. They stopped, unsure of what was happening in the corridor, and scuttled towards the club door. James looked at them, then back at Stella.

With surprisingly feline grace, he slipped through the emergency exit door.

In the club, Stella stood towards the back and took her time scanning the room. He was here, James, he had to be. The next act took the stage: a barely clad woman dancing suggestively with a snake that looked incredibly realistic. Stella had to look twice.

Ravosky's table was front and centre in the room. There was no hiding him. A door to the right of the stage, unlabelled and ordinary, opened, disgorging several well-dressed men. They've no doubt made use of the other side of the club, thought Stella. They went and sat at the table next to Ravosky's.

The snake dancer removed more clothing, not too much, just enough, as the music picked up pace. Like the belly dancer, she swirled her hips. She bent over, her arse in the air, and looked at the audience through her legs. It's amazing she doesn't break an ankle wearing heels that high, Stella thought. The door by the stage opened again and this time James appeared. He made his way over to the table and handed one of the men their wallet. He leaned forward as he did; the other man smiled and patted him on the shoulder. James left through the same door. It took no more than a few seconds. Stella watched Ravosky as he scanned the room. He's in it, she thought. Christ, I'll have to meet him for drinks.

Back at her table, Stella squeezed herself next to Lassiter. He poured her another glass. More people had joined them. Brian and Fifi had left.

'They had to get home to the babysitter,' said Lassiter.

'You're kidding? I hadn't picked that one,' she said.

'Happens to us all, eventually.'

'What? Kids?'

'Not necessarily kids, but y'know, settling down.'

'Fuck that for a joke,' said Stella and drained her glass.

There were more toasts to Teri. More food arrived. There was laughter and applause for the performers. Kate came over and regaled them with a few backstage stories then left for the second set. Stella felt herself relaxing for the first time in a long while. The alcohol warmed her. It took the edge off the sharp corners. Eventually she'd have to get home – but not just yet.

Lassiter got his phone. 'I'm ordering you an Uber, my treat. Your parents are number twenty-eight, right?'

She looked at him and nodded and started to say something.

'Don't argue, Stell,' he said. 'You're exhausted, you need to sleep. I'll come and wait with you.'

'Thanks, Lassie, that's a lovely offer. I'll accept the Uber,' she said, 'but you stay here and finish your drink, really. I'll be fine.'

He gave her a long hug. 'Look after yourself, we'll talk soon, okay?' He checked his phone. 'You'd better hurry – the Uber's only two minutes away. Pick up is at the corner of the mall and Ghuznee. I'll flick you a screenshot so you can ID it.'

She nodded, swallowed, a lump forming in her throat.

The cool night air jarred as she stepped onto Cuba Street. The Bucket Fountain sloshed water, the buckets tipping with a hesitant, slightly apologetic sound. She walked up a block, checking the doorways in the hope she might see Mad-Dog, or Beanie. Nothing. The buskers had left for the evening – the street was dotted with a few hardy souls still trying to find meaning in the night. Her Uber was waiting for her, right where Lassie said it would be.

Her parents' street was narrow and winding. Cars lined either side. The driver turned down the street.

'Don't bother going all the way,' she said. 'Just drop me here.' She closed the door and started off down the street. The moon was behind the clouds, and when it did appear it was an ineffective sliver of pale fingernail. One of the streetlights wasn't working. That snake charmer in the stilettos wouldn't stand a chance out here. Christ, I hope I don't break my neck.

Stella stopped for a minute and leaned against one of the old pōhutukawa trees that lined the street. In the heat of summer, it was a ferocious display of crimson red proclaiming *I am here, I am alive*. Now, in the autumn months, it was a dull green. A faint breeze lifted the leaves, making a gentle rustling sound.

A rūrū called out.

Silence. Then called again, a soft cooing sound. Lassie was good to her, he always had been. It never mattered what she dished out, he'd stood by her. Part of her felt she didn't deserve it. There was an imbalance of generosity and not just of the fiscal kind.

She didn't see him.

She didn't even hear him. But he was there, in front of her, barring the footpath. His fists clenched at his side.

'What the hell do you think you're playing at, cunt?' he snarled.

Now she was very awake and very sober.

'James – it's James, isn't it? – you can fuck off, I haven't done anything.'

'My boss isn't happy.'

'I was at the club to see my friend perform, that's all.'

She went to sidestep him. If it was James who'd messed up Digby, she'd seen what he was capable of.

'Nice try, Stella.' Fuck, he knew her name as well.

'Who's your boss, *James?*'

He stared, unblinking.

'I know there's shit going on at the club,' she tried again.

'You know fuck all.' He moved closer. He was coiled, standing close enough for her to see the tension in his neck.

She stumbled on the path. He shoved. She felt the rough bark of the tree against her back. His mouth was by her ear. His shoulder pressed against hers. His weight pinned her. She couldn't move, his breath on her face, his hand on her waist – then higher, squeezing her breast.

'I could hurt you, Stella,' he said. 'I could fuck you till you split in two.'

He was standing too close for her to get a knee in his groin. Her hands went up to his chest to push him away. His fist landed in her stomach, a direct hit. Doubled over, gagging, coughing, she hugged her arms around herself. He grabbed a handful of her hair, yanked her upright.

His hands were at her throat.

Pressing.

Her hands on his, trying to prise him lose. He was pulling her up. She was standing on her toes, mouth open, eyes wide. In one sharp movement he pulled her away from the tree then slammed her up against it. She hit her head and her back with full force. Then again. She heard a crack.

'I know who you are, Stella.'

Her hands were still at her neck, grasping, trying to loosen his grip. She could hear herself struggling for breath. She was gagging. He was squeezing, forcing her head back. In the distance the sound of a police siren wailed. Not for her, but enough of a sound to break the moment. His grip loosened just a little.

She coughed, gasping for air. 'Why?' she managed to say. 'I don't have to fucking tell you anything.'

He let her go, but not before he stomped his boot hard onto her foot.

Stella unlocked the front door and stumbled into the hallway. Touching a hand up to the back of her head, it came away with blood on it. Damn. Her stomach felt tender. Her foot ached and her neck would bruise. In the kitchen she put her hands flat on the bench and leaned forward trying to calm herself. She was shaking. Furious at herself for letting that shit beat her. Furious she'd been caught unawares.

She found a bottle of the whisky her father kept for 'medicinal purposes'. Pouring herself a generous glass she downed it in one gulp. The coughing made her ache. What she needed, more than ever, was Teri's phone. Pulling hers out of her back pocket, she thought about sending a text to Lassie.

A thin spiderweb crack radiated out from the centre of the screen. That fuckwit had slammed her so hard against the tree the phone in her back pocket had taken the brunt of the force. She plugged it into the charger on the bench and dragged herself upstairs. It was almost 2 AM by the time she fell into bed. She'd had more whisky with a couple of Panadol. At least it's not for my tooth, she thought.

He'd said his boss wasn't happy. She'd have to face him tomorrow.

33

'THERE'S COFFEE IN THE PLUNGER,' said her dad when she appeared in the kitchen the next morning. 'Sometimes easier to make a pot than use that machine of your mother's.'

She poured herself a large mug and took a mouthful. Her throat hurt. Everything hurt. She found some paracetamol in one of the cupboards, quickly downing a couple. The back of her head felt tender, her spine bruised and her chest ached. She didn't know what to think. Ravosky had sent her a message, she'd received it loud and clear. That bastard James had made his point. She flexed the toes of her foot, bruised as well. At least they didn't feel broken.

Her dad was engrossed with the Saturday paper, spread before him like a fungal growth over the entire surface of the table. He refused to get his information any other way. His hair was almost all grey now, and ruffled from sleep. With his reading glasses perched on the end of his nose, he had the air of a wise owl. His green-and-red tartan dressing gown looked a little the worse for wear. He'd had it her entire life – weekend mornings wouldn't be the same if he got a new one. It was fraying around the neck and one of the pockets was coming unstitched. The belt tie, in the same fabric, had disappeared long ago, replaced with a serviceable belt. 'No sense wasting a good dressing gown for the sake of a belt,' he'd said. Her mother said she had given up. 'If he wants to wear that old thing, that's fine with me. As long as he doesn't wear it anywhere in public.' God help him if he ever ended up in hospital, thought Stella, Peace would replace his entire wardrobe.

Carefully she pulled her own dressing gown collar around her neck and sat down at the table opposite her dad. The painkillers would do their work eventually. She'd debated whether or not to tell Lassie what had happened last night. No surprises how that conversation would go.

'You've been beaten up two metres from your home.'

'I know.'

'This isn't random, you know who did it.'

'I know.'

'You need to go to the police.'

'And tell them what, exactly.'

'Tell them what happened.'

'Good one, Lassie. Other than the bruising I've no proof and yes, I know bruising is proof, but it would be his word against mine that he was the one that did it.'

They'd go around and around – he said, she said. The end result would be a stand-off. No. She needed to work this one out herself. She sipped her coffee.

'Can you believe it?' her father said. 'They're still not saying how that wee girl ended up in the water. Her poor parents must be broken.'

'Maybe they did, but you just missed it,' she said.

'Hmmm … maybe.'

'Is there ever anything good in the news?' asked Stella.

'Hardly ever, and another homeless man's been beaten up. What's the world coming to?'

'Really?' She sat forward. 'Where was this?'

'Central city again.'

'Do they give a name?'

His eyes were still glued to the paper. 'Um, let me see, yes, they have named him, he's Charles Andrew Mulgrave. Why? Friend of yours?'

'No, it's just something I have a hunch about that's all.'

'That sounds all very cloak and dagger.' Her father looked up. 'Good god, Stella, sweetheart. What happened to you?'

Instinctively her hand went to her throat. Damn, she should have worn a scarf.

'Nothing much, truly, Dad.'

He stood up and came round the table, his hand gently pulling aside the collar of her dressing gown. 'That doesn't look like nothing to me, Stella love, that looks serious. Who did this to you? Do you need the police?'

'It's okay, I'm okay,' she said.

'What on *earth* happened?'

'Not really sure. I got jumped last night, coming home.'

'You're kidding? You mean someone attacked you? That's it – where's the phone?'

'Dad, look, it's not a police matter.'

'Don't be silly, of course it is,' he said, rummaging through the newspapers on the table for his phone. 'They need to know my daughter has been attacked. They need to catch them and press charges, imagine if this happened to anyone else.'

'Please, stop.' She reached for his hand. 'Please,' she said again. 'Come and sit down.'

She pulled out another chair next to her and patted the seat. Her father sat down, still holding her hand.

'Listen,' she said. 'I'll fill you in, but promise me you won't call the police. If you do I'll deny everything, okay?'

She waited until finally he said, 'Okay … I don't like it, but … okay.'

'Thanks, Dad,' she said. 'Here goes. I don't believe Teri's death was suicide.'

Silence ricocheted round the kitchen. 'What? … But …' Her father faltered.

'I believe she was helped over that balcony. I'm following some theories, ideas really, and I've met some nasty people.'

'And your being attacked was part of it?' he said.

'Yeah, it proves there's something going on, something

227

that someone doesn't want me to find, but I need to find it. For Teri. For her family. If I don't,' she said, 'they'll go on living with the idea that their daughter and sister committed suicide when she didn't.' She squeezed his hand. 'I'm okay, really. It's not as bad as it looks. You know how I bruise. There's no need to worry – I'm a big girl.'

'But I do worry, I will always worry,' he said with his bewildered look. 'I don't like it and I still think you should call the police.' He kissed her cheek and gave her a hug.

'Ow, not too hard,' she yelped.

'Why?' He sat back. 'What else is going on? Have you broken a rib? At the very least you need to see a doctor.'

'My ribs are fine, just a bit bruised, and I fully note your dislike of the situation.' She smiled at him.

'Does this,' he said, pointing to her neck, 'have anything to do with that crack on your phone?'

'Yeah, it was part of it. They don't make them like they used to, eh, Dad? And please don't tell Mum. She'll go overboard.'

'She'll have to know eventually.'

'I know, but can we wait a couple of days?'

'Okay,' he said. 'You know I never liked your being in the police.'

'I know.'

'And now this and you're not even *in* the force anymore. Whatever you're involved with, whatever it is, it doesn't sound right.'

'Yes, Dad, you've made your point.'

'Just you be careful, love, I couldn't stand to lose you. It's bad enough Tim being AWOL ...' He coughed.

'You won't lose me.' She leaned forward and hugged him.

He patted her back and kissed her again. They were both quiet for a moment. He cleared his throat, rubbing his hand across his eyes.

'Still no word from him?' she asked.

'Not really, the last I heard he was in Nelson. Charlotte may have a better idea. He's an adult.'

'Yeah, but he's your son.'

'He can do what he likes.'

'Doesn't stop you worrying though, does it?' She smiled at him. 'Any idea where I can get my phone screen replaced?'

'Not sure, but I can find out for you.'

'Thanks. Has Mum left?'

'She sure has. She asked if you could drop in sometime this morning, she may have more deliveries for you. And make sure she doesn't see that,' he said, pointing to her neck. He smiled at her, a rueful look.

Stella drank her coffee to the faint rustle of the turning pages. It's happening, she thought, that time in life when the relationship between parent and child changes. You begin to see them as frail, in need of protection, your protection. It's where the child becomes the carer. They'd need to move soon. This house was already too big for them. Maybe a townhouse, with a small garden. That was all in the not-too-distant future.

'So, here's a question for you,' she began. 'Have you ever come across a company called Crossfield Holdings?'

Her dad peered over the top of his paper, 'Yes, regularly, why?'

'You're kidding.'

'I'm an accountant, I never joke,' he said. 'Why the interest in Crossfield?'

'I'm not sure. How do you know them?'

'Crossfield Holdings owns the building that houses your mother's shop along with a couple of others on the same stretch. It's the company owned by Audrey in the antiques shop.'

'How can she afford that business?'

'She inherited it from her parents, I believe. Around fourteen or fifteen years ago. I used to do her accounts. It was a favour to her really – she got a bit stuck one year and I offered to help. I did so for a couple of years. After a while she wanted to go with a bigger firm so I handed it over.'

'So it's all legit.'

'Of course it is. I hope you're not casting aspersions on my accounting practice?'

'Course not, Dad.'

'Mind you, I don't know about now. I've had nothing to do with it for years.'

'What about Ravosky? Is there any involvement with Maurice Ravosky and Crossfield Holdings?'

'Not to my knowledge. What's going on, Stella?' He asked, folding up the newspaper. 'What have you got yourself into?'

'I'm not sure. I'll let you know if anything comes to light,' she said. 'So what else does Audrey own?'

'You can look all this up online, you know.'

'Yeah, I know, but tell me everything you know first.'

'My information is old. I stopped doing anything for Audrey a long time ago. But what I remember was that when her parents died, she was the sole beneficiary of several major properties and she invested well with any profits.' He took a hanky out of his dressing gown pocket and started to clean his glasses. 'It all helps to keep that antiques shop of hers afloat – that's her first love, she'd be lost without that. But as I said, I've had nothing to do with her accounts for years.'

'I like Audrey,' said Stella. 'I had an amazing chat with her the other day.'

'Yes, she's been very good to your mum and to Charlotte.'

Stella finished her coffee. Her phone buzzing on the bench split the quiet. An unknown number flashed on the screen under the crack. She answered it. 'Hello?'

'Good morning, Stella, this is Maurice Ravosky.'

Stella arranged to meet Ravosky later that afternoon. She contemplated asking Lassiter to come with her, but he, no doubt, wouldn't approve of her questions. Like everyone else, Lassie was still going with the suicide theory.

It was a cool day. The wind was light. Low grey clouds raced across the sky. Those without children mooched around Tinakori Road. Saturday was for brunch or shopping, taking time and relaxing from the rigours of the week. The roads, however, were choked with massive off-road vehicles that had never seen dirt: parents traipsing their kids across the city to soccer, netball and hockey games. Stella borrowed a scarf from her mother's collection to wear around her neck; she wanted as little comment as possible about the bruising.

She stopped in to Bloomin Gorgeous to see her mum.

'Darling, that colour looks fabulous on you, you should always wear it,' said Peace when she walked into the shop.

'Thanks, Mum.'

'You're limping. Why are you limping?'

'I'm fine, Mum, really, I'm fine. Dad said you needed a hand with deliveries.'

'Absolutely. I've got a couple that need doing. I'll have them sorted in a minute.'

'Sure,' said Stella. 'Can I borrow your car this afternoon?'

'Of course, but I'll need it back for this evening. Where are you going?'

'I need to take a quick trip up the coast to visit someone. I won't be long.'

'Don't tell me, you're going to that spa again. I knew it,' said Peace triumphantly. 'As soon as you experience that level of pampering there's no going back. Good on you,

Stella. How about you have a facial as well, your skin looks a little dry. My treat.' She patted Stella's cheek.

'Thanks, Mum, but I'm honestly just visiting someone.'

'Really, are you sure?'

'Yep, you know all that facial stuff isn't me.'

'I know, but I just thought …'

'Thanks for the thought. Look, I'm just going to pop over to Audrey's, then I'll come back for the keys.'

Stella opened the antiques shop door to the tinkling sound of the doorbell. Soft music was playing. Several customers were pottering around the edges. Audrey was busy with someone making a decision between two large mirrors. She turned at the sound of the door and smiled at Stella.

'Lovely to see you again. I'll be with you in a minute.'

'No rush.'

She could smell furniture polish, age and quiet. It wasn't surprising Charlotte loved working here, she thought. Some of these things were really beautiful, being surrounded by them must be good for the soul. Easing her way between the goods in the store Stella stood in front of the glass counter. The pin her mum had been eyeing sat on a black velvet tray. Audrey was clearly going to be a while, so Stella thought she'd have a quick look upstairs.

The carpet runner was well worn, the staircase steep and narrow. The polished wooden railing felt smooth under her hand. At the top of the stairs was a hallway running the length of the building. The first door was open and Stella walked into a large front room that faced the street. This would have probably been a bedroom at some stage, now it smelt of old leather. High sash windows let in a shaft of light that fell on an assortment of items jumbled together.

A couple of large chairs, one with the stuffing leaking out from under cracked leather, some rickety bentwood kitchen chairs stacked to one side. An ornate wooden coat stand stood alongside a rack of heavy, vintage fire tools. The walls were covered with more large mirrors and framed paintings. It was the item hanging in the corner that caught Stella's eye. She walked over and touched it. It swayed gently under her hand.

A wooden birdcage. It was square, made of highly polished red wood. A carved spire sat on top. Inside were perches for the birds, the little door held shut by an ingenious twist of wood. She'd seen them before, on her holiday years ago with Teri. This city was full of her friend, even here, upstairs in a musty-smelling shop. Fuck, she'd better not lose it in front of Audrey again or she'd think she was a basket case.

Every move Stella made carried an image of Teri. Every corner held a memory. The cafés, the streets, the waterfront. The funeral was a blur. She'd been so intent on shutting it out she could only remember sketchy details. The music, the excessive calm. Ravosky pulling out that tissue. Stella had no idea what she was going to say to him, no idea at all. Meathead McCarthy was right. She no longer had any jurisdiction here, so anything Ravosky said to her would be inadmissible. She could record the conversation, but some smart-arse lawyer would have her up for entrapment, or defamation.

She took one last look at the birdcage and went back down the stairs. Audrey's customers had left. Stella felt hot in this space and unwound the scarf from her neck.

'Oh, my dear,' said Audrey. 'What on earth happened to you?'

Stella's hand went to her throat. 'It's all part of that long story,' she said.

'Well, I'm due for a break. How about I swing the closed sign around and make us a hot drink. I'm sure we could both use one.'

Stella talked and while the tea was brewing, Audrey rustled around and found a packet of biscuits. Like the other day, it all came tumbling out again.

'So, why do you think this James is following you?' Audrey asked.

'I'm not sure. It's something to do with the club. My friend Kate who works there reckons he's a nasty piece of work. So does Birdie – she works the bar. Beating me up just proves that.'

'But I don't understand, what's he after?'

'I think he knows about the phone. Don't ask me how. I've no idea. Maybe he thinks I've got it.'

'And how does Ravosky fit in to it all?'

'Teri, my friend who was killed, she worked for him,' said Stella. 'My guess is that she found something out. Possibly about him and that there's something on her phone. Something that he needs back.'

'Enough to get her killed? That seems a bit extreme.'

'I know.'

'Well, part of me hopes you never find out. I'd hate for the same thing to happen to you.'

Later that afternoon Stella parked at the spa and switched off the engine. There were several other cars there. She had a quick look but Ravosky's wasn't there. Large glass doors were open onto the deck. Voices drifted over from the café, accompanied by the monotonous drone of flute music being piped into the warm air. It was a mild afternoon, definitely warmer up here than in Wellington. Tables shaded with softly coloured umbrellas dotted the deck. Feeling hungry, she wondered if she could get something more substantial than the sprouts she'd had last time. Worth a try, she thought. She strode into the building, looked at the menu and ordered.

Sitting at one of the tables outside, Stella thought about Audrey. Once again she'd been amazing. She'd just sat there, asked a few pertinent questions and Stella had ended up telling her pretty much everything. Humans are strange beasts: quick to accuse or hurt and slow to find good in people. Audrey broke that mould – she was kind with a real warmth to her.

Unable to take much more of the flute music, Stella hurriedly finished her lunch. She folded up the napkin and decided now was the time to take a stroll around the buildings. She skirted around one side, but not before she'd spotted a CCTV camera. Fuck it. If anyone asked she could always say she got a bit lost. She should have made an appointment, gone in the front way, but there wasn't time for that. She just needed to satisfy her curiosity.

Around the back of the main building the place was quiet, empty. Every door was closed: the laundry, the garage, the doors into the main building. She went up and tried one. It was locked, they all were. Stella stood there, her arms folded. She scraped the toe of her boot in a small patch of loose stone. *Those wee girls had come out of that door over there. That part sounds like the kitchen area.* This was hopeless. There was nothing here. Over to one side, a couple of sparrows were having a dust bath. Feathers ruffling, tiny bodies wriggling, preening.

A voice, harsh and commanding, split the quiet. 'Why you back here?'

It was the same fierce woman as the other day.

Startled, Stella said the first thing that sprang to her mouth. 'Sorry, I was after Corrine. She's one of the massage therapists who works here.'

'Well, she not here and you shouldn't be either.'

'I didn't know it was out of bounds,' said Stella. 'I saw you the other day. What is your name?'

'That none of your business.'

Stella tried again. 'How long have you worked here?'

'Long enough. Now you must go. Back around the front. This area not for clients.'

'Your daughters, how are they?'

'My daughters?'

'Yes, the ones I saw you with. You said they were off school because they were sick.'

'Yes, they much better, thank you. Now you must go.'

Back at the car, Stella leaned against the bonnet, the metal still slightly warm from the drive. She shivered. The breeze had got up and she'd parked in the shade. She wondered if there were visa issues, maybe poor working conditions without a decent employment contract. That would be enough to make anyone grumpy. What she needed to do now, she thought, was to form some questions for Ravosky. She was only going to get one decent shot at grilling him.

Stella dropped her mum's car back at home and walked down to Courtenay Place.

She checked her phone. Only a few minutes late, she thought. Let him wait. It won't do him any harm. She needed to treat this like a police interview, except there was only one of her; she'd need to be both good cop and bad cop. Teri had trusted him. She worked for him, knew him, but something had gone badly wrong, enough for him to want her dead.

She pushed open the door to the Firefly Bar. The door was heavy, but once inside she was enveloped by the warmth and atmosphere of the room. The highly polished horseshoe bar dominated the central space. Mirrored glass cabinets reflected low light. A scattering of patrons sipped late coffees and early cocktails. A couple sat at the bar. Stella caught sight of a foot being eased up the curve of a shin, laughter. The waiter behind the bar shook a silver cocktail shaker with the flourish of a seasoned performer. Like the Ferris wheel at the fun fair, the night was winding into motion. This end of town would soon fill up with those happy enough to be out and those sad enough to want to drown their sorrows. Stella looked around.

Ravosky was sitting at one of the corner tables, tucked away, nursing a glass of wine the colour of gemstones. Holding out his hand to her, he stood up as she walked over. She shook it, standing close enough to be enveloped in the embrace of his aftershave.

'What can I get you?' he asked.

'Just coffee, thanks.'

Ravosky nodded to the waiter, who came and took his order. Stella placed her jacket on the back of the chair but kept the scarf on. There was no way she was going to let Ravosky see what James had done. She removed her phone from her back pocket and sat down.

'What happened to your phone?'

'Nothing. I dropped it, that's all.' She scooped it up again and slipped it into her jacket pocket.

'Would you like something to eat?' he asked.

'No, thank you. I'm fine.'

'Well, I took the liberty of ordering a plate of hors d'oeuvres earlier. Perhaps you'll join me?'

The waiter came back with the coffee and the plate of food. The sound system played something with a bass beat she could do without.

She drank her coffee.

'You wanted to talk,' Stella began.

'You must try these,' he said, holding up a minute square of toast topped with a swirl of pale pink and a sprig of green. 'They're quite delicious.'

'What did you want to talk about?'

Ravosky sighed. He sat back in his chair and took a sip of his wine. 'You're all business aren't you, Stella?'

'But this is a business meeting, isn't it? I don't imagine we're here for a social get-together.'

'I suppose not, but I would like to say again that I was very fond of Teri. She was a great asset to me at work. She's irreplaceable. Her funeral was quite lovely, don't you think?'

'Yes,' she said. They were both quiet for a moment.

'Suicide is such a brutal act,' said Ravosky.

'Her mother is convinced it wasn't suicide.'

'I know. A difficult situation for any parent to come to terms with.'

'What do you think, Mr Ravosky?'

'I think that no parent should have to sit through their child's funeral.'

'I agree.'

'How nice that we can agree on something.'

'What did Teri do for you?'

'At work? She looked after my schedule. Dealt with correspondence, organised meetings. Generally looked after the day-to-day running of my life. She used to call herself my Girl Friday. On occasions where I was required to attend a dinner she would often accompany me.'

'Did you know she was moonlighting?'

'At the club? Yes, I did know that.'

'So, what you paid her was crap?'

'What Teri chose to do in her spare time was entirely her business.'

'Of course.'

'What's your interest in the club?' he asked.

'My friend Kate works there.'

'The singer?'

'Yes,' said Stella.

'So nothing else. There's nothing of interest for you there?'

'You tell me. Did you know Teri was unhappy?'

'What do you mean unhappy?'

'Well, if it was suicide, she must have been in a bad way. So, did you know she was unhappy?' Stella sipped her coffee, wincing at the bitterness.

Ravosky stopped chewing. 'You need to be careful, Stella.'

'Of what, exactly?'

The corner of his mouth lifted slightly, a small twitch.

'Of finding the truth,' he said.

'But that's precisely what I'm after,' she said. 'What about at Teri's parents' house, Mr Ravosky? Did you find what you needed?'

'Maurice, please. And yes, I did find the bathroom.'

'Really?' She leaned forward, her elbows on the table. 'Are we going to play that game? I know you want Teri's phone. I heard you talking.'

Ravosky sat completely still. Her trump card was Christophe, Mad-Dog.

'Do you have children?' she asked.

If Ravosky was surprised by her question, he didn't show it. 'No,' he said. 'My late wife and I weren't blessed.'

'Adoption wasn't for you?'

'No. We briefly investigated inter-country adoption but it wasn't for us. We had a mere twelve years together. I miss her.'

'Your wife or Teri?'

He laughed. 'Both of them, they were both formidable women in their own way. Why do you ask about children?'

'Not sure. Just curious to know a bit about you, some of your background.'

'Well, let me fill you in.' He sat back from the table. His

manicured hands cupped his wine glass as he slowly swirled the liquid. 'I'm currently single. Teri and I were not lovers. I am a childless widower. I own several businesses and travel regularly. I visit my dentist regularly,' he said. 'My religion is my business. My politics lean towards the left with an occasional sway to the right depending on the business side of things. Shall I continue?'

'Please do.'

'There's no point. It won't get us to where we want to be.'

His blue eyes stared at her, unblinking. Like a game of tennis, the volleys were sharp. Each had their eye on the other, neither content to give away their position. Thwack, backwards and forwards, without so much as breaking a sweat. Eventually a ball would drop into the net.

'You visit that spa up the coast, don't you,' she said.

'As you have, I believe. Did you happen upon anything interesting?'

'I'm not sure. I was there with my sister – what's your excuse?'

'I go there often,' he said. 'What I can tell you is they have the most marvellous masseuse by the name of Corinne, quite magical.'

The door to the bar opened, a cool rush of air followed, then a chorus of greetings as they found their tribe of friends and ordered drinks.

Stella sat back in her chair. 'Teri used to go to that spa.'

'Yes, she was the one who introduced me to the place. Can I trust you?'

'That depends what with?'

'Let's get to the point,' he said.

'I'd like that.'

'Teri's phone, have you located it?'

For a brief moment Stella considered lying to him, telling him that she had the phone. She wanted to see what his reaction would be. Would he be pleased, angry, relieved?

'No,' she said. 'I haven't found it. Now, your turn.'

'My turn?'

'Yes, your turn to answer my question. What's so important about Teri's phone? What did she have on it that you want? You see, *Maurice*,' she said, 'I've got the feeling that Teri knew something about you that you didn't want out in the world.'

'About me?'

'Yes.'

'And you think I killed her for it?'

'I never said that.'

'No,' he leaned forward, his elbows on the table. 'But your implication is clear.'

'That isn't an answer,' said Stella. 'What about the police – have you asked them about the phone?'

'They've told me as much as they're able to. No offence, but I don't think that DI McCarthy is terribly bright.'

'No offence taken. I happen to agree with you about McCarthy.'

'This conversation is starting to have the feel of an interrogation,' he said. 'Are you interrogating me, Stella?'

'The term *interrogation* implies you have something to hide.'

'Does it?'

'By its definition, yes. So, what are you hiding, Maurice?'

'We live in strange times, Stella.' He offered her the platter in front of him. 'Really, you must try one of these.'

Stella picked up a morsel of food and put it in her mouth.

Ravosky needed the phone just as much as she did, but this was going nowhere. Stella had had enough and decided to go in for the kill.

'What can you tell me about Crossfield Holdings?' she asked.

He coughed, then dabbed at his mouth with a large linen napkin. 'Crossfield Holdings.' He pursed his lips.

'It's a name that's come up. You're a businessman, what do you know about the company?'

'You and I are at a delicate place in the proceedings. I don't wish danger upon you, but I would caution you to mind whom you talk to.'

'Sounds ominous.'

He sat back in his chair and sighed. His eyes held a faraway look. Eventually he focused them directly on her.

'Be careful, Stella. That's all I can say.'

34

THE MEETING WITH RAVOSKY unsettled her.

They both wanted the same thing but for different reasons. Stella felt the door of the bar swoosh close behind her. As she walked towards Cuba Street, a voice from a darkened doorway called out,

'Hey, any smokes?'

'Beanie. Hi, how are you?'

'Not so bad – any smokes?'

'Do you have any info on Mad-Dog?'

'Nah, haven't seen him all day. He's been really low key.'

Stella was quiet for a moment. 'I guess you heard about the latest bashing?'

'Yeah.' His face brightened a little. 'It wasn't Mad-Dog though.'

'That's good, well, not for the bloke that got bashed of course, but I'm pleased it wasn't our guy.'

'We're all a bit buggered out here,' said Beanie. 'The night shelter is chock full. The Sallies had some space, but that goes real fast. I know some guys who were going to head up the back of Wadestown. Safest place if you ask me.'

'You look after yourself, Beanie, and thanks,' she handed him an almost full packet from her jacket pocket. 'Don't smoke them all at once,' she said. 'They'll stunt your growth.'

Courtenay Place was humming. People were either leaving the movie theatre or going in. Arriving for dinner invitations, or drinks before a party. Hunting entertainment, sex, love, booze. Stella smiled to herself. For the first time in a long while she felt at home. She could go back to London, back to her flat, her flatmate and her PI job.

But really, Europe was a cesspool, albeit a cultured one. And then there was family. Her parents were okay for now, but how long would that last? And Charlotte pining for a baby and Tim perpetually absent. He'd been on her mind as well. She needed to find him, just so she could see for herself that he was all right. She started walking. Several of the deeper doorways housed those sitting under jackets and blankets, sitting on flattened cardboard boxes, signs at the ready. The busking guitar player was tuning up, girls in packs roamed, boys salivated. It was the same the world over.

The entrance to the Chandelier Club was controlled again by the massive doorman. He went through his whole routine with the couple standing in front of her. Eventually, he found their name on his list, unhooked the red velvet rope and let them in.

'Stella Weston,' she said when it was her turn.

He ran a sausage finger down the list. 'You're not listed,' he said.

'Not again.'

'Sorry, I'll need to make a call.'

He tapped numbers into his phone. 'Yep, Stella Weston. Yep, she's here in front of me.' He looked her up and down. 'Yep, yep, okay.' He finished the call and turned to her. 'Your name's not on the list.'

'Yes, I know. You've already said that,' she said. 'So, who was that you were you talking to?'

'My boss. He says your name's not on the list.'

'Okay, I get that bit—'

He interrupted her. 'And your name won't ever be on the list.'

'What the fuck? I just want to get into the club.'

'Well, I guess what you want isn't what my boss wants. You're not on the list.'

'Can you please stop saying that – I get it.'

'Clearly you don't, because you're still standing here.'

Stella stared at him. He stared back, then over her head to a couple standing behind her. 'Can I help?' he asked them.

Back on Cuba Street, Stella phoned Kate. 'What's going on, Kate? I can't get into the club. You have to get me in.'

'To do what, Stell? You're not police anymore. Look what happened to Teri.'

'Exactly, we need to do it for Teri. She found something. Something about the club or the brothel, I don't know.'

'I can't …' began Kate.

'Whatever it was, she was killed for it. Get me in.'

'I can't. I can't do what you're asking me,' said Kate.

'What's going on?'

'After we talked last night, I asked a few questions, just quietly. I didn't get much. No one wants to talk,' said Kate. 'You're not safe in here, Stell – if they find out you're here you'll ruin any job prospects for me in the future.'

'I can look after myself. If anything happens, I promise I won't mention your name. I just want to chat to a few of the staff, get a feel for the place, nothing sinister. Please, Kate.'

Kate was silent.

Faint sounds from the nightclub filtered through the phone. A door slammed in the distance. 'Okay,' she finally said.

'You're a star,' said Stella.

'There's the back entrance off Dixon Street. It has a number keypad. They change the number pretty often, but they let their regular workers know by text what it is. It's where we come if the front entrance is locked during the day.'

'Can you get me that number?'

She could hear Kate talking to someone in the room. Stella only heard part of the conversation.

'I have to go,' said Kate. 'I'm due on stage really soon. I'll text you the number when I find it, okay?'

'Sure. Take care and thanks.'

Stella pocketed her phone, pulled open the door to the Bristol and headed for the crush at the bar.

'Whisky,' she said. 'With a splash of ginger.'

Keeping an eye on her phone she sipped her drink. Bloody hell, she thought, maybe Kate's got caught up in something as well. No, she wouldn't. Not Kate. Even if she managed to get into the club, Stella had no idea what she was looking for. James would most likely be there; he was her biggest problem. What she needed to do was to try and talk to some of the workers. Find out anything they might know.

Alley off Dixon. I think it's cx129.

The text from Kate. Stella breathed a sigh, if Kate were any way involved with shit, there was no way she'd help her into the building. She put her phone on silent and slipped it into the back pocket of her jeans. Teri had found something, Stella was convinced of that. Something that was enough to get her killed.

Stella finished her drink and made her way through the crowd to Cuba Mall. A fire-breathing street performer was in full flight. People gathered around, oohhhhing and ahhhhing as flames shot from her mouth, a modern-day dragon in tight black leather. She had a quick scan of the crowd but couldn't see Christophe.

Stella cut though a car park that ran along one side of the alley. Apartment blocks lined part of the throughway. Directly off the alley was another smaller entrance. It smelt of stale piss and rubbish. The back door of the club was down the far end. The alley was partly lit, but the light was on the blink, flickering intermittently like the hand of a detoxing addict. Stella began to wonder if she'd accidentally stepped into a bad noir film. There were a couple of doors. Both had keypads, and she had no idea which one led to the club. The only thing to do was try them. I'm in bloody Wonderland again, she thought, pushing the keys: cx129. She twisted the knob. Nothing.

She tried the other door. Same thing.

Stella pushed the buttons again – firmer, slower this time. Still nothing. Shit.

'They've changed the number again,' came a voice from behind her.

Stella looked over her shoulder to see a woman standing there. She looked young, in her early twenties maybe.

'Yeah, can you believe it,' said Stella. 'I've just tried cx129 but no luck.'

'That was last night's number. You're new, aren't you?'

'Yeah I am. I'm Stella.'

'Jill,' she said. 'Nice to meet you.'

'You too. Thanks for your help.'

'Who hired you?'

Shit, she'd better get this right. 'Um, James, I spoke to him a few days ago. He was the one who told me to come around the back, rather than going in where the public go. Then he gives me the wrong keypad code.'

'Fuck that. They get really antsy if you use the main entrance during performance hours – they want to keep us as far away from the punters as possible. Helps to maintain the illusion,' said Jill. 'I've got the new code on my phone.'

'Have you worked at the club long?' Stella asked.

'On and off for a couple of years.'

'Good place to work?'

'Yeah, better than most. Here it is.' She scrolled through her texts.

'Did you ever work with someone called Teri? She was a waitress.'

Jill tilted her head to one side. 'Nope, name doesn't ring any bells. Mind you, lots of them don't use their real names. What do you want with her?'

'She was a friend of mine, we've lost touch and I'm not sure where she's working at the moment.'

'Yeah, some of the girls move around a fair bit.'

'Anything or anyone I should be careful of?'

Jill punched the numbers into the keypad; the door to the rabbit hole opened with a rush of warm, thick air. 'I'd steer clear of James – he's a fuckwit.'

'Yeah, I got that impression,' said Stella, letting Jill go ahead of her up the stairs.

'Come on,' said Jill. 'I'll take you to the room out the back where you can leave your stuff. Where's your things?'

'I travel light.'

Stella scanned the hallway. Her hearing ramped up a notch. She had perfected the art of alert nonchalance and a saunter that held every fibre ready for fight or flight. Around each corner she filed a mental floor map into her head. If she needed to get out fast she had to be sure where she was going.

Industrial-style linoleum covered the floor. The walls were shit-brown. There was an underlying antiseptic smell laced with cigarette smoke, patchouli and dope. Stella could hear the performance on stage: it was Kate singing.

They passed a lounge area. It was empty.

'This is where you can leave whatever you want,' Jill said. 'I'm going to get a coffee before my shift starts, would you like one?'

'Thanks, that'd be great.'

As soon as Jill left, Stella made her way towards the music. Through a gap in the curtain she could see the stage, the smoky sounds of 'Diamonds are a Girl's Best Friend' seeped to the back. The tempo was ultra slow, the song almost unrecognisable, but the voice wasn't. Stella waited. It was cramped and airless. As Kate finished, the applause gave Stella a long enough break to move.

'Can I help you?' a deep voice asked from behind her.

She was being watched through a face of thick makeup, by someone over two metres tall and built like a prop forward. Stella admired the glitter on the face and the swirl of the gown. Christ, she thought, you've got to have a serious pair of balls to do that.

'No, thanks. I'm new. I just wanted to watch a bit of the show, then I'll be outta here.'

'There's not much room, but we make do.'

'Yeah, it's pretty cramped,' said Stella. 'I'm actually a friend of Teri's, do you know her?'

'Sorry, love, doesn't sound familiar. She part of the show?'

'No, she's one of the waitresses.'

'Oops, we're just about to go on, 'scuse me.'

Kate came backstage. She wore a large red-feather boa around her neck, fishnet tights and a skirt that looked as if she'd spray-painted it on. Catching sight of Stella she looked at her, then over at the drag queen. Two more massive drag queens shimmied past them, 'Sorry, girls, we're late on,' said one of them with a flourish of a satin-gloved hand. They flicked open the curtains, took the stage and acknowledged the applause. Some risqué comments were made and the beat of 'Boogie Woogie Bugle Boy' hit the air. The crowd was cheering, clapping; the queens were in their element. Stella wasn't.

'Can we talk somewhere else?' she said. 'I can't hear myself think.'

Kate grabbed her arm and pulled her to one side, behind a rack of costumes. 'What the fuck are you doing here?' she whispered, her voice fierce. 'How did you get back here?'

'You gave me the wrong code.'

'Of course I did,' said Kate.

'Kate, tell me, are you involved in some kind of shit?'

'You're kidding, right? I was trying to keep you safe. I wanted to make sure you didn't bloody get back here. Who let you in?'

'Jill, one of the working girls. I promise I didn't use your name.'

'If James finds you ... you have to leave. Now.' Still holding her arm, Kate tried to pull her towards the door.

'Why are you so frightened of him? What are you hiding?'

'I'm not hiding anything.' Kate said. 'It's just I've heard he can be ... difficult. He likes things to be separate. Us lot back here, the punters through there.'

'What the hell does that mean?'

'You have to go,' said Kate, tugging on her arm again.

'I can't. I'm here,' said Stella. 'I need to know what Teri found out.'

'Well, I don't,' said Kate. 'I keep myself to myself. I do my job. You're going to get me into a shitload of trouble. Please, Stell, go.'

'Teri knew something about this place. She had evidence on her phone, that's what got her killed.'

'She worked here for a while, waiting tables, that's all.'

'No, it's more than that. I've just come from a meeting with Ravosky.'

'So?'

'He knows something.'

Kate looked at her. 'You're scaring me,' she said.

'I don't think you're in danger,' said Stella.

'Not that. You're scaring me because you sound like you're losing the plot. Stell, you need help. You're going all weird, creeping around, making people suspicious of you. It's just performers and hookers back here. That's all,' said Kate. 'What could it possibly be? Drugs? Guns? I mean seriously, what do you think is going on? Look, I love you to bits, you know that. But if you don't leave, this won't end well.'

Kate was right, this wasn't the way to go, this wasn't the way to find out what Teri knew.

'I'm back on stage soon. I have to use the loo and you have to leave.'

'I'm sorry, Kate. You're right.'

Kate gave Stella a quick hug then a push towards the door. 'Off you go.'

Stella left to find the alley door again. Around a corner and she saw him. She ducked back out of sight. *Shit! I'm screwed.*

His boots were quiet on the lino.

He stopped. She heard his voice.

'Where's Jill? There's a client requesting her.'

'Dunno,' came the reply. 'She was showing some new chick the lounge last time I saw her.'

'There's no one new starting tonight. What the fuck's she playing at?'

Stella tried a door.

It was locked. She tried another.

Sweet baby Jesus, let this one open, she thought. It did. Quietly closing the door behind her, she paused – it took a couple of seconds for her eyes to adjust to the low light. A faint red glow lit the room.

She put her ear to the door.

She couldn't hear him.

There was no telling if he was still out there. I'm stuck, she thought. There's got to be another way out. The room smelt of stale whisky and cigarettes. The wall to her left was draped in a floor-length velvet curtain. She sidled past a couple of couches and pulled the curtain aside. There was a door. She tried the handle, locked.

Another wall was covered by a pleated shorter curtain. There was no way that was an outside window. A pull cord hung down one side. She pulled it. The curtains opened onto a window that revealed another room. In the centre was a four-poster bed. There were no covers, only a red satin sheet tucked neatly into each corner. Well-stuffed pillows were stacked at the head end. The walls were covered in a rich, flocked wallpaper; ceiling lights were recessed and dimmed. Thick opulent rugs tracing intricate oriental designs carpeted the floor. Stella realised the room she was standing in was elevated, giving a better view through the window. She pulled the curtain closed.

Fuck, she heard voices. One of them sounded like James.

'Right this way, gentlemen. I'll leave you to your pleasures. Don't hesitate to let me know if there's anything I can help you with.'

They were outside the door. Hoping like hell they were drunk and had their minds on other things, Stella slipped behind the curtain that went to the floor. The handle of the locked door dug into her back. The door out into the corridor opened. She listened as the men came into the room and settled themselves on the couches.

'Is the sound on?' said one.

'I'll check,' said another. 'Yep, we're all good. I'll pull the cord.'

There was a swish as the other curtain was pulled across. She peered out from her hiding place. Three men, all with their backs to her, were sitting on the couch. A full bottle of whisky was on the low table next to them. One lit a cigar.

'You're meant to have that afterwards,' said his companion.

'Before, during, after, who gives a crap. When's this going to start? I paid fucking good money for this. I want my entertainment.'

The smoker leaned forward, shrugging off his jacket and throwing it over the back of the couch. She held her breath. The room she could see through the window gave the appearance of having no entrance or exit.

A seamless box.

The door in the wallpaper opened. A woman of an indeterminate age walked in. She was dressed in a black G-string and short lingerie top. Lying down on the bed, she raised her arms above her head. Twisting her hips, she sprawled, her legs apart. The men watched, grunting in appreciation.

'Get your tits out properly, bitch,' said the smoker.

The wallpaper door opened again and the room saw the arrival of a man wearing nothing but a towel around his waist. He was older, reasonably well built, with a tan and only the hint of a middle-age spread.

For the next while Stella stayed behind the curtain. All she could think of was Amsterdam. A bank holiday weekend trip she had taken a couple of years back. Her married boyfriend wanted to take her – his mistress – for a mini-break.

'I've told the wife it's a business trip,' he said.

'And she believed you?'

'Who cares. We've got three nights and three days to get stoned, drunk and whatever else we fancy.'

And they had. Like two people swimming through a calm sea, they'd taken in all the sights the city had to offer. They'd hired bikes and cruised the cycle ways. The trees alongside the canals glowed autumnal colours in the thinning light. The evenings were for food, wine and sex. Not always in that order. They'd kept busy. They'd had fun. He was generous with himself and his money.

On their last night he'd looked at her. 'Let's go and see them,' he said.

'No, thanks, that's not for me.' Stella said.

'Go on. It's a bit of a turn-on, don't you think? All those women behind glass, streets of them. It's hilarious, some of them even sit there and read.'

'I've seen it before. It's not that great.'

'And I've seen it too, but not with you.' He looked at her. 'Come on, honey, do it for me.' He crawled over the bed on his hands and knees towards her. 'What about a peep-show, they have those as well.'

'I'll tell you what,' said Stella, 'why don't I sit here and read while you watch.'

'That's not the same, babe,' he said stroking her thigh. 'You're not for sale.'

She smiled sweetly at him. 'You've just paid for this trip. Sex is involved, isn't that the same thing?'

'Don't go all fucking serious on me, Stella. I can go home for that shit.'

Stella didn't bother watching the room with the bed. The audio was enough. At times she wished she could plug her ears with something other than her hands. Eventually the moaning, grunting and squealing stopped.

'When's the main event?' one of the men asked.

'Patience, all in good time,' said cigar man.

The first performers exited the room. She heard the clinking of the bottle as the men poured more whisky into their glasses. The room was full of smoke now – it was all she could do to stop from coughing.

At one point she contemplated making a run for it. She had the element of surprise. They were pissed, sitting down and had no idea she was there. The trouble was she wasn't exactly sure who was out in the main corridor. She didn't fancy running into that dick, James – she'd seen and felt what he was capable of.

Careful to shield the light with her hand, she checked the time on her phone. Hell, she thought, the crack across the glass perfectly covered where the time would be. By her reckoning the performance behind the window had lasted a good twenty minutes, but the light from her phone gave her an idea. Carefully, she looked from behind the curtain over to the bedroom. The door opened and closed – this time a towel-draped man was the first to enter.

He was blond. The towel stretched underneath his paunch. He was not tanned. On his left wrist he wore a large silver chain. A tattoo crawled up his right arm. He puffed up the pillows and positioned himself in the centre of the bed. The men on the couches shuffled their feet, 'Yeah, now we're fucking cooking with gas.'

Stella tried to figure out the logistics of making a run for it. She wasn't sure how long she could stand being in the same room with these men as they watched other men having sex with paid partners. Voyeurism is one thing, but this took it to a whole new level. They could potentially be here all night.

Was this what Teri found out about? So what? This wasn't worth being killed over. Maybe she had audio on her phone that she was threatening the men with. But she wouldn't do that; it still didn't equate to the desperation of murder. The flocked wallpaper door opened again.

Stella watched.

Her heart raced. One of the men started to slow clap. 'Yeah,' he said.

Her teeth were clenched tightly together.

The man on the bed slowly peeled off his towel, his penis erect. He stroked himself and looked towards the window. He winked, and patted the red satin sheet beside him.

She felt an icy cold jolt.

This was not happening, not here.

A girl, with jet black hair and a slightly crooked fringe, sat next to the man on the bed. Stella recognised her. It was Sia, who'd hidden behind the skirt of the older child at the spa.

Sia lifted her small legs onto the bed to lie next to the man. Even at this distance, Stella could see she was shaking, trying not to cry. The light from the lamp in the room glinted. It was then she spied the small silver bells hanging from a slim chain around her left ankle.

This had to stop. She stepped out from behind the curtain.

'What the fuck?' said one of them.

The light on her phone was at full glare shining into the men's faces. They shielded their eyes. Stella backed away to the door. They were all standing now. One knocked against the table then stumbled against the window. The bottle of whisky hit the floor with a crash, the smell filling the room. The man on the bed jumped up and grabbed for his towel. He shoved the girl out of the way and barrelled through the door.

'I've seen you,' she said. 'I've seen all your faces. I have audio on my phone and video.'

She turned and grabbed the door handle. Out in the corridor the light was too bright. She heard a scream. No doubt semi-naked towel man had surprised someone. There wasn't time to think. She ran along the short stretch of corridor, wrenched open the door and grabbed her.

She was tiny. Stella half-carried her under her arm.

Behind her were voices, yelling.

She flicked off any switch she could see. The lights in the corridor went out. More voices, more yelling. A scream. Running now, she pushed someone out of the way. They fell against the wall.

'What the hell's going on?'

She'd made it to the stairs. They were in darkness. Clutching Sia under her arm, Stella ran down as fast as she could, pushing open the heavy door to the outside. In the alleyway, she put Sia down.

'Don't move,' she said.

As fast as she could, Stella pushed a large heavy wheelie bin against the door. Then another and another.

35

Picking up Sia, Stella walked as quickly as she could down the alley and away from the back of the building. There wasn't any time. James would be after her. Darting up another smaller alley, she hid behind a couple of green recycling bins. Leaning over she retched.

'Jesus, oh fuck.' She wiped her sleeve across her mouth.

She held Sia close and checked her phone. It had been on silent, but she could see, on the part of the screen that was still working, that she'd missed a voice message. Grabbing Sia by the hand she started moving again. Quickly, almost running, Stella held the phone to her ear and listened to the message.

'It's Gus. Christophe wants to meet you. He said something about liking your name – he's got a thing about stars. Anyway, he's at my workroom but not for much longer. I thought you'd like to know sooner rather than later. I don't know what you're involved with, Stella, but I don't want Christophe hurt.'

The message was received at 9.32 PM. What's the time? thought Stella. The screen on her phone said 9.50-something, but with the spiderweb crack, it could be 9.59. Picking up Sia, holding her on her hip, Stella jogged further along the alley towards Ghuznee Street. It was the long way around, but safer. Soon she was at the corner of Courtenay and Tory. As far from the club as possible. The streets were full of people. She tried to move unobtrusively, as if it was perfectly normal to have a lightly dressed child out at this time on a Saturday night.

Finding the building with the brass plates and polished marble steps, she charged up the stairs and ran awkwardly along the corridor to the workshop.

'Stella.' Gus looked up. 'And who is this wee mite? It's awfully late for a child to be out.'

He picked up a cloth off the counter and wiped his hands. The workshop was warm; something lilting and operatic played in the background.

'Is he here? Where is he?' Stella spoke quickly, trying not to sound agitated.

'What's going on, Stella. What's he done?'

'Christophe hasn't done anything wrong, Gus. He's inadvertently got hold of a phone that may be an important piece of evidence. Is he here?'

'You've just missed him,' he said. 'He took the lift. His knee was bothering him.'

She looked at the girl in her arms. Her head buried in Stella's hair, thin arms clung tight around her neck. Stella tried to prise her arms lose, but Sia held on. 'Will you stay here with Gus?'

She shook her head. 'No, stay with you.'

'Okay, Sia, you come with me. I'll fill you in later, Gus.'

The lift would take forever, so holding on to the banister, Stella ran down two flights as fast as she could without breaking her ankle. Out on the street people drifted to and from their entertainment, like slow-moving fish in deep water. There was no sign of Christophe in the crowds. Shit, shit, shit. She'd lost him again. The marble doorway felt cool against her back. A car burped along the street, the air smelt of fumes and fast food. It wasn't a good idea to be out here; the fiasco at the club meant she was a target as well. She stood on the steps to scan the crowd. Her arm was tired from holding Sia's weight, so Stella moved her over to the other hip.

On the other side of the road waiting to cross at the lights, a group of people jostled for their starting position. Fuck, he was there – there was no mistake. He was scanning the street too. A barracuda in a leather jacket and shaved head. Stella melted back into the doorway, bolted up the stairs. In the workroom, Gus was making tea. Stella could smell toast. There was a ping from the microwave.

He put another slice into the toaster. 'I'm guessing your wee friend might be hungry – I've warmed some milk.'

With Sia still clinging to her, Stella flopped down on the couch. It felt strange to have this tiny body so close. Small thin arms, the feel of her hair against her cheek. The smell of her. They were tied together now. Stella was utterly responsible for a life that wasn't her own. Gus handed the girl a cup of milk.

'Thank you,' she said in a tiny voice.

He found a blanket, wrapped it around them both and went back to buttering the toast.

'Why are you here so late?' asked Stella.

'I needed to finish this,' he said, pointing to the violin he'd been working on. 'Emergency repair work, see here, there's a tiny crack in the bridge and the tension of the strings has …' He looked up. 'But I'm guessing you're not here for another lesson on what a luthier does.'

'We can't stay here, Gus. You'll become a target as well.'

'He's been here before.'

'Christophe?'

'No, James. A couple of days ago. He must have followed Christophe. Wanted to know where to find him,' he said as he poured the tea. 'There isn't a lot in this world that a good cup of tea can't cure, or at least hold off the inevitable, even for a short amount of time.'

Why on earth would James be after Christophe, Stella wondered. Yes, Christophe may have Teri's phone, but how would James know that, unless … unless … he was the one who helped Teri over the balcony. Jesus, no wonder James was all over her.

Mad-Dog stepped into the stream of people walking along Courtenay Place. She hadn't turned up. Gus had phoned and left her a message. Maybe she hadn't got it. Maybe she wasn't interested anymore. Either way, she didn't show. Gus was nice, he kept the room warm for them, made him a mug of tea. He liked Gus, but what to do now? He needed to get back to his camp up the hill.

He felt tired, more tired than usual.

Someone bumped into him. 'Sorry, mate, you okay?' The voice was too loud.

'Yes, yes, I'm fine,' said Christophe without looking up. His shoe flapped. He hadn't got around to repairing it yet. He walked along, pulling his hat out of one pocket; from the other he reached in and found his gloves. That was better. It didn't do to get cold. A small crowd waited at the pedestrian crossing that led over to the Embassy Theatre. Christophe waited at the back, moving when they did. A shoal of humans swimming over the dark street. On the other side, he sighed and started up Majoribanks Street. The steep bit at the end was always the hardest part.

Just before the street tilted up the hill, he stopped. Someone had a radio on, or a CD playing. Bach Cello Suite No. 1. He stood there listening as the sound wound itself around him, music was such a comfort, a familiarity that gave him hope. He continued walking. Catching his breath again at the top – one of the streetlights wasn't working. Not to worry, the dark suited him. The way was familiar. Clouds hung low in the night sky. Occasionally they drifted apart to reveal a few stars.

It's funny, he thought, how we all look at the same moon.

Mad-Dog waited at the gate of the communal garden. Coming down the path towards him was Thomson, his tail straight in the air in greeting. 'Ah, you're a lovely wee thing,' said Mad-Dog, bending down to stroke the soft fur. Thomson's warmth transferred to Mad-Dog's hand, he could feel the rattle of his purring. It's all we want really, he thought, rubbing the cat's head and chin, warmth, kindness, someone to believe we're worthwhile.

With Thomson sauntering along beside him Mad-Dog made his way through the garden area. Part way across he heard something. A flash caught him on the side of his head. He staggered off the path, falling onto the grass. His hat askew, he reached up to straighten it away from his eyes. It was then he saw the man in the leather jacket.

'What are you doing? What do you want from me?'

Mad-Dog held up his hands in supplication. He struggled to right himself onto his knees. Before he could, a boot landed around his middle, another kick onto his head. He fell back again, pain shot across his body, he whimpered.

Putting his hands up to shield his head and face, one of his gloves came off, a boot caught his fingers. Mad-Dog heard a crack. He tasted blood.

'Please, please, stop,' the sounds gurgled in his throat. Mad-Dog felt the stranger's hands in the pockets of his jacket, his trousers. Pulling, tearing the fabric.

'What do you want?' He tried again. 'I don't have money.' His words slurred through the blood in his mouth.

A boot caught his head again, then his arms. He was on his back now, pushed onto the grass. A face peered at him. He recognised the shaved head, the glint of silver rings in his ear.

'Money? You old fucker – I want the phone. Where's the *phone*?' Hands over him, grabbing into the pockets inside his jacket. Mad-Dog heard the lining rip. Blood was dripping into his eyes. There was a heaving, dull ringing in both ears. 'I don't have it,' he groaned with the pain, a soft keening sound. 'I don't have it. I took it to the …'

More boot into his spine. The backs of his legs – just above his knees. Over and over. Mad-Dog curled, fetal. A searing, stinging pain climbed up his back, every nerve end on fire.

'You fuck.' The boot landed. 'You great big fuck.'

Mad-Dog's arms were grabbed, pulled away from protecting his head. He was being dragged, off the grass and onto the concrete path. His feet scrabbled for a foothold on the damp grass.

He felt himself being pulled up.

He's getting me to stand up, he thought, he wants to take me somewhere. He's going to stop; please make it stop.

He was pulled up only a few inches and slammed down again. Up, then down, his head against a hard surface.

He blacked out.

36

THEY LEFT GUS'S via the back service lift. Another alley, dark and filthy, greeted them, a rotten smell coming from the bins at one end. Sounds of Saturday night filtered from the main streets. Slurred voices, high heels clipping the pavement, the sounds of a party. The alley was a wind tunnel. Discarded fast-food wrappers bounced along like urban tumbleweed.

'My car is over here. Are you sure you know what you're doing, Stella?'

'No. But I'll work it out. Just promise me you'll let me know if you hear anything from Christophe. The longer he has that phone, the more danger he's in.'

'I have your number,' he said. 'I'll call.'

She knocked and waited. Sia, like a limpet, still clung to her neck. Stella looked over her shoulder just in case they'd been followed. Skylark opened the door.

'Is he here?' Stella asked pushing straight past her.

'Yeah.'

'You're the niece, right?'

'And you're the one who broke his heart,' said Skylark, closing the door.

Stella stared at her. '*Excuse* me? Did he say that?'

'He didn't have to. I can tell. And who is this?'

'This is Sia,' said Stella, 'and I admire your powers of deduction.'

'I want to be a writer.'

'That explains it.'

'He's in the lounge.'

Stella climbed up the stairs. Skylark followed.

'Mitchell,' sing-songed the young woman behind her. 'You have a visitor. Or should that be: *Uncle Mitchell, you have visitors.*'

She flicked her long hair and skipped up the last couple of stairs.

He stared at her. 'Oh, no. Stella, what have you done?'

'We need to talk.'

'That's pretty bloody obvious.'

Skylark raised her eyebrows and glanced first at Mitchell then over to Stella and Sia. 'Well, this is awkward and my cue to leave.' She shrugged on a jacket and grabbed her bag. 'Yes, I've got my key and no, I'll be staying at my flat tonight. Have fun, you two.'

They went into the lounge. 'Okay,' said Lassiter. 'Start talking.'

Stella opened her mouth just as Sia began to pee. She felt it, warm against her skin, trickling down her hip and soaking into her jeans. Sia's eyes were wide with fear, a whimpering sound in her throat.

'It's okay, sweetheart. I guess you've been holding that in for a good long time.' She looked over at Lassie. 'I'll tell you everything, but can we get this sorted first?' Stella tucked a strand of hair behind Sia's ear. 'Let's take you off for a bath and get us both cleaned up.'

Sia sniffed and nodded. 'Yes.'

Lassie provided a dressing gown for Stella and a small T-shirt for Sia. 'It's one of Skyla's,' he said. 'She left it here. Give me your clothes. I'll chuck them in the machine.'

In the bathroom, Stella helped Sia as if she were delicate and precious. Each movement was slow and gentle. She helped her out of her meagre clothes and into the large tub. As she sponged the girl's back she could smell Lassie's cooking and realised just how hungry she was.

*

Lassie had made pasta with a mushroom sauce. Sia managed a few mouthfuls, chewing slowly. She said nothing other than, 'Please, drink water.' They didn't talk much, just ate, then Stella carried Sia down the hallway, staying with her on the bed in the spare room until she fell asleep. She watched her breathing, the way her tiny hands curled around each other, dark eyelashes rested on downy cheeks. In the bathroom Stella had removed the anklet.

Lassie was in the lounge. 'Is she asleep?'

'Finally.'

'Did she tell you anything about herself, where she's from?'

'No, I didn't really try either, she's pretty shell-shocked. I'll ask some questions in the morning. There's plenty of time for that.' She pulled out a chair and sat at the table. 'So, that's Skylark?'

'You've bought a kid to my flat and you're leading with that?'

Stella was quiet.

'Okay, yeah, she worries about me,' he said. 'It's cute really. There are times when I get the distinct impression that she is directly channelling my sister.'

'Is she the one that helped with your decorating?'

'She's quite good at spending my money,' said Lassie. 'She's young and very enthusiastic. Not much more to add to that. Seriously, why are we talking about decorating?' he asked. 'I get the feeling I'm going to need a drink as well.'

'Yep. Something strong,' she said.

It didn't take long. Stella laid the story out like a pack of fortune-teller's cards. Each one peeled off the deck, before being placed carefully, image side up, on the table.

Lassie made no comment, his face was unresponsive. But with each new piece of information, she waited while he took it in. Stella got to the part about the voyeur room, detailed her hiding – the men arriving.

'Adults watching adults have sex isn't a crime,' he said.

Stella looked down at her glass. She drained the last drop before placing it back on the table. 'I haven't finished,' she said. 'That's what I thought as well. It's creepy and just a little sad that people find entertainment in it, but you're right, it isn't illegal.' She sat back and crossed her legs. 'I waited, trying to figure out how to get out of there without getting caught by that thug James. Another man came in and lay on the bed ... shit—'

'What, what went on?'

She looked around the room.

It was warm, the light was soft.

Stella picked at a loose piece of skin around her thumbnail, pulled the collar of the dressing gown closer around her neck. The clock ticked over to 12.43 AM. There had been things she had witnessed: the wife of her lover hanging from a rope; the mangled bodies of accident victims; people in desperate situations. The body of the girl under the wharf. But this, this was something else. Like a strange rainfall, pennies had been dropping one by one, right the way back to the trip she and Teri had taken to Thailand. She'd seen it, Teri had, she knew that now. She'd witnessed the depravity of human nature. The violation and destruction of young lives.

Stella peeled the last card off the deck and placed it face up, not able to look at him.

'Another man came in,' she repeated. 'Then Sia.'

For a few moments they were both quiet.

'So, if you think that for one – single – moment I was going to leave her there, you must be joking. I couldn't. I

267

just *couldn't*,' she said. 'The thought of what was going to happen …'

'This is what Teri had on her phone?'

'Yeah, I imagine she got some kind of evidence and was found out.'

'And Ravosky?'

'I don't know. I'm guessing he's somehow behind the business. He must have discovered that Teri had evidence against him and had her killed. If he was ever found out for being involved with child prostitution and trafficking, he'd do serious jail time.'

'I know.'

'It's bad enough knowing that groups of men are going to these countries to violate the kids—'

'That's why they brought in harsher penalties, to stop the groups going.'

'But now it's here, in this city.'

'It'll be other places as well,' said Lassie. 'Wellington won't be unique. Mountains and Mohammed, I guess, where there's a market …'

'It's sick. The girl in the water had an ankle bracelet too,' said Stella. 'She was probably a runaway from the brothel.'

The whisky bottle was almost empty. He leaned forward, pouring the last of it into her glass. 'I suspect your need is greater than mine,' he said. 'I'm sorry for not believing you.'

'I don't blame you. I was sounding a bit crazed. That's why I was so desperate to get Teri's phone. Whatever it was, she presumably filmed or recorded it.' She sipped her drink. 'How much would it cost for those men to watch, to do what they were doing?'

'I've no idea, but it's bound to be quite a lucrative business they've got going on, as well as obviously highly illegal.'

'You have to go,' said Stella.

'What?'

'The club, you have to go. I can't, they won't let me in the door, especially not now. I'm not even safe on the street.'

He leaned back into the couch and contemplated her through half-closed eyes. 'And what, exactly, do you expect me to do? All of this, Stell, should be handled by the police.'

'Handle what, exactly? McCarthy would laugh me out of the room. We've no evidence without that phone.' She drained her glass. 'If the police turn up at the club that bastard will say exactly what he told me, that the kids are the children of the workers, or they'll whisk them out the back door and up the coast.' Like lights on full beam, Stella's eyes opened wide. 'That's what they do, *don't you see?* They bring them into the country – fuck knows how they do that – they must keep them at the spa. That woman I spoke to looks after them before they get taken to that club. Lassie, you have to go,' she said. 'We can't go to the police, not yet. You have to get into the club.'

'Then what?'

'Oh, for god's sake,' she stood up and started pacing the room. 'Why do you have to make things so difficult? As much as I hate to admit it – you've got a better chance of finding stuff out. You're male, you've got money. Sit there, drink whisky, ask questions. Come on, it's not rocket science.' Her eyes glinted with fury. 'The more you find out, the better placed you'll be to get in to one of those rooms. Teri was killed for this.'

'From what you've told me, they will have shut things down. If not for good, then at least for tonight. These aren't amateurs, Stell. These guys clearly know what they're doing. They have a slick operation bringing these kids in – it's potentially worth hundreds of thousands of dollars.'

'And it's going on right under everyone's noses.'

'Forget the club. That's a dead end. We need to focus on the phone. If you reckon Christophe has it, he's the person we need to find. It's late, it's dark and it isn't going to happen tonight.'

Stella stopped pacing. 'Okay, fine, point taken.'

'And besides, we have another problem.'

'What's that?'

He tilted his head towards the door. 'The girl.'

'What do you mean?'

'She can't stay here.'

'Why not?'

'You've just kidnapped a child, Stella. I'm a lawyer. I can't be involved in aiding and abetting a kidnapping.'

'I didn't kidnap her, I saved her.'

'That's what you think, but as far as the law is concerned you've kidnapped her.'

'You're already involved,' she said. 'Whether you like it or not.'

'You can both stay tonight, but tomorrow she's got to go somewhere else.'

Stella flopped onto the couch next to him, then leaned forward her head in her hands. 'I can't take her to Gus's, or Mum and Dad's. That fucker James knows about both places.'

'What about Charlotte?'

'I can't leave the child with Charlotte, that's not a good idea.'

'Okay, where else?'

'Oh, god. I don't know. I'll think of something in the morning.'

They were both quiet. 'We should get some sleep,' he said.

'I can't, I'm too wired. I think I'll sit up for a bit.'

Muted traffic sounds came from the street below: a car door was shut a little too firmly, then silence again. She reached out and took his hand. It was warm. She loved his hands, the shape of them, the feel of them. She traced a finger over his palm.

'What does it tell you?' he asked.

'I've no idea.'

'Do you think we'll ever get our shit together?' He reached out to brush a strand of hair from her face.

'You mean falling into each other's arms and sailing off into the sunset?'

'Yeah, something like that.'

'Nah, we don't want to be like one of those TV shows where they spend the first two seasons glaring at each other with unbridled sexual passion. Once they get together, the series goes downhill and gets axed.'

'Righto,' he said. 'I guess we'll just try and get some sleep.'

She didn't let go of his hand. 'Lassie …'

This time he didn't push her away. His hands were at the tie of her dressing gown. Her hands tugged his shirt up over his head, reached down for the zip and belt of his jeans. He lifted his hips and she tugged them down. She sat astride him, as urgent as he was, her mouth on his, tongues and teeth.

She wanted him. She needed to feel something other than death.

When they finished, her heart was racing.

'I needed that,' she said.

'I think we both did.'

They stayed like that for a while. Her head on his shoulder, his arms around her. He stroked her back. 'Careful you don't get cold,' he said.

'I need to go back to Sia. I don't want her to wake up by herself.'

'So you're going to leave me to wake up by myself,' he said, smiling at her.

'You're a big boy, you'll cope.'

'I'll take that as a compliment.'

It was late when she woke. The clock on the bedside table glowed 10.23 AM. This is strange, she thought. She lay on one side, Sia curled up against her, under Stella's arm. She felt her steady breathing. Such a tiny body. What was her life? Where was she actually from? Indonesia, Bali, Thailand? Did her parents know, had they agreed to some arrangement but were misled?

The musical tone of Stella's phone ringing in the other room bought her back. She heard Lassie's voice as he answered it. Her mind raced through the events of last night, then settled on the sex. She scrunched her eyes shut.

That wasn't a good idea.

She didn't deserve someone like him. What she preferred was no strings, no love and no commitment. She'd just fuck him up. Maybe not straight away, but she would, in the end.

Stella eased her arm off Sia and started to sit up just as Lassiter, with two mugs of coffee and a plate of toast, came into the room. She rested her head against the headboard; Sia curled up as small as she could by her side.

'I answered your phone,' he said. 'It was Gus.'

'What did he want?' She sipped the hot coffee. 'Has he heard from Christophe?'

'No, he'd been phoned by the police, early this morning.'

'Why did the police call Gus?'

He stared into his coffee. 'Christophe has been found—'

'But that's great, we need to go talk to him.'

'—beaten to death. Gus made him wear a tag around his neck engraved with *In case of emergency, call this number.* It was his way of keeping tabs on him if anything should happen.'

'Fuck, you're kidding.'

'Yeah.'

They were quiet. 'Who found the body?' she asked.

'A woman from the apartment block, she was taking her dog for an early walk and she saw him lying there, next to the bench. She thought it was odd that he wasn't actually on the bench, so she went and checked. He must have crawled there after he was beaten. His arm was wrapped around a cat,' he said. 'She called the police; they contacted Gus. He's been asked to go in later to formally identify the body.'

'Did you ask about a phone?'

'No,' he said. 'Whoever beat him up would have gone through his pockets, just like you said they did with Digby. So, if he had it on him, it's gone.'

'So that's it then? Without the phone, we have nothing.' She couldn't look at him. 'The brothel will clean up its shit. The children will be hidden and Teri will have been murdered for nothing. So, other than someone taking months to get behind the scenes at the brothel, that's it. Who knows how many children will be raped before that happens?'

'Let's face it, I'm never going to be accepted in that club.'

'Why not?'

'As soon as someone looks into my background, especially if you still think Ravosky is involved, they're going to connect me with you. It's a dead end.'

'So that's it for you? You're going to give up, just like that.'

'It's not about giving up ...'

Stella looked down at Sia, who was beginning to stir. Stella stroked the girl's silky coal-black hair off her forehead; her head felt hot. 'There are children, ' she whispered, 'let me repeat – *children* – who are being systematically abused by men who pay for the privilege. We have the start of something here and you're going to roll over and pretend it isn't happening. There could be a whole string of these brothels up and down the country.'

'That may be and I'm sorry to keep banging on,' said Lassie, 'but, whether you like it or not, you're going to have to involve the police.'

'McCarthy would be in charge and he's got it in for me. He'd probably think I was winding him up,' she said. 'All I have is a crack-pot story, a couple of Asian girls with anklets and fuck-all else. I wouldn't believe me, there's no way he will.'

'So, it's over?'

She finished the last of her coffee and put the mug on the table beside the bed. Her voice was firm and steady. 'No, it's not over. I refuse to believe Teri died for nothing. If she was killed over this, I will get the bastard that did it.'

Sia was wide awake now and sitting up, nestled into Stella's side. She looked intently at both of them.

'We have this problem as well,' he said nodding towards Sia. 'She can't stay here.'

'I know where I can take her. Audrey. She'll keep an eye on her for a couple of hours, I know she will.'

'Are you sure?'

'Yep, she's been good to Mum and Charlotte. She let me rattle on about Teri and goodness knows what else. She's got the time and the space.'

'Okay, sounds like it could work.'

'Hand me my phone, I'll give her a call,' she said. 'You can drop us both there this morning.'

'What about Christophe's camp? Maybe his phone is there.'

'I don't know that we've got any chance of finding that now,' Stella sighed. 'I think the main thing is to make sure Sia is safe, then try to think of a long-term plan. There's going to be a hole in these guys' defences, we just have to find it.'

'One other thing,' said Lassie, resting his hand on her arm. 'I don't want last night to be the end of things.'

Stella finished her coffee and handed him the mug. 'First things first, eh?'

37

LASSIE WENT DOWN and waited in the car. Eventually Stella and Sia arrived; Stella pulled open the back door.

'What took you so long?'

They got in the car and sat together on the back seat.

'She was too frightened to leave the flat. I had to assure her I wouldn't leave her. We'll just have to see how it goes with Audrey.' Stella buckled Sia in.

It was after midday and Wellington was well and truly awake. The Sunday traffic was heavy in all directions. Stella had phoned Audrey, who'd been quick to say she was happy to help. 'You must bring the wee girl here,' she said.

The day was perfectly clear and still. Sia held her thin arm over her eyes to ward off the bright light. As they drove Stella's phone buzzed in her pocket.

'Gus, hi, how are you doing?'

'Ah, Stella. I'm drinking coffee,' he said. 'I have pastries.'

'Sounds lovely.' She could hear the rattle of china cups. They stopped at the lights. The traffic was particularly heavy at Tory Street. Streams of people carried bags loaded with their weekly shop of fruit and vegetables from the Sunday markets.

'Today is a sad day,' said Gus.

'Yes, it is.'

'How's the girl this morning?'

'All right, I guess. It's hard to tell.'

The car took off again, towards the waterfront.

'Stella, I have news. Earlier this morning, after I got the phone call from the police, I stopped by my workshop. I wanted to take Christophe's violin to the police. It is his property; they would know what to do with it.'

'Did he have any other family here that you know of?'

'None.' Gus paused. 'I checked all was well with the instrument.'

'Everything okay?'

'Yes. It's French, a very good one,' said Gus.

'Do you know if he had a will?'

They drove past the Michael Fowler Centre and headed under the massive sculptured wooden bridge that ferried people from Civic Square to the lagoon.

'As far as I'm aware there is no will and no next of kin. I will talk to the police about donating it to a worthy violin student, or maybe selling it and setting up a scholarship in his name.'

'I'm sure he would have approved of that,' she said.

'There is something else. I checked the violin. I looked in the front pocket of the case, where the rosin for the bow is kept,' said Gus. 'He left it in the case, Stella. He must have slipped it in there and I never noticed.'

'You have the phone?' She practically yelled it. Beside her Sia shrank at the sudden noise. 'It's all right, sweetie,' said Stella. 'It's good news, really good news.'

'Yes,' said Gus. 'I plugged it in before I went to the mortuary, just to see what would happen. The screen is badly damaged, but the battery seemed to be okay. So, when I got back I ...' He paused. 'I mean it's not that I don't trust you, Stella. I guess I was curious to see what my friend had been killed for.'

Lassie was driving up Bowen Street towards Tinakori Road. He stopped at the lights, waiting for the change to green, looked around with a big grin on his face. 'Gus, the violin guy? He has the phone? That's brilliant news, Stell.'

Stella nodded at him and kept talking, 'Hang on a minute, Gus, we're just trying to park.'

The lights changed; a car horn sounded behind them.

Turning into Tinakori Road the traffic was backed up. Cars were parked bumper to bumper on both sides of the road: people arriving to shop, visit the art gallery, mooch around the recycled clothing stores and meet up with friends for a late Sunday lunch. The Botanic Gardens were behind them but that stretch of the street was lined with cars as well.

'I'll turn around and drop you off – that'll be easiest,' said Lassie. 'You can let me know when you want a pickup.'

Stella and Sia got out and closed the door, and Lassie drove off into the stream of traffic. She scooped Sia up onto her hip. 'Hi, Gus, you still there? What did you find?'

'I used my computer to see what was on the phone. The screen was too damaged to see anything. I don't fully understand what's going on but there's nasty stuff here.'

'What's that? The traffic's too loud.'

'I said there's some nasty stuff,' he said again slowly.

'Yes, I'm sorry you had to see that. Is the name Ravosky mentioned at all?'

'No. The one that speaks a lot, James – I recognised his voice from when he paid me a visit.'

'No surprises there,' said Stella as she pushed open the door to Audrey's shop.

It closed with a loud click behind her.

The shop looked empty of customers. It was quiet and cool. The traffic noise diminished to a soft rumble. Sia felt heavy in her arms. Stella bent down and put her on the floor. The girl clung to her leg.

'Some other people are mentioned as well,' said Gus. 'There is quite a lot of video, but there is audio as well, and one name that James refers to a lot.' Audrey gently slalomed through the piles of items for sale and stood in front of her.

'He calls her boss.'

'Her?'

38

'James,' called Audrey over her shoulder. 'I'm going to need your help in here.'

Stella quickly picked up Sia and swung her onto her hip. James appeared from the back room – same dark shirt and boots, same smirk.

'What the fuck is he doing here?' she said.

'James works for me,' said Audrey, a smile playing on her face.

Stella held her phone to her ear. 'Gus,' she said quietly, 'I have to go now.' She ended the call and slipped her phone in the back pocket of her jeans.

'I don't understand,' said Stella. The girl buried her head in Stella's hair.

'Why ever not?' said Audrey. 'Your naïvety and ignorance was charming. For a short time even slightly amusing. But we now have a problem on our hands and I dislike problems intensely.'

Stella felt her heart beating. How well do you really know someone? 'You own the club?' she asked.

'Is that a statement or a question?' Audrey tilted her head to one side, stepped past Stella, locked the door and changed the sign around to read *closed*. Gently she pulled down the blind over the door. 'There, now,' she said. 'I think we'll close a little earlier today, I wouldn't want anyone interrupting us.'

'Audrey, really. I think it's best if we leave now,' said Stella.

'Well, that's clearly not going to happen.'

If Stella hadn't had the girl, she could have easily overpowered Audrey and got out the door. Not this time.

James stepped forward.

'Take the child, James. Stella and I need to talk.'

'With pleasure,' he said.

Sia started to scream. A high-pitched wailing sound and tightened her grip.

'No,' said Stella.

'Yes,' said Audrey. 'She's my property and I will do as I want. James, take the child.'

'*Property*. She's a child, a human being.'

'You're too emotional. When will you learn that it hinders you?'

James grabbed Sia around the waist, wrenching her from Stella's grip.

'No, no, no,' Sia wailed.

'If you hurt her, I'll—'

'You'll what?' said Audrey. She moved between them. 'Take her to the back room, James. Do whatever you have to and keep her quiet. I don't want the neighbours disturbed.'

Stella stood there, impotent. She could run, but that would mean leaving Sia. She had to stay.

'I don't think you quite realise what kind of position you're in, Stella,' said Audrey, brushing a fleck of cotton off her sleeve. 'And now I'll have your phone.'

'You're making a huge mistake.'

'Your phone, please.'

Stella fished it out of her back pocket and handed it over, slapping it down on Audrey's outstretched hand.

Shit, shit and more fucking shit. How was Audrey caught up in all of this? James was the one to help Teri over the balcony. He knew about the phone, that's why he'd targeted the men on the street. He must have been responsible for the death of Christophe. If he was capable of that, fuck knows what he'd do to her.

James arrived back.

'Take Stella upstairs,' said Audrey. 'I'm going to make us both a nice cup of tea.'

'Don't touch me, dickhead,' said Stella as James walked over to her. In one swift move he reached out and, wrenching her arm behind her back, marched her up the stairs and into the room at the top. The single sashed window let in little light at this time of day. It was cold up there; she shivered. Pulling a chair around he gave her a shove. 'Sit.' As if she were a dog. He left the room, and she heard a key turn in the lock.

Jumping up, she tried the window. It was jammed shut. She double-checked to see he'd locked the door. What the fuck was happening? Her mind was racing. Why would Audrey be involved in this kind of thing. Money? Was that it? What else would it be? No one knew, no one would suspect. It was the perfect cover. Audrey and James in some kind of sick arrangement to bring children into the country. Did Charlotte know any of this? She can't have. Oh god, what happens if she's somehow been roped into it all?

Teri's phone was her bargaining chip, the one chance of getting herself and Sia out of this. She needed to keep calm, think rationally, carefully. She looked around for anything to use as a weapon. Dull footsteps came slowly up the stairs.

Stella sat down, resting her hands on her knees. The sound of teacups rattling. The key turning in the lock.

'I've got some tea for us,' said Audrey. James put a flowery tray down on one of the tables. 'Off you go now,' she said. 'I'll call if I need you.'

He turned and clumped down the stairs. Audrey fussed over the tray. 'I do so hope he didn't break anything. Let me pour you a cup and I'll add a little sugar. You look as if you could use it.'

Only Lassie knew she was here. She'd said she'd call when she needed a ride. Her parents were having lunch with her aunt and uncle. Kate wasn't currently in communication with her. And Ravosky? God knows how he fitted into all of this. Audrey passed her a cup of tea and sat on one of the chairs.

'Okay,' said Stella. 'You go first.'

'Stella, such a pretty name, Latin for *star*,' said Audrey, 'but you already know that. You're so young, Stella. You have so much of your life in front of you. I, on the other hand, don't.' She smoothed her hair, then lightly touched the string of pearls at her neck. 'I have no family. What do you want to know? Where should I begin? Shall we play twenty questions? I did love that when I was a child.'

Stella tried the tea, wincing at the sweetness of it. She was trying very hard to control her breathing; she needed to sound calm.

'How long have you owned the brothel?' Stella asked.

'Oh, I don't *own* it,' Audrey replied. 'A company owns it. Mind you, I own that company. Brothels are legal – you are aware of that?' She sipped her tea.

'Yes, I know prostitution is legal, as long as the workers are consenting adults.'

'Of course they're consenting adults, both workers and clients.'

Stella stared at her.

Audrey stared back. Her unblinking eyes were hard ice-blue pools.

'Quit waltzing, Audrey, and get on with it.'

'Always in such a rush. Let's just enjoy our tea, shall we?'

'I'm not here to drink tea.' Stella put the cup and saucer back on the tray. 'I'll answer your questions, then you'll answer mine.'

'What on earth makes you think I owe you any answers?'

Stella looked at Audrey without blinking. 'My friend is dead,' she said. 'It was not suicide. She was helped over that balcony. Others have been brutally beaten. There is a child in the other room who has no say in her future. If I do nothing she will be raped repeatedly. All of this I know – the least you can offer me is an explanation.'

'She was clever, your friend Teri. But not clever enough,' said Audrey. 'She got herself a job at the club. Saw some things, heard some things. She went places she shouldn't have. Everyone's a witness these days with their mobile phones; Teri thought she'd play detective. James took care of it for me.'

'He didn't get her phone,' said Stella.

Audrey sipped her tea. 'Well, we're close to finding it.'

'But you haven't yet.' Stella smirked.

'No. You came along and decided to play your version of detective. But you got emotional and tried to rescue the girl.'

'Yes.'

'Do you want children, Stella?'

'I'm not sure.'

'They can be such a joy,' said Audrey. 'So I'm told.' She gently placed her teacup on the tray. 'Do you love your parents, Stella?'

'What do my parents have to do with this?'

'Nothing really, but you see much of my life was spent in the company of my parents and the monotony of their ill health,' Audrey began. 'The interminable wait for them to die. Years of it. They insisted I be the one to care for them.'

'I'm not seeing the problem here. What on earth have your parents got to do with the brothel and the girls?'

'Patience, Stella.' Audrey sighed, and Stella caught a trickle of possible humanity.

'I'm sorry, Audrey, but I really don't have time for your stories,' she said, and stood up.

As quick as the tongue of a snake Audrey was on her feet.

Her hand shot out, backhanding Stella across her face.

'Jesus, what the fuck was that for?' said Stella, holding her cheek.

'Sit. Down. Now.'

Stella stumbled slightly and sat back on the chair.

'Let me continue,' said Audrey. 'I've listened to you, now have the decency to listen to me.'

'Decency?'

'Yes. Not every story has a Cinderella ending – I could have left my parents to it,' said Audrey as she sat down. 'But by then I had nothing. No career, no real job, no partner, no money of my own. All I had was this shop my parents owned and a load of guilt. They blamed me,' she said, her face suddenly hard. 'They said I should have been watching him. I carried it for so long, it became truth.' She moved slightly in her chair and crossed her feet at the ankles. Stella caught sight of red Louboutin soles. 'It was years later,' Audrey continued, 'I realised it wasn't my job. They used me as a scapegoat for their own guilt. Guilt is such a powerful tool. Have you ever been in prison?'

'As a visitor, yes,' said Stella, her cheek still stinging.

'I was in a prison without bars. When they died, I inherited everything. Including my freedom.' She stood up and went to the window. Her back was straight, her fingers ran over each smooth pearl in her necklace. 'There are some clouds coming in, it looks like rain,' she said. They were both quiet for a moment. 'It turned out my parents had been pious little squirrels and I became a wealthy woman.'

'We all have choices – you could have chosen to do something good.'

Audrey's voice was quiet, steely. She kept her eyes on the street. 'Yes,' she said. 'I tried that first. I rather rashly decided I wanted a child. I was too old to have one of my own, so I looked at adoption, but I was considered too old.

I went further afield and what I found wasn't a child but an opportunity. With that opportunity, I decided I wanted to experience life.'

'You wanted to experience life by trafficking children into the New Zealand sex trade?'

Audrey laughed. 'No, not at first. But it became simply a matter of economics. Supply and demand. On one of my holidays to Thailand I met a fascinating man.'

'Let me guess,' said Stella. 'Maurice Ravosky?'

'Dear Stella, your ignorance is charming. Ravosky is nothing but a nasty thorn,' she said laughing. 'He started off as a customer, claimed to be interested in military memorabilia. I believed him at first – he seemed harmless enough. But I did some investigating of my own. Turns out he works hush-hush, behind the scenes for some humanitarian group that wants to put a stop to inter-country adoption and people trafficking.'

Oh my god, the NGOs he was listed on – he knew all about it.

'So, you see, he was tailing me,' said Audrey, 'and all the while I was tailing him. Foolish man. This other man I met – I'll call him Charles – was full of interesting business ideas. All I had to do was to make a decision. Just like that. Simple really. It's a fine line that divides us in the end.'

So Ravosky knew why Teri was killed, thought Stella. Was he trying to protect me? Why the hell didn't he say something earlier? Audrey moved away from the window, sat down and again crossed her feet neatly at her ankles. From where she was sitting, Stella couldn't see a way out.

Overpowering Audrey would be a piece of cake, getting past James to find Sia wouldn't. Unless she could do it quietly, take James by surprise. Then what? There was no proof this conversation was happening and there was no way she could corner Audrey. Her records would be clean. For all her twinsets and pearls she clearly ran a slick operation. The only thing Stella had left was Teri's phone.

'To start with, Charles and I organised tours,' said Audrey. 'Men from all over the world, Germany, Australia, UK, Sweden, even the US. They would visit New Zealand, have a wee holiday here and make their way home via Thailand. Always in small exclusive groups. They liked it that way. Eventually it became too dangerous, we had to shut it down.' A private smile swept her face; she raised her chin just a little. 'But,' she said, 'I kept the client list, I made a huge amount of money. Men didn't want their significant other finding out they'd been on child sex trips to Thailand, instead of business meetings in Sydney. They lie, you see. Men lie. That list paid for my apartment in Dubai. It's how it's done,' she said. 'Buy property in Dubai, hold on to it for two or three years, then sell it and bring the money back home. Laundry has never been so easy.'

'So, it's just about the money?' asked Stella.

'Of course not.'

'Then what?'

'It's about what's possible when you *have* money, Stella. Money equals freedom,' she said. 'Safaris in Africa; art galleries in New York City; the opera, ballet, theatre in London. When my parents died I realised I hadn't lived. At the grand old age of fifty-two, as I was then, I understood that life was short and I wanted a piece of it.'

She leaned forward and poured herself another cup of tea. She held the pot towards Stella and raised her eyebrows in a question.

Stella shook her head.

Audrey started speaking again. 'The business I have here is pocket money. An excuse to come back to my little bolthole in Wellington. The brothel just keeps me in shoes. The real money these days is in the couples desperate to

286

adopt. Desperate for their own slice of family life,' she said. 'It's the picture we paint, isn't it? An ideal. Mum, Dad, the two-point-five kiddies. You see it all the time.' She sat back and sipped her tea. 'Those horrid little stick figure families pasted on the back windows of vehicles. The proclamation of one's ability to breed. That's what people want. It didn't take me long to realise the burden of a child wasn't for me. But I could sell it to others.'

'Most people don't see children as a burden,' said Stella.

'Maybe, but the people my business deals with are more than happy to exchange a small life for some cold, hard cash.'

'This business of yours, where is it based?'

'My main office is in Shanghai, where I employ a number of people. We have ties with Europe and South America. People want choice, we try to accommodate that.'

'It doesn't matter how you dress it up, it's still trafficking. The buying and selling of life.'

'Don't you see? Helping each other is a waste of time. It's an illusion of humanity.'

'What about the spa?'

'James told me you'd been there,' said Audrey, 'you and Charlotte.'

'We visited. I saw some girls.'

'We keep them there, tidy them up, give them good food.'

'Then place them in your brothels to be raped.'

Audrey sighed. 'It's easy to be black and white, isn't it?' she said. She shook her head slightly. 'I knew I had to be careful. The authorities were hounding us, clamping down on sex tourism. But there was still a need, money to be made, shoes to be bought.' Audrey laughed and looked down at her feet. 'So, instead of going to the mountain, we started bringing the mountain here. We have a network now: Melbourne, Sydney, Auckland, Wellington, Christchurch. The Rugby

World Cup was very lucrative for us. We're investigating Hamilton at the moment – it's so close to Auckland, very convenient.'

'And convenience is something that's clearly important to you.'

'Who was it that said sarcasm was the lowest form of wit? I forget now. It's what happens when you age, your memory softens and melts like ice cream on a summer's day.'

'Your memory seems just fine.'

Stella shuffled in her chair. With her left hand she brushed a piece of fluff from her jeans. Her right hand closed around the handle of the cast-iron fire shovel she'd put beside her chair.

'What's important, Stella, is the ability to take emotion out of the equation. Emotion makes people weak. We beat our chests, look for solutions. Like the fall of the Roman Empire, we are in decline,' she said. 'America is dissolving, Europe is slowly breaking and the world as we know it is collapsing.'

'Isn't it our job to try and help?'

'Help or hinder? All those organisations, any NGO you wish to name, all they do is delay the inevitable.'

'It's only inevitable if you see it that way.'

'How else could you see it?'

'Like this,' said Stella.

She stood and swung the metal shovel at Audrey's head. It connected with her shoulder with a dull thud. Audrey fell to the floor. The look of shock on her face didn't last long.

'You little bitch! James. *James!*' she screamed, clutching at her shoulder as she tried to get up.

Stella hit again, harder this time, connecting with the knuckles on Audrey's hand. She screamed again.

Stella kept hold of the shovel and waited for the door to open. When James rushed towards Audrey, still on the floor, Stella hit the back of his head. He lurched forward, stumbled, then righted himself.

'Grab her,' yelled Audrey.

James lunged at Stella, who was already out the door and halfway down the stairs. He caught her up, pushed her. She fell against the banister, tripped and landed at the bottom.

Scrambling to her feet she realised her ankle had twisted badly underneath her. Damn him, she thought. She swung the shovel, James caught it mid-flight, yanked it towards him and grabbed her arm, twisting it up her back. She cried out in pain.

'This is only the start of it, bitch,' he hissed in her ear.

39

AUDREY CAME DOWN the stairs, breathing heavily. One hand she held in front of her, like an animal with a wounded paw. Her hair was slightly messed; a thin streak of blood trailed down her white blouse. Stella had cracked Audrey's hand hard, but not hard enough.

'What now?' asked James.

'Give me the shovel and take her to the room with the girl.'

James twisted Stella's arm further up her back and pushed her towards the rear of the store. They went through the small room used as an office and into another part of the building. Opening the door, he let go of her arm and shoved her in. She stumbled slightly, her eyes adjusting to the low light.

The room was almost dark, a blind covering the narrow window. There was a day bed along one wall. Sia was on the bed, cowering in the corner, her knees pulled up under her chin. She didn't move. She pressed herself as small as she could. James roughly pushed Stella onto a chair. Audrey followed behind them. She'd found a scarf and wrapped it around her injured hand.

'I want Teri's phone,' said Audrey. 'And you will give it to me.'

'No,' said Stella.

'Tell me who has the phone,' Audrey repeated.

'It's not that simple.'

'Of course it is.'

'What do I get in return?' Asked Stella.

'You're not in the best position to bargain.'

'I want the girl.'

Audrey looked at Sia and back to Stella. A smile played on her lips. 'I hadn't pictured you as the sentimental type. That seemed more the territory of your sister. As I said, emotion will always get the better of you.' She pulled up another chair and sat down. 'So, here's what's going to happen. James will very slowly do as he pleases with Sia. You will sit and watch, like you did at the club. But this time, if you want to rescue her, he will stop only when I ask him to.'

'That's fucking sick.'

'Maybe, but I will get the phone.'

'You can't be serious.'

'Well, let's see how much you want the girl. James? You may begin.' Audrey smiled at him.

He went over to the bed. Sia didn't make a sound. She wasn't crying. Her eyes were closed, arms wound around her head, knees drawn up to her chest. James knelt on the bed and pulled her arms away. Stella closed her eyes. A searing pain savaged her shoulder. Audrey had hit her with the shovel.

'Fuck!' yelled Stella.

'Keep your eyes open,' said Audrey calmly.

James pulled Sia's legs away from her chest. He started to undo the buckle of his belt.

'Stop, stop it!' Stella jumped up, grabbed hold of James's arm and tried to pull him off Sia. With one quick movement he sent an elbow sharply into her stomach. She fell back onto the floor.

'I'm having my fun, bitch,' he snarled at her.

'I'll tell you,' Stella said. 'I'll tell you where the phone is. Get him off her!' She started to stand up. He kicked her leg. It buckled underneath her, she landed heavily on her knees. 'Audrey!' she yelled again.

He swung his fist. It connected with Stella's jaw and ear.

Her head whiplashed to one side and she fell again, against the chair, blood dripping from the gash on her temple. The metallic taste of blood filled her mouth. His boot landing in her chest, winded her. She gasped for air.

Stella curled up, hands over her head, knees to her chest. She tried to turn her back away from him, but he was practised, each kick landing precisely at the base of her spine. 'I – will – have – my – fun – ' each word resounded with his boot in her back. There was ringing in her ear. The pain of each kick shot up her spine.

'Okay, James,' said Audrey finally. 'You can stop now.'

Stella rolled over to face Audrey. Her eye caught the glint of a short-bladed knife in James's hand.

'Lassie,' she managed. 'Mitchell Lassiter has the phone.'

'Ah, yes. The lawyer,' said Audrey. 'There now. That wasn't so difficult, was it? Put that knife away, James.' She readjusted the scarf around her injured arm. 'Stella, you will phone him, assure him everything is all right. You will hand the phone to me and I will set up a meeting at a place of our choosing,' she said. 'We will then manage a cold-war style hand over. How exciting. The girl for the phone.'

Audrey gave Stella her phone. 'Call him, now, put it on speaker,' she commanded. 'And don't try anything stupid.'

Slowly Stella scrolled through her contacts, found Lassie's number and listened to it ringing. 'Mitchell,' she said when he answered. 'Mitchell, this is Stella … Yes, I'm okay. You're on speaker. Mitchell, Audrey knows you have Teri's phone. Listen carefully to what she has to say to you.'

Audrey took the phone and, with James, left the room.

Stella slowly eased herself off the floor and onto the bed. She was doubled over, the pain up her spine was excruciating, her ankle throbbed. She swallowed several times to calm the nausea and tried to wipe the blood from her eye. There was a sharp click as the key turned in the lock. She pulled Sia towards her and wrapped her arms around her small frame. 'I'm so sorry, my love, so sorry.'

Like a bruised piece of fruit, the sky was darkening by the time James took them out to the car. Opening the passenger door he bundled them into the backseat, then whisked a pair of cuffs out of his pocket and slapped them over her wrists.

'You won't get far with these on,' he said.

Stella looked at them. There wasn't any point in trying to pick them; she remembered from experience that was a dead end. She held Sia in the circle of her arms.

'Where are you taking us?' she asked.

'I have my orders.'

'Okay, I get that, but where—?'

'Shut the fuck up.'

He flicked the central lock, then gunned the accelerator and turned sharply onto Tinakori Road.

Stella leaned back.

She had to think and fast. She had no phone, no money and no weapon. He was strong. But she was clever. She needed to get him off balance somehow. They drove up past the Botanic Gardens – like a canopy, great wide branches of old pōhutukawa extended over the road. The tyres squealed around the sharp bend at the top. The car was a late-model BMW and James had little regard for the speed limit. It was just the sort of wide-boy, dick-extending vehicle he would drive, she thought. They shot through the tunnel, past Birdwood Street and through the lights just as they turned red. Veering left he kept on Chaytor towards the main Karori Road.

They drove through the affluent end of the suburb, past the shopping centre, the post office, Pilates studio, organic juice bar, all closed for the weekend. They were driving in a leather-smelling, boy-racer bubble. Stella watched a woman scooping up poop her expensive dog had deposited on the pavement, a man battling with a cycle rack on the back of his SUV. Soon there was the cricket oval and the playground.

James kept driving. They shot through the less affluent end of the suburb and up the hill. There was nowhere left but Makara and the coast. All he needs is access to a boat thought Stella; he could dump us both overboard. At this time in the afternoon, in this weather, there wouldn't be anyone out there.

The road was newly finished and smooth. James indulged his Formula One fantasies and sped up Makara Hill, each corner reminding Stella of the pain in her back and side.

'Jesus, slow the fuck down,' she called out.

He pulled over in the lay-by at the top of the hill. In the distant skyline the wind turbines turned in slow motion, their blades stark against the fading light. Keeping the engine running, he swivelled around to look at them.

'Nice view,' he said.

'You bring all your dates up here, do you?'

'No, but we're going to have a bit of fun before the serious bit.'

'Fuck you.'

He sneered. 'I didn't get what I wanted before, so I think I'll be the one doing the fucking.'

Unclipping his seatbelt, he reached towards them. Stella put her hands up to push him away from Sia.

'I like the feisty ones,' he said.

'Handcuffs turn you on?'

'Shit yeah.' His phone beeped. He sat back in his seat and checked it. 'Christ.'

James turned the car back onto the road and started down the hill towards Makara Beach. Stella breathed a short sigh of relief. Her wrists were beginning to hurt; he'd done the cuffs up too tight. She was sweating, but Sia felt cold at her side.

This poor child, she thought. She's in the middle of a nightmare. Her small body was shaking in the thin clothing, no sound came from her mouth. Stella knew there was a limited window in which to defeat this guy. There was also the chance they'd screwed with Lassie and sent him off in the other direction. Fucked if we're going to die up here, thought Stella.

James revved the engine.

The road was narrow on the Makara side, a thin slice cut from the steep hillside. Gorse covered the hills, fighting with native plants that were exerting their dominance. Loose rock, which had tumbled down with the rain, had been swept into piles along the roadside. A pine plantation stood dark and silent down the steep valley to their right. James shot round another sharp bend and slammed on the brakes. Stella felt the back of the car fish-tail. In front of them was a double horse float with both stalls filled.

'Jesus, fuck, could you go any slower!' yelled James at the gently undulating arses.

There was no way he could pass. He sat there as close as he could, moving out into the oncoming lane, revving the engine every so often to let the horse-float driver know he was pissed off. Sia whimpered and started shaking again. Shit, thought Stella, I should have got a rug or something for her. She looked around the interior of the car. Nothing. She pulled her closer trying to exchange as much of her own body warmth as she could.

Ah, Teri, she thought, why didn't you say something, anything, even a hint. I would have understood. Now I've got *this*, a child, another life ... London wasn't great but fuck this for a joke.

Eventually, just before the Makara village, the horse float peeled off.

'About bloody time,' yelled James, flooring the accelerator. He ratcheted up to race mode again but didn't make for the beach. Instead, he swung the car off to a side road.

The tyres crunched over the gravel as he pulled into the car-park area. He stopped the car and turned the engine off.

The car park was empty.

The last of the day's sun glinted off the massive turbine blades as they turned with slow regularity. Like sentinels, they faced the sea. Shredded cabbage trees dotted the ridgeline. Hardy sheep huddled together in small groups, their backs to the wind. Stella looked around, her mind a mess of tangled thoughts. There wasn't much up here and certainly nowhere to hide. A couple of portable toilets sat along the road; over from the car park were the remains of the old post office radio station.

But that was it.

The cliffs on this part of the coast slipped vertically down to the beach. There was one road in and one road out. They were fucked.

There was a huge gust of wind. She felt it pushing against the car.

'So is this where it ends?' she said.

He said nothing.

'What are your orders from Audrey?'

He looked at her. 'No one orders me around.'

'No, you just do as you're told. You're a good little lap-dog.'

'Fuck you,' he said.

'You're like one of those de-sexed fluffy dogs. The sort that society girls carry in their handbags. You're a handbag dog.'

'Shut up, bitch.'

He opened his door and got out, slamming it shut. Stella could see him rummaging around in his pocket for the keys to the cuffs. He found them, looked up with a slow grin and dangled the keys in front of his face. She stared at him through the car window. Her eyes followed him as he walked around to the other side of the car. He pulled open the door and grabbed Sia's arm, yanking her up off the seat.

'No!' yelled Stella. 'You're not taking her!' She grabbed her arm and held on. James stopped.

He let her go.

Another car was driving up the road to the car park.

40

As instructed, he was alone in the car. He parked a short distance from where James had stopped. Stella watched as Lassie got out and stood by the car door, holding his hands out in front of him. The wind slammed the door shut.

'I've got the phone,' he called out, the wind whipping his words around. 'Audrey told me to give it to you in exchange.' He stood there waiting. James didn't move. 'But first I want to see they're both okay.'

James opened the car door on Stella's side and pulled her out. Sia followed, holding on to Stella's leg.

'Stay there,' he said. 'You'll go when I'm satisfied it's the right phone.'

He walked a few steps over to Lassie, who met him halfway.

'The battery is stuffed,' said Lassie.

'So, how do I know it's her phone?'

'You can see the screen is cracked, from where it hit the side of the skip.'

'What skip?'

Lassie stared at him. 'She threw it off the balcony, just before you helped her over.'

'You expect me to admit to any of that?'

'I don't expect a bottom feeder like you to admit to anything.' Lassie and James locked eyes. 'But it was you, wasn't it? You were there in the apartment with her. We have an eyewitness.'

'No you don't, not anymore.' James laughed and looked away, then he stopped. 'You fucker, you're wearing a wire.'

'God, you really think you're in some kind of hardcore police movie. I'm not wearing a wire, I'm not recording anything. Look, see for yourself – here's my phone. It's not on record.' Lassie reached a hand into his pocket.

'Keep your hands where I can see them.'

'I'm not about to shoot you,' said Lassie.

'Shut up, just give me her fucking phone.' James took it in his left hand, jiggled it up and down, turned it over, his thumb massaging the cracks on the screen.

There it is, thought Stella. Teri's phone, the end of the line. If we don't get it, there's nothing left, just the memories of a night witnessing the brutality of men. Teri died for that.

Christ, I've completely cocked it up, she thought. Teri believed in something enough to try and help. Without that phone, the police would have nothing to go on. There might be a paper trail, or a money trail, but Audrey wouldn't be that careless. And what about the children, what would happen to them?

Jesus fuck, I should have spoken to McCarthy, gone the official route. Maybe then Christophe would still be alive.

The wind was picking up now, buffeting them.

He will not win, she thought. *He will not win.*

'Okay,' said James finally. 'I'll buy it. This is the bitch's phone. You know, she had us going for a while there. Wanted to screw her myself, but little miss whiter-than-white wouldn't have it. All the while she was feeding me bullshit about wanting to learn the business, she was recording everything.'

'Well, I guess you'll have to learn to stop thinking with your dick,' said Lassie.

James stared at him, long and hard.

'You think you're better than me. You and that godawful shonky detective,' he glanced over at Stella. 'Thought you had us, didn't you? Me and Audrey, we're better than that. We're too bloody clever for arseholes like you.'

'I don't know you,' said Lassie. 'All I want is for you to

take the cuffs of her and let them both go. You have the phone, you've got what you wanted.'

James slowly tapped the phone against his cheek, then slipped it into his jacket pocket. He curled his lip and started to laugh. With a flash he lashed out with his right hand and hit Lassie, just under his ribcage. Lassie clasped his side, folding forward and landing on his knees.

'You fucker!' Stella yelled.

James walked back towards her.

'Get in the car,' he said.

'What did you do that for?'

'I said, get in.'

'With you? No bloody way,' said Stella.

Lassie was still kneeling on the gravel. He looked up at her, then down to his hands, they were red with blood. That's when she saw the knife in James's hand. Oh, Jesus, thought Stella. He's really going to finish this.

'Get back in the car,' he said again.

Stella bent down towards Sia. 'Run to the other car,' she said, pointing and giving her a push.

'What the—' James reached out to grab Sia, and in that split second Stella's cuffed hands went straight up, full force, under his chin. His head snapped back. She pushed him in the chest. He landed, heavily, against the open door of the car.

He stumbled.

She ran.

That was it.

That was her chance. She ran as fast as she could, up the slope, over the grass towards the old radio station building. Crunching over the loose gravel path, she gripped hold of the metal railing and ran up the stairs to the second floor. The whole place had been gutted, an Eastern European concrete shell, made into a viewing platform.

At the top she paused, breathing heavily.

Fight or flight, her body was wired, shot through with enough adrenaline to take on the Olympic mile. She stood on her good foot, taking the weight off her twisted ankle. From here she could see the car park, Lassie still on the ground, his arm around Sia. James wasn't in sight.

The wind was howling now. A faint mist rose up the cliffs from the sea, spilling onto the grass. Soon it would be dark, really dark. There were footsteps on the gravel, then quieter as he made his way up the steps.

'I know you're up there,' he called in a sing-song voice. 'There's no way out of this. Your boyfriend's fucked, you're next, then the girl.'

Stella waited in the shadows.

He reached the top and came round the corner. Her foot went out, and he tripped and landed heavily on the hard surface. She lashed a foot out towards his head, he grabbed her. She twisted away, half-limping, half-running, leading him away from Lassie and Sia, buying time, buying anything.

Her ankle howled in pain.

Stella stumbled out on the top floor, at the same level as the slope and onto the grass. A closed wooden gate was ahead of her, leading to a plantation of large silent pine trees on the other side. If she could get to the trees, maybe she could do a loop and double back to the car park. Running was awkward. Her hands were still cuffed in front of her.

She had to get to the trees – then she was falling forward, hit the ground hard, and felt her shoulder crack.

He'd reached her and tackled her from behind.

Stella had fallen awkwardly with a sharp thud, her left arm bent underneath her side.

Rolling sharply onto her back she kicked her foot out at him. It found its mark on the front of his face. He screamed, a high-pitched noise, putting both hands up to his nose.

'You bitch, you bitch.'

Scrambling to her feet her shoulder felt numb. The thigh of her right leg stung. Christ, she thought, he must have sliced me when he made that tackle. Stella started the limping run again towards the gate. She just needed to get through, but it was like moving through quicksand. She stumbled, her leg not wanting to hold her full weight.

It was bad.

Fuck it was bad.

He was right there, on the grass in front of her, barring the way.

'You're a thick bitch,' he said, blood running down his chin. 'You really don't get it, do you?'

The knife was in his hand – he lunged towards her. She turned her shoulder, but the knife found its mark into the muscle of her upper arm. '*Olé*,' he said with a sly grin.

He lunged again but missed. Then again and again.

With each lunge she backed up the slope towards the gate. She swallowed; her vision was blurring. She clenched her fist, slippery with blood. The wooden fence post was at her back, he was right in her face. His hands went around her throat.

She couldn't breathe; she could see the blade of the knife.

He was pressing his thumbs into her windpipe. She felt her eyes bulging. Her cuffed hands were just low enough … for her … to grab his dick and twist.

He screamed and fell back onto the grass.

The cops arrived without the sirens or lights on.

There are moments when time itself stands still.

There are moments when it speeds up, like a silent movie reel – flickers of images, without sound.

She remembers bits. Stumbling down the slope. Falling, the smell of damp grass. Voices.

'Stella, Stella, can you hear me? You're okay now, can you hear me?'

The lights, the yelling and confusion. The ambulance.

Drifting in and out of consciousness.

The pain in her leg, her arm and shoulder, her head.

Then no pain.

Nothing.

41

WHEN SHE WOKE, all around her was white and still. Muffled hospital sounds filtered through. She closed her eyes against the bright and tried to remember. All she could see was the green slope and flashing lights, wind rushing and voices, lots of voices.

Slowly she opened her eyes again and moved her head. Charlotte was sitting in the chair beside the bed. Stella tried to speak but her throat was sore – all she could manage was a hoarse 'Hey.'

Charlotte smiled. 'Hey,' she said. 'You managed to give us a fright.'

Stella tried to smile back, but the side of her face hurt. 'I aim to please,' she croaked. 'What about Lassie and Sia? Are they okay?'

'They're both fine. Lassie lost a lot of blood, but the knife missed all the vital bits, thank god. He's been in surgery, he'll be okay.' Charlotte leaned forward and gave Stella's hand a gentle squeeze. 'You lost a lot of blood as well.'

'Don't tell Mum and Dad – they'll freak.'

'Too late for that I'm afraid. They've both been here,' she said. 'Dad's taking Mum for a coffee and to get flowers. She keeps worrying there are no bouquets in your room, or in Lassie's. She's bordering on hysterical. It's not a pretty sight.'

'Don't make me laugh,' said Stella. She lifted the sheet and tried to swing her leg out. She stared at the bandage on her thigh. 'Shit,' she said. 'I need to see Lassie.'

'You're not meant to be up.'

'I need to see him.'

'Later,' said Charlotte gently. She stood up and started to tuck the blankets around her. 'You can see him later.'

*

When Stella woke again, Charlotte had gone. She'd been replaced by Meathead McCarthy.

'I ought to throw the book at you,' he said, taking off his jacket and flinging it over the back of a chair.

'Metaphorically, I hope,' she said. 'Do people still do that kind of thing?'

'You are in so many kinds of shit, Weston. I don't know where to start or what to start throwing.'

'Come on, give me a hand.'

He helped her to sit up, plumping up a couple of extra pillows behind her head.

'Is Sia okay?' she asked.

'The girl, yes, she's being cared for. You can see her soon if you want.'

'And James? Please tell me you got that bastard?'

'Yes, we did, eventually.'

'Eventually?'

'He did a runner through the trees, but we got him in the end. I presume you'll want to lay charges. He'll be done for assault and kidnapping.'

'That's only the start of it.'

'Yeah, you'll need to make a formal statement.'

'Of course.'

He looked at her, shaking his head slightly.

'What?' she asked.

'We'll have to figure out what to charge you with.'

She stared at him. 'You've no idea, do you? What about the phone? Did you find the phone?'

'Well, you're right about that. I have some ideas but not the full picture.'

The sun was streaming straight into Stella's eyes. McCarthy moved over to the window to adjust a blind, then turned to face her. 'So, how about *you* start at the beginning.'

She did. All of it. Teri, the phone, Audrey, Christophe, the spa, her suspicions about the girl under the wharf being a runaway from the brothel. McCarthy pulled up a chair, sat down and listened. He leaned forward, his elbows on his knees, head in his hands.

Eventually he looked up. 'We're not completely hopeless you know, Weston. We did have some idea there was shit going on in that place. We had an undercover in there a while back, but she had to ditch it, she was feeling really unsafe. We were starting the idea of recruiting that kid Birdie, the one on the bar. Then you came along – now we're even further down the toilet.'

'I should have been able to do something, but I didn't and my friend is dead.'

'What, exactly?' said McCarthy, interrupting her. 'What could you have done? You should have come straight to me, or someone else. Now we've got to clean up this bloody mess. When you found that body in the water, Weston, you withheld important information from us.'

'Maybe,' said Stella. 'But at that point I didn't know what was important, I wasn't sure what was going on. Teri's death, I don't know ...' she faltered. 'And let's face it, McCarthy, you weren't exactly dancing a jig to give me a fair deal.'

He nodded. 'You have a point. Well, we could put James in a line-up and see if any of the guys who were beaten can ID him.'

'The ones still alive, you mean? What about the phone, he might still have it,' she said hopefully.

'Fat chance, Weston. You and I both know he'll have ditched it. We've set up a search in the area, sniffer dogs, the works, but it'll be real needle in haystack stuff. We didn't get him till he was out on the cliffs, for all we know he could have chucked it in the sea. We'll be lucky if we find it.'

Stella sighed and closed her eyes. 'Yet again I've cocked it up.'

They were both quiet for a while. McCarthy cleared his throat. 'Yep,' he said finally. 'You sure did. You could have been good, you know?'

'Yeah, I know. I fucked all that up too, didn't I?'

'Don't be too hard on yourself.' He stopped and coughed again. 'There's no easy segue into this – he remarried.'

'Who?'

'William. It took a few years; he left the force soon after you went tripping off on your sad-sack OE.'

'You make it sound like I was running away. It wasn't a holiday.'

'I know, I know. "Running", "a holiday", call it what you want, I'm just pulling your chain. Anyway, he said he couldn't stay here, not after what happened with Dee. He moved to Nelson. I caught up with him a few times when I was over there. He's got a kid, even.'

'Great, that's good,' said Stella. 'I'm pleased for him.'

'Blamed himself for it all, y'know, in the end.'

'That's not what he told me,' she said, wincing slightly as she tried to find a more comfortable position in the bed. 'He made it pretty clear it was all my doing.'

'He didn't think she'd go and kill herself. He was angry, shocked. We all were.' McCarthy took a deep breath and slowly puffed it out. His teeth worried a piece of loose skin on his lower lip. 'Clichéd, I know,' he said, 'but time does make a difference. He realised it was both of you doing the horizontal tango thing – that he was equally to blame.'

Stella closed her eyes.

'Her name was Mai,' he said eventually.

'Whose name?' she said.

'The girl under the wharf was Mai.'

She would not cry in front of McCarthy. He leaned over and tapped a box of tissues against her arm.

'Here you go.'

'Fuck you,' she said gently and pulled a couple of tissues from the box.

'Been a rough week all round,' he said.

There was a soft knock on the door. Ravosky came into the room.

'Good to see you're awake and sitting up,' he said, and holding out his hand to McCarthy, 'Maurice Ravosky.'

'DI McCarthy,' he replied.

'A pleasure to meet you and I'm so very pleased that you're all right, Stella.'

'Why didn't you tell me what you knew,' she asked.

'And have the same thing happen to you as happened to Teri? I was trying to steer you away from it all. I didn't want you hurt,' he said, 'but you just wouldn't leave it alone.'

'Yeah, it's a bad habit of mine.'

'I'm sorry,' said McCarthy. 'But how exactly do you fit into all of this?'

'McCarthy, I'm sorry,' said Stella. 'I haven't got to the Ravosky part yet.'

Ravosky smiled at him. 'I see you're playing a bit of catch-up, Detective Inspector. I had some idea of what was on that phone,' he said. 'Teri worked for me, she showed me her phone the night before she was murdered. I knew she'd been working at the club. I knew what she was trying to do and begged her to be careful.' Ravosky pulled up a chair and sat down. 'I wanted to go through more conventional means, but she was so determined. She had photos, video, audio. She had names, places, she got people to talk to her. Even Audrey let her guard down – she said Teri reminded her of herself when younger.' He lowered his head. 'They must have realised she was onto them. Do you have any idea how difficult it was to keep it from you?'

'Keeping me in the dark hurt me, if I'd known I could have—'

'It was all a bit of a stuff up,' said Ravosky. 'That brothel will be clean by now – the word will have gone around their networks to lie low for the foreseeable future.'

'They'll surface again, scum always does,' said McCarthy.

Ravosky's voice was quiet. 'Teri was killed for this,' he said. 'We have to continue; we have to find another way. This operation has been stopped, but there will be others to find.'

Stella looked at them both. 'You forgot about Gus,' she said.

'Who on earth is Gus?' they said in unison.

Charlotte wheeled Stella into Lassie's room. He looked pale; his hair was ruffled against the pillow. He smiled at her.

Charlotte parked the wheelchair. 'I'll leave you to it.'

'Hey,' said Stella. 'I hear you lost a lot of blood, but they managed to stitch you up okay?'

'Yeah,' he said. 'They assured me I didn't get any of your mad-cow blood when they transfused me.'

'Nah, we're incompatible.'

'Only in the blood department I hope.' He made a sound that might have been a laugh.

'How's the pain?'

'Only when I laugh, Stell, only when I laugh,' he said. 'What about you?'

'I'm fine. That bastard beat me up, but nothing I can't cope with.' Stella wheeled the chair a bit closer to the bed and took his hand. 'You'll be happy to know Sia is okay and being well looked after.'

'Great.' He gently squeezed her hand. 'McCarthy wants to talk to you,' he said.

'I've already spoken to him and Ravosky.'

'Is this how it's going to be?' He laced his fingers in hers.

'What do you mean?'

'Me sitting at home, getting calls from crazy women wanting to arrange cliff-top assignations to exchange you for a phone?'

'Probably,' she said softly.

'Seeing you in handcuffs,' he continued, 'and me getting stabbed?'

'Ah, go on! You loved it. It's much more exciting than your usual lawyer stuff. Why did you call Meathead McCarthy?'

'When you phoned from Audrey's, you called me Mitchell – three times. You never call me Mitchell.'

She grinned at him.

The hospital gown gave him a fragile look. 'I figured there was bound to be some turds hitting the fan,' he said. 'Especially if you were involved.'

'Right again. It's just that the name Lassie suits you better.'

'Well, I didn't manage to rescue you this time, did I?'

She wheeled herself over to the window. She wasn't sure how many floors up they were. She could see the main road, buses, cars, people going in and out of the hospital. In the distance the hills rolled and shimmered, green under the sharp light. Life goes on, she thought, it always does.

'I didn't even have the phone,' said Lassie. 'I had to wrangle it from Gus, and he's one tough dude under all that facial hair.'

Stella laughed.

The room filled with people. Stella's mother arrived with a massive bunch of flowers for Lassie.

'I've already put one in your room,' she said, and gave Stella a long shaking hug, her face wet with tears. She started fussing around for a vase and water. Stella's dad gave her a quick hug and kiss. 'You'll be the death of me,' he said close to her ear. She patted his hand and smiled at him.

Charlotte arrived, then Lassie's brother and father showed up. Ben came in and gave Stella a hug before seeking out Charlotte. People were introducing themselves to each other; it felt like a party but without alcohol. Stella watched them all, their ease, their affability. London was never like this. There was always that air of cool indifference. The sheer volume of humanity living on top of each other; always leaning forward to the next thing.

What a shitty disaster it's all turned out to be, she thought. Audrey's probably left the country; Sia might follow. A young girl has drowned in a foreign country far away from her family. Teri was murdered. Christophe was murdered.

Stella listened to the hum of conversation and wondered if she could ever truly be happy to live back in London, or here. Like all her history, like anyone's history, it didn't go away just because you willed it to.

She closed her eyes.

Maybe she should try. Maybe she should turn around and face them, face this city. Learn to live in it again.

Gus showed up. He stooped over the chair and gave Stella a warm and enveloping hug. 'I knew Christophe had that phone – well, I suspected as much. But if I'd known that this would happen,' he said, 'I'd never have let you have it.'

'It's okay, Gus, really, you did the right thing. We're all going to be fine. I'm only sorry Christophe got so badly caught up in it all. He didn't deserve that.'

'Even so ...' He wiped his eyes. 'We will be holding a funeral for him in a few days, I'd like you to be there.'

'I'll be there,' she said. 'Try and stop me. Just one quick question,' she said. He crouched down so his face was near hers. He was close enough she could smell the wax he used to polish the instruments. 'When you looked at Teri's phone, did you happen to copy it onto a computer?'

'I am a musician …' he said gravely – then he smiled. 'I'm not stupid. Of course I did.'

'All of it?'

'Yes, all of it.'

Stella felt a smile form on her face too. A large dopey grin. She rubbed the heel of her hands into her eyes. The room was so busy, no one noticed her crying. Gus patted her arm.

Peace had found a place for Lassie's flowers – unable to resist fussing a little with arranging them.

'I couldn't bear to lose you, my darling girl.' Peace pulled out a tissue from her bag and wiped her eyes. 'Losing Teri was bad enough,' she said, leaning forward to hug her.

'I'm okay, Mum. Really, I'm okay.'

A nurse came in and started to hustle them all away. The patients needed their rest, she said, wheeling Stella from the room.

Yes. Stella needed to rest.

ACKNOWLEDGEMENTS

I haven't got the space to thank everyone who helped get this manuscript off the page and into your hands. But here's a few.

Huge thanks to the team at The Cuba Press: Mary McCallum, for her thoughtful and careful editing (I will never comma splice again, I promise); and Sarah Bolland and Paul Stewart, for their comments and eagle-eyed edits. You have all made this a much better book.

Mandy Hager, for her wonderful, insightful teaching, and the Whitireia creative writing class of 2015.

Tim Jones, for the many literary conversations.

Pip Adam and Paddy Richardson, for being honest and encouraging first readers.

Wendy, Margaret, Andy, for their enthusiasm and support.

Massive thanks go to Jane, for being extraordinary, in all ways.

And my family, Simon, Isabelle and Elliot, who put up with my many absences and more than a few odd questions.

ABOUT THE AUTHOR

Anne Harré has studied music, literature, publishing and creative writing, and been awarded an NZSA/Hachette mentorship for the manuscript of *The Leaning Man*.

She works now as a school librarian, but has also been a music teacher, bookseller, freelance editor and reviewer, and editor for the New Zealand Poetry Society anthology. She has worked for the New Zealand Book Council and as a trustee for the Randell Cottage Writers Trust.

Anne lives in Wellington and *The Leaning Man* is her first book.